A Viking Maiden for the Marquess

Michelle Willingham

A MOST PECULIAR SEASON

Published by Michelle Willingham
www.michellewillingham.com

ISBN-13: 978-0-9906345-5-3

Cover by Carrie Divine/Seductive Designs
Photo by Period Images
Interior formatting by Author E.M.S.

Published in the United States of America.

Her Irish Warrior
The Warrior's Touch
Taming Her Irish Warrior
"The Warrior's Forbidden Virgin" (novella)
"Voyage of an Irish Warrior" (novella)
Surrender to an Irish Warrior
"Pleasured by the Viking" (novella)
"Lionheart's Bride" (novella)
Warriors in Winter

The MacKinloch Clan Series
(Medieval Scotland)
Claimed by the Highland Warrior
Seduced by Her Highland Warrior
"Craving the Highlander's Touch" (novella)
Tempted by the Highland Warrior
"Rescued by the Highland Warrior" (novella in the
Highlanders anthology)

The Accidental Series
(Victorian England/Fictional Province of Lohenberg)
"An Accidental Seduction" (novella)
The Accidental Countess
The Accidental Princess
The Accidental Prince

Other Titles

"Innocent in the Harem"
(A novella of the sixteenth-century Ottoman Empire)

"A Wish to Build a Dream On"
(time travel novella to medieval Ireland)

"A Dance with the Devil"
(in the *Bedeviled* anthology)

ChAPTER ONE

Katarina Larsdottir strode along the rocky shoreline, the cool summer air biting her skin. The sun was descending into the sea, its rays gleaming upon the dark waters brushed with crimson. With every stride, she kept her hand upon the blade at her waist.

For she dreamed of vengeance.

In her memories, she could see the faces of her enemies. Geilir, son of Jósep, and Jokull, son of Áfalstr. Although both of the Norse warriors had left the shores of Rogaland, Katarina had sworn to the gods that she would find them…and they would die.

Her steps slowed as she reached the small cairn of stones upon the hillside. Bitter remorse flowed through her, and she rested her palms upon the limestone, dropping to her knees beside her sister's grave. One day soon, the men would regret what they had done.

Even now, after a year, she could not forget what had happened. Gentle Ingirún had barely reached the age of thirteen. Her beautiful sister had been ravaged by those drunken men, and she'd died at their hands.

1

A hard lump formed in her throat, and Katarina clenched her fingers against the cool stones. "Odin, grant me vengeance," she whispered. "Let me bathe my blade in their heart's blood." She would give anything in exchange for their deaths...anything at all. One day, her sister's enemies would pay for her death with their own lives.

Perhaps then, Katarina could forgive herself.

When footsteps resounded behind her, she spun, her blade in hand. But it was only her brother, Hrafn. He wore a cloak, hiding the stump of his missing right arm. "You should not be out here alone, Katarina. It will be dark soon."

She only shrugged and shielded her eyes against the setting sun. "If I choose to visit with our sister, what harm is there?"

"You are watching for ships," he predicted. And in that, he was right. Each day, she watched to see if the striped sail would arrive, unfurled in the wind as the boat crested along the waves toward the shore.

"None of them has returned," she said.

"Not yet," he agreed. But her brother knew she would never stop searching. Her enemies had gone a-viking to East Anglia...but when they came back, she would be waiting.

Hrafn's gaze narrowed, and he remarked, "Leave it be, Katarina. If they do not return by next summer, I will find their settlement and bring them here to face judgment."

"If you go, I am coming with you."

"No. This, I will not allow. You cannot travel with us," he insisted.

She said nothing but turned back to walk toward their settlement. Hrafn didn't understand. He had not been there, never suspecting that his sisters would fall prey to men of their own tribe while he was away.

Katarina closed her eyes a moment, pushing back the dark memories. Her sister had been attacked and raped by the raiders before she could save her. When she had found Ingirún, her sister was lying motionless while blood streamed from her head.

And then Katarina had been attacked. The men had beaten her, tearing at her clothing. She'd been battered and bruised, trying in desperation to fight them off. Thankfully, Valdr, the *jarl* of their tribe, had arrived, along with Leif Tormundsson, before she was harmed.

Katarina's eyes blurred with hot tears. Even when she'd tried in desperation to bring Ingirún to the healer, it was impossible to save her sister. She'd never awakened, for the men had struck her head against a stone during the attack.

She slowed her pace, fingering the scar at the corner of her mouth. *One day they will die for what they did.*

Katarina continued walking toward the settlement before she cast a look back at Hrafn. Her brother had remained near the rocks, letting her return alone while he kept watch. He had looked after Ingirún and her during the past year, ever since their father died after a hunting accident. Their mother, Kolla, had died a few years earlier, from illness during a long winter.

Although Hrafn was only three years older, he considered himself responsible for her. He had hardly left her side since the night their sister had died, and Katarina had never told him that she, too, had been attacked. After Ingirún was dead, it had seemed unnecessary. He carried his own burden of guilt for not being there—and she saw no reason to make him feel worse. Especially when she had been rescued before any true harm was done.

Just inside the walls, she saw *Móðir* Gerda. The old *volva* was seated upon the dirt, her legs folded beneath her skirts. Both of her palms faced the setting sun, and she was chanting to herself in words Katarina had never heard. A strange chill crossed over her back, and the hair stood on end at her nape.

3

The *volva* was chanting a name, she realized. Arik Thorgrim.

Without meaning to, Katarina took a step backward, her face flushing. As a young girl, she had been deeply in love with Arik. She had once dreamed of sharing a life with the stoic warrior. She had twined locks of her hair with charms, hoping that one day he would look upon her with interest. But he had left the settlement, traveling across the sea with another woman, Svala.

Why would the *volva* speak of him? A cold fear slid over her spirits, for she was certain that Arik was dead.

She remained frozen in place, wondering if she should leave. But an invisible force seemed to draw her closer until she knelt beside the old woman.

"He is coming," the woman said, her eyes opening. One blue eye was already blind, and she seized Katarina's arm. "You must be ready. At dawn, he comes."

"What do you mean? Arik is dead."

The old woman closed her eyes again, rocking back and forth. "No. He will be the shield to protect you from what was never meant to be. But his life lies in your hands."

The seer's words troubled her. She tried to tell herself that *Móðir* Gerda was caught up in a vision, one that might not be true. There was no denying that Arik Thorgrim had once held more power than any man of this tribe. As the son of the *jarl,* he had been the one who was meant to rule them all.

But how could Arik's life be in her hands? And what was she meant to do?

"At dawn, by the edge of the sea," the old woman prophesied. "You must be there when he comes."

OFF THE COAST OF NORWAY
ONE THOUSAND YEARS LATER

The moon glowed blood-red over the dark waters of the sea. It hung within the sky like an omen of death, and more than one sailor sent up a silent prayer for protection against evil. Eric Fielding, the Marquess of Thorgraham, knew it was only the moon—and yet this night held an otherworldly aura.

A cloud slid across the sky, and the winter wind began to shift and blow. The hair rose on his forearms, and the waves grew rough. Though he supposed it was only weather approaching, an air of tension tightened among the men. Eric approached the bos'n and asked, "Do you need help with the sails?"

"Mr. Thorgraham, stay out of the way," the bos'n warned. "Our sailors know how to handle a storm. Go below deck where it's safe."

None of these men knew of his true identity as a nobleman. Eric had allowed them to believe that he was a merchant's son, an ordinary passenger of no consequence. He preferred working among men who were content to earn their living with the sweat of their brow. They didn't know what a gift it was to have that freedom. Many of his friends had envied his place as a future duke—he knew that. And yet, that life had never felt like his own.

The wind's intensity heightened, whipping the sails and increasing their speed. The ship began to toss in the waves, and the night sky had turned so black, they could hardly see where the heavens met the sea.

"You need the help of every man," Eric told the bos'n. "It's not safe for any of us."

After the man nodded permission, he joined one of the sailors and helped pull a rope tight, tying it off. But the ship lurched against a wave and tossed him backward. Eric struck his head hard against a barrel, and violent pain resonated through his skull.

Now the storm raged higher. The sea had become a monstrous being, spewing icy water while the wind howled.

You're going to drown, an inner voice taunted. *You turned your back on your estates and your father. Was this what you wanted?*

No. But the idea of spending his days in Parliament, arguing over the laws and learning to become the Duke of Somerford, seemed like an excruciating fate. All his life, he'd been trapped among dusty ledgers and books, learning to govern the estates that his ancestors had built. The need for adventure, the fierce desire to sail across the sea, had burned within his veins. Even now, when he inhaled the sharp tang of the sea air, it held the scent of freedom.

It was possible that he might die this night if the storm continued to batter the vessel. He should have been afraid. But instead, Eric stared up at the moon, and a strange calm descended over him.

He ignored the throbbing in his head and seized a piece of rope. The hemp cut into his palms, but he tied himself to the upper deck, while the waves tossed the vessel within the tempest. An icy spray drenched him, and he shuddered against the frigid ocean water.

If the ship could not withstand the storm, all of them would die. And still, his uncertain fate felt preordained somehow.

The winds battered at his face, and he wondered if he would ever see his father again. His death would devastate Gregory, and Eric didn't want to imagine how that grief would consume him. Regret cloaked him, along with stinging rain. He tried to imagine Gregory's face, tried to hold the vision in his mind, as if it could push back the horrors of this night.

Bitter winds ripped the sail in half while waves pounded

against his ship. The ship's captain shouted orders to his men, but to no avail. The mast cracked, the wood shattering into jagged pieces. Salt water covered the deck, and all around him, men were praying for mercy.

But no pleas came to his lips. Instead, Eric turned his gaze to the clouded skies, his thoughts in turmoil. If the sea took him, there would be no redemption, no chance to see his father again. His father was the only family he had left, and he didn't want to die with enmity between them.

A large wave crashed against the ship, and salt water sloshed against his mouth and nose. His ropes had come loose, and before he realized it, a second wave swept him overboard. The frigid water iced his limbs, dragging him under. For a moment, all grew still, and the cold seemed to freeze his very bones. Beneath the water, he saw the reflection of the moon, and the light was tinted red.

Eric clawed his way upward, fighting to break the surface. *I will not die.*

An unseen force seemed to hold him beneath the water as he struggled for life. The cold darkness surrounded him, like a ghostly embrace. He knew he ought to be terrified, but within his consciousness came the realization that he was not alone. Someone was with him, an unknown presence, speaking words in a foreign tongue.

He churned his arms, finally bursting through the waves and sucking down gulps of air. His body was numb, and when he looked around him, the storm had abated. The waves grew calmer, and the blood-red moon rose high above him, the rosy amber light illuminating the water.

Not yet, a woman's voice whispered.

Eric took more breaths of air, not knowing if he'd imagined the sound. His skin tingled with awareness, as if something had parted the veil between life and death. Was this real? Had he survived the storm? Or was this his first glimpse of the afterworld?

He struggled to swim, not knowing where he was going. The water's surface gleamed with the reflection of the blood moon. In the distance, the sky was transforming from dark blue to lavender. It would be dawn within an hour.

As he continued swimming, he grew somber at the realization that there was no ship remaining—only floating bodies and shattered pieces of wood.

I'm alive, he thought. Somehow, he had survived this shipwreck, though his friends and shipmates had not.

If he didn't reach land, the ocean would become his watery grave. Eric continued swimming, trying to conserve his remaining strength while he searched for something to hold on to.

There. A large piece of the ship floated nearby, and he swam as hard as he could to reach it. His fingers seized the wood, and he crawled upon it, his heart pounding. He held tight, praying that the tide would bring him to land.

His cheek rested against the wood, and he shivered violently against the cold. Yet, he clung to life, refusing to surrender. He floated for what seemed like hours, until a tiny light caught his attention.

Was it the flare of a torch or a fire? The crushing fears lifted, for it meant land was surely nearby. Eric closed his eyes with thankfulness. He let himself drift toward the shore...and when dawn broke, he saw the light more clearly. It was indeed a flickering torch, though he could not see who held it.

The ocean waves slid across the sand and a rocky beach, while behind it, taller gray hills dotted with limestone rose up. He didn't know where he was but suspected Norway. They had been sailing near the country on the way to England when the storm had struck.

The view of land encouraged him to swim harder, still holding on to the makeshift raft. When his feet finally touched the ground, he lifted his face to the sky. *Thank God.*

Today was not his day to die.

Eric trudged through the water until he reached the shore. He sank to his knees, digging his hands into the wet sand. For a moment, he steadied himself, so thankful to be alive. He longed for home, wishing he could see his father again and apologize for all that he'd said and done.

He'd been so angry at the legacy of his forebears closing in around him...of his obligation to sit in the House of Lords, debate laws and, of course, marry an heiress from a good family.

Now, he didn't care.

He would bind himself to the life he didn't want if it meant he could see his father sitting by the fire, reading his favorite book, *Gulliver's Travels*. He could envision the older man seated in his wingback chair, a cup of cold tea on the table beside him. And he imagined the joy on Gregory's face when his only son returned.

And he would return to England, as soon as he could hire a new ship and a crew.

The wind whipped at his skin, and Eric forced himself to stumble forward along the rocky shore. His first priority was to find shelter and get warm.

As he walked, the sense of familiarity grew stronger, almost as if he'd been here before. Which was impossible, since he'd never set foot in Norway...or wherever this was. But he couldn't shake the premonition that he knew this place somehow. He'd dreamed of it.

A narrow pathway led north toward the open meadow, tempting him to follow the road. Yet he'd seen the torch flare on the west side. Through the rocky hills, he would find shelter—he was convinced of it.

He trudged through the sand, realizing that his shoes had fallen off during the shipwreck. His clothing was in tatters, soaked and torn. But strangely, his head no longer hurt. When he studied his palms, they had healed, with no trace of the rope burns. An uneasiness caught him, for he couldn't understand it. Another injury plagued him—something upon his back. He didn't even remember being cut, but his spine burned as if someone had stabbed him.

Eric climbed through the rocks, and beyond them, he saw green grass and trees covered in leaves. Again, the disquiet passed over him, for it was February. There should be no leaves on the trees, nor green grass. If they were in Norway, he expected to see snowy fields. Instead it seemed to be…summer.

He gripped his hands together, willing himself not to imagine the impossible. Either he was dead and this was his new existence…or he had somehow lost the memories of the past two seasons.

There were too many questions, and he felt a dizzying sense of apprehension. But if he allowed himself to think too much, he would lose his grasp on control. *Find shelter,* he reminded himself. *And food.*

Eric took another step forward, and a dark vision came over him, of being struck down with a battle-ax by a…Viking. His spine burned with agony, and he nearly dropped to the ground from the force of the phantom ache. And yet, no one had touched him. With effort, he caught his breath and steadied himself. What was happening?

Strange words mingled within his mind in a language he'd not heard before…but somehow he could understand them.

Svala betrayed me.

His skin tightened with fear. Who was Svala? Was he hearing voices now and had he gone mad? Or was he, in fact, dead? Eric knew that the seasons didn't change within hours. And he most definitely should not be hearing voices in his head. He blinked a moment, forcing himself to continue walking through the rocky sand.

You hit your head on board the ship, he reminded

himself. Perhaps he was unconscious right now and dreaming. Yes, that was it. He had to be imagining all of it. The thought calmed him, and he decided to continue on with the dream, letting it take him where it would.

But with each step, he felt the sense of foreboding heighten. He stopped a moment to touch his head, trying to force back memories that did not belong to him. God above, what was happening to him?

He was Eric Fielding, the Marquess of Thorgraham. And yet…he was not. Another name came into his consciousness, Arik Thorgrim.

That's not who I am.

He wondered if the violent storm had caused him to see and hear things that weren't there. It was as if his life had been unseated, torn apart at the seams.

Before he could question it further, a beautiful woman emerged from the shadows. Her golden hair hung unbound below her waist, and several braids were pinned like a coronet across her head. Never had he seen anyone like her. She was taller than most women, and she moved like a warrior goddess, a torch in one hand.

Her blue woolen gown hung in folds, and a long apron was pinned at her shoulders with two golden brooches. The moment she spied him, she stared at him in shock. "Arik…I thought you were dead."

Katarina couldn't believe the sight before her. Arik Thorgrim was standing outside the settlement, just as the *volva* had prophesied.

A part of her hadn't believed the old woman, but she'd awakened just before dawn, unable to sleep any longer. All night, the wind and the rain had battered her roof, filling her dreams with fear. Without understanding why, she'd hurried outside toward the shore, as if the goddess Freya had commanded her to be there.

Now, she understood why.

She hardly recognized Arik, for his dark hair was cut short. Even his beard was far lighter than she remembered, as if he'd shaved only a few days ago. He had always been a tall, muscular man, but now, he appeared leaner and less like a brute warrior. His clothing was in rags, and he walked barefoot.

But still, the sight of him made her heart pound faster. Only a few weeks ago, one of their kinsmen had returned with the revelation that Arik was dead, struck down by a battle-ax. It must have been a mistake, for clearly he was standing here now. She tried to quell the errant thoughts, pushing back the unbidden feelings. "I cannot believe you're alive."

The words were foolish, but she could not pull them back. *It doesn't matter,* she told herself. She had made a different life for herself now, and her girlish infatuation with him would fade.

Arik's gaze fixed upon her, and his dark eyes drank in her features. For a moment, she remained frozen, not knowing what to think or say. Goose flesh rose over her skin, and she felt her face flush. Why was he looking at her like this? Arik had never been attracted to her. Instead, he'd treated her like a little sister, a maiden to be ignored. He had been far more captivated by Svala, a fiery beauty with a heart of ice.

But at this moment, he was staring at her in a way he never had before. She was spellbound by the intensity of his interest, and her gaze drifted to his firm mouth.

Don't, she warned herself. There was no reason to believe anything was different now. She took a step backward as her embarrassment heightened. "What happened to you? Where is your ship?"

He didn't speak but instead closed his eyes, as if trying to steady himself. When she looked back at the dark waters, there was no sign of any vessel—only fragments of wood. She swallowed back other questions realizing that he'd survived a shipwreck...and the other men were likely dead.

She yearned to ask more questions, but he was likely freezing from the cool summer air. "Come with me, and you can warm yourself at my hearth. We will talk more there."

He gave a nod to indicate that he agreed with her words. Katarina took his arm, guiding him toward the settlement. Odin's blood, his skin was like ice. He jolted at the contact, and she pulled back, realizing that he hadn't wanted her touch.

She never should have reached out to him. He was destined to be their leader, the *jarl,* and she had no right to cross that invisible boundary. Katarina walked alongside him toward the settlement, keeping her head held high, hoping he would disregard the gesture. But her cheeks burned with shame.

She'd known he would return to Rogaland, but she'd been unprepared for the emotions that had risen up within her. His very presence brought back a flood of memories she'd tried so hard to forget. Once, this man had been the reason to make her smile, the one she'd adored from afar. He'd been strong and bold, the warrior she'd dreamed of.

And now, she was a broken woman, haunted by nightmares. Her life had shifted, changing in ways she'd never anticipated.

It does not matter, she told herself. *All that matters is bringing Geilir and Jokull to justice.* She fervently hoped that they hadn't drowned on board Arik's ship. A death by drowning was far too good for either of them.

They crossed over the rocky hillside, the path winding toward their settlement. The sky was deep purple with creases of pink along the horizon. The torch she carried cast a faint glow upon the grass, and Arik followed her in silence.

Her brother stood guard outside their settlement walls. The moment Hrafn spied Arik, his features turned grim. He sent Katarina a questioning look, and she shook her head in warning. Neither of them knew what had happened, but Arik would tell them soon enough. Right now, he appeared confused, as if he had barely survived the shipwreck.

Worst of all was his silence. He hadn't spoken a single word since she'd found him. It made her uneasy, wondering if his tongue had been cut from his mouth.

Hrafn stepped in front of them, blocking their path. Her brother's gray eyes held no welcome—only suspicion. To Arik, he said, "I heard that Björn killed you." His voice held a trace of doubt, as if wondering why that tale had been spread. "If that is untrue, then what happened?"

Katarina wanted that answer as well. She held her breath, waiting for him to speak, but again, Arik said nothing. Her brother stepped forward to demand an answer, but Thorgrim moved aside, causing Hrafn to stumble.

She was startled when Arik moved in front of her…as if to guard her from Hrafn. His dark eyes gleamed with an unspoken challenge, and her brother reached toward his weapon with his left hand.

"Don't." Katarina stepped between them, holding her hands up. "This is not the time for a fight. We will hear more about what happened once Arik has dry clothes and something to eat."

Hrafn's expression didn't change. "He should go to his father's house. Not ours."

She knew that. But Arik and his father had argued fiercely before he'd left, and she suspected Valdr had not forgiven his son for leaving. It was better to wait a little while before Arik confronted the man.

Katarina touched her brother's chest with a palm. "So he will. In a little while." *After I've had the chance to speak with him.*

But when she looked back at Arik, she felt the strong sense that something terrible had happened. It was as if he had returned from the afterworld after being struck mute by the gods. Katarina wanted to know why he would not speak, but she had a feeling he would not tell her. She intended to delay his return to his father, Valdr, until he was prepared to explain the reports of his death.

Hrafn's expression tightened, and he leaned down to whisper in her ear. "I do not want you alone with him." Both of them knew he was not permitted to leave his guard post until the next sentry arrived for duty.

"I will be fine, Hrafn," she reassured him, resting her hand upon her own blade. "I promise you that." She had known Arik all her life and trusted him. But if he dared to raise a hand to her, their *thralls* would come to her aid. With a slight smile, she added in her own whisper, "Else I will gut him."

Hrafn seemed unconvinced. "Send him away until I am there." She understood that her brother trusted no one anymore—but she wanted answers and would not wait until later in the morning.

Instead, she took a step back and stood at Arik's side. "Arik Thorgrim will not harm me." She turned to face the man. "Will you?"

He eyed her and then Hrafn before he shook his head. She guided Arik toward her home, thankful the dwelling rested on the outskirts of their settlement. It was still early, and only a few folk had arisen. "Come quickly," she urged, not wanting anyone to see him. She led him inside the wooden longhouse, closing the door behind them.

Inside the dwelling, her *thrall*, Astrid, was preparing a hot porridge, along with oat cakes. The young slave's eyes widened at the sight of Arik, but she was wise enough to hold her tongue.

"Stoke the fire hotter," Katarina ordered, and the girl

added wood to warm the space. Arik remained quiet, and there was only the sound of the oak log cracking as it caught fire. She lit an oil lamp near the far end of the dwelling and moved to stand by the curtain that divided the living space. Though there was no reason to be nervous, Katarina wasn't quite certain how to begin. She wanted to know how he had arrived back at their shores, where the ship was now, and which men had traveled with him. And most of all, whether any of them were still alive.

"Are you hungry?" she asked, stalling while she gathered her thoughts. Without waiting for his answer, she retrieved a hot loaf of barley bread and gave it to him. "Here."

Arik paused a moment before he took it, but he nodded his thanks. Then he spoke in a language she had never heard before, foreign words that made no sense at all.

Katarina frowned and shook her head. "I do not understand you." A cold chill washed over her with the worry that something wasn't right. Arik Thorgrim wasn't acting like himself. Although it looked like him, could she have been wrong? Her instincts heightened, that something was amiss.

He ate the barley loaf and closed his eyes a moment, lost in his own thoughts.

"Is your name Arik?" she asked softly, not even knowing if he understood her words.

He gave a single nod but did not speak again.

"What happened to you?" She stood before him, studying his features intently. His brown eyes were the same, as was his dark hair, though it was cut shorter. She studied his face and saw that there was no longer a scar across his throat—his skin was smooth, unmarred. Her heartbeat quickened, as she wondered if he had been changed by the gods. What if he *had* died, but Freya had sent him back to her in a spirit form?

Katarina took a step backward, suddenly afraid of this man. She took a step toward her *thrall* and reached for her

16

blade. Discreetly, she unsheathed it and tucked it into a fold of her gown. It made her feel better to have the weapon, though she hoped she was wrong about Arik Thorgrim.

He walked toward the hearth fire and stood with his hands outstretched, welcoming the heat. His hair was still damp from the sea water, and his clothing was soaked. But when she studied him, she noticed that his garments were far different than those he had worn before. Instead of a belted woolen tunic and leggings, he wore a dark tunic closely fitted to his arms. It was unlike anything she had ever seen before.

He traveled to distant lands, she reminded herself. Perhaps it was clothing he had bought from a foreigner. But a strange tingling alerted her senses.

She moved closer and asked, "Do you remember who I am?"

He nodded again. "Katarina."

At the sound of his voice, she let out a slow breath of air. So he *could* speak. And if he remembered her name, then he might truly be Arik Thorgrim. No one else had told him her name—not even Hrafn.

But her doubts lingered. There were enough physical differences that made her question the truth of his return. Scars never disappeared—she knew that, all too well. It set her trust on edge, making her wonder if he was an outsider who only appeared similar to Arik.

He adjusted the sleeve of his tunic, which was soaked, and she understood that he wanted to get out of the wet clothing. Katarina motioned to Astrid. "Bring him dry clothing from my father's belongings."

A flutter of nerves passed over her, for she knew that Arik had other scars upon his chest. Were those gone, too? She pushed back her own uneasiness, gripping the blade in her hand. Her brother had been right. She shouldn't have gone with this man without being certain he was Arik Thorgrim.

"Take your wet clothing off while Astrid fetches you something dry to wear." She sat down on the other side of the longhouse, near the door. Arik didn't move, not even when her *thrall* returned with the clothes.

"Shall I help?" Astrid asked him, and he nodded. The slave tried to remove his tunic, but Katarina noticed that the edges were caught on small, round fasteners. When Astrid tried to pull the tunic apart, he stopped her, and slipped the circular object through a smaller hole. He continued unfastening the garment, and the dark blue outer tunic came off easily.

"Bring that to me," Katarina ordered her slave. She took the tunic and studied it, noticing the quality of the foreign clothing. The stitching was hardly visible at all, making her realize that this was an expensive piece. The round fasteners were made of a strange metal, not gold, but they were so perfectly cast, and she saw the value in them.

Arik wore another layer beneath the tunic, also held together by the round fasteners. This time, he stared at her while he undressed. His dark gaze held hers, and she grew aware of the charged intimacy between them. He peeled off the second layer, but a third garment of linen remained soaked to his skin. It should have frightened her to see him so exposed. Instead, she could not tear her eyes from him.

He had lost some of his muscles, but this was not a weak man. His shoulders were honed, his body tight. She stared at the exposed part of his chest, wondering what it would be like to slide her fingertips over his skin. A sudden flood of heat warmed her, and she could not understand the reaction.

Arik's brown eyes were watching her as if he wanted her hands upon him. His expression softened, and she jerked her attention away. *It isn't real.* But even so, her instinctive response humiliated her. It was foolish, born of her own insecurities and idle dreams.

She was startled to see Arik removing the last garment,

pulling the linen over his head. The sight of the man's bare chest shocked her. The scars were all gone, leaving only smooth skin in their place. Instead of a ruthless fighter, he was sleek and toned.

Her heart pounded at the sight. He was still staring at her, and the sight of him unclothed made her breath seize in her lungs. But she could no longer deny the evidence before her. To Astrid she ordered quietly, "Go and fetch my brother."

Then Katarina faced the stranger and revealed her blade. "I do not know what evil spirit you are. But you are not Arik Thorgrim."

CHAPTER TWO

Eric stared at the woman, recognizing the fear in her eyes. In truth, he had no idea what was happening to him. Weariness had caused him to simply accept what was before him—but this dream was becoming more real than he could have imagined. At first, he'd believed that he had survived the shipwreck and had landed upon the shores of Norway. But now, he was beginning to wonder.

It felt as if his life had been shattered into jagged pieces, put back together in ways he didn't understand. He had never before heard the language this woman had spoken…and yet he understood every word.

How was that even possible? It unnerved him, as if he had stepped into another man's life.

The cold chill that washed over him had nothing to do with the sea water and everything to do with the moments when he'd been drowning. He had felt the presence of someone else within his mind.

Some of the sailors had traveled to the Far East and had told stories of holy wise men who believed that death was only a doorway to another birth. They claimed that all men were brought back into life a second time, to change their mistakes. It wasn't the faith he'd been taught as a child…but what if it were true?

Could his soul have been reborn into another life? Or worse, switched with another man's?

When he studied this woman, he knew her somehow. He searched for memories, and the pieces came together. Katarina Larsdottir was her name, and she had an older brother and a younger sister. More memories came forward, and the sudden surge was overwhelming. He locked away the images, closing his mind against the tide of visions that were not his.

My God, he was going mad. Although he'd had many dreams that had left him shaken upon awakening, this was by far, the most vivid.

It isn't real, he repeated to himself. *None of it is real.* Not the primitive longhouses of this settlement, not the fierce maiden who stood before him, and certainly not the language she spoke. When he'd attempted to speak English, only confusion had flickered in her eyes. And somehow, he had understood the Norse language she was speaking.

It was unlike any dream he'd had before. He could still feel the heat of the fire warming his bare skin. His senses were alert, and the dark aroma of burning wood mingled with the earthen floor. He'd tasted the barley bread, and the food had eased his hunger. Never in his life had he experienced anything like this, and it unnerved him.

He stared back at the woman. Though she was beautiful, there was a sharpness to her. In her hand, she gripped a blade. From the coolness in her eyes, he knew she would not hesitate to strike if she believed he was dangerous.

He lifted his hands to show he meant no harm, but she never lowered the weapon. In her blue eyes, he saw a raw fear that belied her threatening manner. Eric held himself motionless, knowing that the slightest movement could provoke her.

He could not understand any of what was happening, and he didn't know whether any of this was real. But he believed one truth—if he told Katarina that he was not Arik Thorgrim, she would kill him where he stood.

There was no alternative but to try speaking the unfamiliar language and hope that the words held meaning. If this was all conjured from within his mind, then he would be able to speak. He concentrated, searching for the words he needed. But the harder he tried to think of the correct speech, the more he struggled. A sense of unrest heightened within him, and he struggled to find calm.

Let go, he told himself. *Trust that the words will be there.* If it was indeed naught but a dream, he would know what to say.

"I do not know what happened to me," he told her. "But I know this place. And I know you."

He let the foreign words flow through him, not understanding how he knew any of them. It was the strangest feeling, speaking words with the fluency of a man born to this place. And yet, she *did* seem to understand him.

The chill that washed over his body was a fear beyond any he had known. He was a man who needed to be in command of his life and in this, he had no control at all.

Katarina's fingers trembled, and for a long moment, she remained silent, almost unwilling to trust him. "Your scars are gone. What happened to them?"

"I do not know." He wanted to tell her the truth, that he had no scars—but he suspected that his life depended on his ability to become the man she called Arik Thorgrim. Until he awakened from this madness, he had to go along with it.

Katarina moved closer, still holding the blade. With one palm, she moved her bare hand over his chest, down his ribs. The light touch seared him, and he tried to hold back his response. But this woman fascinated him, for he'd never met anyone like her. Her face held the exotic beauty of a foreigner, and those blue eyes held the fierce strength of a goddess. Her long blond hair drifted around her hips as if it had never been cut.

Her fingers grazed his ribs, and his skin tightened as she continued to explore his chest. "Arik Thorgrim was in many battles. His flesh was scarred, the way yours is not." With a swift motion, she jerked the blade to the underside of his throat.

The coldness of the iron blade was all too real. He forced himself not to pull away while Katarina held the knife to his throat. Never in his life had he been faced with a situation like this. The women of his acquaintance were shy and well-mannered. Although they might have been irritated with their fathers or brothers, they would never dream of pulling a knife.

Swiftly, he stepped back and caught her wrist, tightening his grip. "Drop the blade, Katarina."

Her face held only fury. "Who are you?"

"You know who I am." He twisted her wrist and forced her to surrender the knife. Then he spun her around and held her against his chest. "I will not harm you, but neither will I let you try to kill me." She tried to wrench free of him, but he held her steady. In her eyes, he saw frustration blended with fear.

"What happened to you?" she asked. "Why did they say you were dead?"

Eric had no notion of how to reply. He was convinced that he had to be dead or dreaming, for this experience lacked all basis of reality. He softened his grip upon Katarina and said, "There is a great deal that I do not remember. Some memories were taken from me."

"What about the men who traveled with you? Where are they now?" she demanded.

"All are dead, save me."

"What of Geilir and Jokull?"

There was hatred in her tone when she spoke of the men.

But he did not remember either name and simply shook his head. "They were not traveling with me." He didn't know what else to tell her, but she seemed disappointed that they had not drowned.

Her head lowered, and he kept his hands upon her wrists, to prevent her from behaving in a rash manner. With her standing so near, the scent of her skin enticed him, like crushed flowers. Her slender body fit against him, but she seemed apprehensive.

For a moment, he stood before her, willing her to become calm. When she seemed less likely to kill him, he let her go. He took a moment to study his surroundings, and the sight of her dwelling brought back the feelings of uncertainty. The floor was earthen with straw scattered upon it. While the table and chair were both sturdy and clean, there were no carvings upon them. He saw no silver, no glass of any kind.

His mind fixed upon the details, and he studied the woman again. She could have stepped out of an oil painting from long ago, like Athena, the goddess of war. Her clothing was colorful and well made, but even the blade she'd held was primitive.

It was as if he'd fallen back a thousand years in time. He shook the thought away, knowing that all of this was only part of his dream.

"What else do you remember?" Katarina asked.

Eric struggled to think of what to say. He didn't want to say anything at all, but her insistence made it difficult to refuse. She wanted answers he could not give. And so, he allowed the foreign memories to intrude, searching for one that would silence her questions.

"You are Katarina Larssdottir," he said quietly. "And I remember that you had feelings for me long ago."

She wouldn't meet his gaze, but he saw the tell-tale flush upon her cheeks. "I was only a child then. A great deal has changed." Her denial held a trace of bitterness and an emotion he didn't recognize. Perhaps regret. "Just as you have changed. So much that I do not know you anymore."

He lifted his shoulders in a shrug. "I cannot answer why, for I do not know the reasons."

She did look at him then, and in her blue eyes, he saw the doubts. "I heard that you were struck down by a battle-ax. Eyker's brother, Björn, killed you. It was a lie, was it not?"

Eric gave her no answer, but he searched the memories. In his mind, he beheld the horrifying vision of a red-haired giant releasing a war cry, before a violent blow had struck his spine. His men had carried him on board a ship bound for his brother's home in East Anglia. And that night, a blood red moon had risen above the earth. He had seen the same moon last night as well.

He spoke again, but the words did not feel like his own. "Freya," he heard himself murmur. "I heard her voice."

With that, Katarina jerked free. She stepped backward toward the wall of the longhouse, apprehension in her eyes. "I don't believe you."

"Believe what you will." He was not a man who held any faith in the supernatural, but everything he'd encountered thus far had defied logic. There were no words to explain any of it.

He had heard a woman's voice on the wind. *Not yet*, she had said. And whether it was the voice of an angel or the voice of a Viking goddess, he couldn't know.

But what he did know was that he had somehow crossed into a different world. The only question was whether this was a dream or an afterlife, perhaps purgatory. Or even a reincarnation that the holy men of the East had spoken of. None of it held any meaning—but he was stranded here until he awakened.

He needed to understand what had happened, what had become of his father and his home. It was the only way to make sense of it. He intended to find a ship bound for

England and gain passage upon it. In the meantime, all he could do was make a place for himself.

Katarina remained far away from him, her expression guarded. In time, she straightened. "I do not know if you are Arik Thorgrim or a liar. But if the gods brought you back from death…" Her words trailed away, as if she could find no other explanation.

The thought sobered him, for he didn't know how to respond. It was far easier to deny all of it, to let himself believe it was only a dream.

She lowered her knife and tossed the dry clothing to him before turning her back. "Put those on."

Eric pulled the long-sleeved undershirt of linen over his head, and it fell down to his knees. There were no buttons—only a few ties to draw it closed. There was also a blue woolen tunic to cover the shirt. He guessed that the leather cord was meant to be a belt, and he fastened it. The trousers were shapeless and ended at his knees, though she had given him long socks. As he drew them on, the primitive clothing reminded him of the Viking age. The thought entered his mind that perhaps when he'd fallen into the ocean, he'd crossed through time on his journey toward death.

But no. Such things were not possible.

A strong scent of smoke caught his attention after he'd finished dressing. Eric turned toward the hearth. "The oat cakes are burning," he warned Katarina.

She let out a low curse and seized the hot pan from where it lay close to the hearth. The moment her hand touched it, she yelped, dropping the pan on the earthen floor.

Eric searched the dwelling and found a bucket of water in one corner. He dipped a wooden bowl into the container and brought the cool water to her. He took her hand, submerging it in the water. She inhaled sharply, but he forced her to keep it there. "The pain will pass."

"The pain is nothing." But she closed her eyes as if to

push back the discomfort. For a moment, he held her hand, letting the water cool her burned skin. At last, she faced him and tried to remove her hand from the water. "I will be all right. Let go of me."

Her eyes met his, and in them, he saw her embarrassment, joined with nervousness. It was clear that his very presence made her uncomfortable.

"Katarina, you have nothing to fear from me." He would never dream of harming a woman. To underscore his words, he released her hand, and she shook the water droplets away.

"I am *not* afraid of you." Even so, she turned her gaze to her burned fingers, as if she didn't want to see him watching her. Her eyes remained troubled, but it was the beginning of peace between them.

After he set the bowl down, Katarina went to the door. "When Astrid returns with my brother, she will send word to your father so he can prepare a place for you."

In other words, she wouldn't allow him to stay here. It wasn't surprising, and yet, he found himself unwilling to be in the company of more strangers. He needed answers before he faced anyone else. Although Katarina did not yet trust him, she was his best hope for finding a strategy to navigate this place with their unusual clothing and customs. He held his ground and crossed his arms. "I would be grateful for a little more time before I go." A few hours, at the very least. If he made any more blunders, his ignorance could cost him his life.

"What do you mean?"

He crouched down near the hearth, considering his words carefully. "I have no doubt my father will want to see me. But before that, I would like to better understand what has happened since I left."

She seemed to relax, nodding her agreement. "For a little while, then. But since you were chosen to take his place as *jarl* of our tribe, you will have to go soon."

Eric didn't know what to think of that, for he could not be leader of these people. He hardly knew where he was, much less anything about their tribe. And he wasn't ready to trust another man's memories.

Katarina offered him the burned oat cakes, along with barley bread and porridge. She picked at the cakes, but her thoughts seemed to drift away. Eric tried to ask a few questions, but she gave one-word answers. Something was weighing upon her, but he could not guess what it was.

The spoon she gave him was carved from a sea shell, not made of silver or tin. He had never seen one like this. Nearly all of the dishes were made of wood, save the horn she'd used to pour him a cup of mead. There was no porcelain or crystal. Not even any candles—only the oil lamps, which appeared to be burning rendered fat. He didn't know what to think of her manner of living. More and more, this existence appeared to be ancient.

Her servant, Astrid, returned and behind the woman stood Katarina's brother. The warrior entered the space, his left hand resting upon his belt. He wore the fur of a wolf wrapped around his shoulders, along with leather trousers and a shirt. An enormous battle-ax hung at his waist, and his right arm was a stump below the elbow. Despite the loss, Eric knew not to underestimate the man's fighting skills.

Don't move, a voice seemed to warn from within him. *Or he will cut you down.*

It seemed a logical conclusion, and he met the man's gaze evenly. Within seconds, the name came to his memory, and he greeted Katarina's brother. "Hrafn."

He knew with certainty that Hrafn had a vicious temper. From the way the man was staring at him, the man appeared to be contemplating how best to kill him. "Has he harmed you?" he asked Katarina.

"No," she answered. "But Arik has changed since we saw him last."

28

It became clear that they intended to discuss this in front of him, and Hrafn appeared to be the sort of man who would kill first and ask questions later.

Eric stood slowly and faced the man. "Will you sit and join us?"

Hrafn eyed him for a moment, and then turned to his sister. His hand rested upon his battle-ax, and his expression darkened. "What do you want me to do, Katarina? Shall I throw him out?"

Chapter Three

Katarina didn't know how to answer her brother. She had known the man sitting beside her all her life—and yet he was a stranger. His clothing was foreign and his mannerisms were nothing at all like Arik Thorgrim's. All his scars had vanished.

It's not him.

In her heart, she knew it—and yet, if she told her brother this, he would slay him in a heartbeat. Despite all that had happened in the past year, every time she looked at Arik, she saw the man she had once adored.

She could not watch him die—at least, not until she had the answers she needed. "It is Arik Thorgrim," she lied. "I believe he was brought back from the afterworld by Freya." The words slipped freely from her lips, though she inwardly questioned what was real and what was not.

Hrafn's tension didn't diminish, but he took a step forward. To Arik, he demanded, "If what Katarina says is true, tell me how I received this scar." He turned and revealed the jagged edge of his throat. The scar was a mottled red and white color, and she held her breath, wondering if Thorgrim would give the correct answer.

There was a slight moment of hesitation, then Arik spoke. "A wolf tried to kill you. You're wearing his pelt now." He paused a moment and added, "You lost the arm when we were boys. A raider struck you down."

Hrafn's shoulders lowered, and a faint look of approval crossed his face. He exchanged a look with her as if to say— You were right. Katarina couldn't quite muster a smile, for her own thoughts were too confused. But she did nod to her brother, and that seemed to be enough.

He moved in and gripped Arik's hand. "Welcome home, Thorgrim."

Katarina poured cups of ale for the men and retreated back a short distance, hoping they would forget her presence while they talked. She sat at a small weaving loom and began working over the threads.

The mindless task helped to calm her troubled thoughts. Her brother and Arik had been friends for many years. It was only in the last two years that there had been tension, when she'd confessed her feelings for Arik. Hrafn had been angry with him for not wanting to wed her, but then Arik had left. She had been heartbroken, but now she believed it was better this way.

It made it easier to concentrate on revenge.

Leif had asked her to wed him, and she was considering it. She did not need a marriage based upon love or affection. Protection was what she wanted now, and he had proved himself worthy when she'd been attacked.

She closed her eyes to fight back the memories. That night, she had been surrounded by drunken men who had beaten her when she'd tried to fight them off. She had no doubt at all that she would have been raped by all of them, had it not been for Leif's arrival. He had saved her from the men, and for that, she would always be grateful.

He kept pressuring her to wed him, but she would not agree. At least, not until he helped her find the men who had killed Ingirún and bring them to justice. It was a means of delaying their joining, for Leif's physical size made her wary. After being attacked, she needed time to get over her fears. But at least she trusted that he would keep her safe.

Katarina glanced down and realized that she'd woven a snarl of colors into the wool. With a sigh, she began untangling the threads, wishing she could as easily smooth out the uneven edges of her life. The past was finished, and she could only look toward a future where no one could ever threaten her again. All she had to do was please Leif, and that was simple enough. He was very clear in his expectations of a wife.

But when she shifted her gaze back to Arik Thorgrim, she remembered what it had felt like to see those brown eyes staring back at her. His skin, though cool, had been a welcome comfort, and it had drawn her imagination down a path she hadn't expected. From the moment Arik had returned, she'd been drawn closer. Even when she'd touched his bare skin, she had not been afraid of him—not the way she was with other men.

Let him go, she reminded herself. If she allowed her feelings to weaken, it would only hurt when he left again.

"What became of Svala?" she heard her brother ask.

Katarina's hands stilled against the wool she was weaving. Even the name sent a wave of annoyance through her. Svala, the blond, blue-eyed woman, had followed Arik to the Anglo-Saxon shores. And though to everyone else, she appeared to be virtuous, Katarina had never trusted her.

Like as not, it was jealousy. But she was glad that the woman no longer had her claws in Arik.

"She betrayed me," was all Arik said.

Katarina was glad to hear it, though it shouldn't matter. Why should she care what happened between them? It was over and done with now.

The need to be outside, to walk away from the uncertainties building inside her, was growing far too strong.

She rose from her loom and went to the door. Before she could leave, Arik asked, "Where are you going?"

She didn't truly know, but answered, "Just outside the door." Lifting her chin, she opened the door. But a moment later, he was at her side.

"Not alone."

She stared at him in disbelief. "My brother and you will keep me safe." There was no danger here; of that, she was certain. "If I go anywhere, I will take Astrid with me or another thrall."

He sent a look toward her brother as if he didn't believe that. "A female slave cannot defend her. Katarina should go nowhere without a man to guard her."

Her brother's mouth tightened, and he gave a stiff nod. "I agree."

Arik glanced back at Hrafn. "Or I will walk with her." There was a silent agreement exchanged between them.

"I do not need a guard at every moment," she protested. She had her own weapon and knew well how to use it. It had taken time to regain the courage to walk alone, but she rarely went anywhere beyond the settlement walls. There were always men and women nearby.

Right now, she wanted some space from both of them and a chance to think. She took a step back. "Perhaps I will go and see Leif. Then, at least, you needn't worry about the need for someone to guard me."

Her brother's expression darkened. "Katarina, not now." Although Hrafn had not forbidden her to wed Leif, neither had he supported the match. It was likely because Leif came from lands far away, and his customs were different from their own.

"If I want to go and see Leif, I will." Her words came out harsher than she'd intended, but she didn't want her brother to begin shadowing her. She refused to allow herself to be ruled by fear.

She signaled for Astrid to accompany her and left the longhouse, letting the door fall shut behind her. Once she was outside, the tension tightened within her. Her mind was filled with such turmoil at Arik's return.

Why did one man have such an effect upon her? She had never anticipated the old feelings coming back. But when Arik had come to stand beside her, a flare of interest had returned. His very presence was dangerous to her heart— especially when his eyes fixed upon her. And that was why she had decided to go to Leif. Right now, she needed the reminder that she should marry someone else, not the man who had sailed away and left her behind.

Leif had never mistreated her and had always been kind. And the sooner she set aside idle dreams of Arik Thorgrim, the better.

"Your father has reclaimed the tribe for his own," Hrafn said. "You will have to see him tonight to take your rightful position as jarl."

Eric searched through the visions in his mind for memories of the jarl. The man was Thorgrim's father, and he vaguely recalled that Arik had been chosen by the people as the successor. But Thorgrim hadn't wanted the position and had left Rogaland.

His head was aching while he tried to make sense of his surroundings. He was beginning to recognize this place from the Viking era. An icy chill filled his veins, unnerving him.

"Were you listening to what I said?" Hrafn demanded, interrupting his thoughts.

Eric shook his head. "Forgive me, but my mind went astray." He knew the man had been speaking about their leader, and he offered, "I will go and speak with him if you wish."

That seemed to pacify Hrafn, and Eric went to stand near the door. Despite his promise, he was still concerned about Katarina. It did not seem that her brother approved of this man called Leif.

"Who is Leif?" he asked Hrafn. "I do not remember him."

Hrafn shrugged. "He asked Katarina to marry him. But I don't like the way she changes around him. She becomes nearly a servant to him, and she was never that way before."

His expression held wariness, and he added, "Leif says all the right things, as if he knows what you want him to say. Have you ever met a man who appears to be perfect and wonder if he can be trusted?"

No, he hadn't. Usually men like that were trying to hide something. And although it wasn't his concern, Eric considered whether he should meet her intended. "Do you want me to follow her and ensure that she is safe?" Then, he could determine if there was any cause for worry. Eric started to open the door, but Hrafn stopped him.

"My sister grieved for you. She was not the same after you left, and she hardly ate or slept. Unless you plan to take her as your own wife, do not interfere with this. Let me handle Leif."

Eric met the man's gaze, understanding her brother's protective instincts. Although he had not been the one to break Katarina's heart, he recognized the need for distance. It was a vivid reminder that this was not his life—not truly. It didn't matter what broken memories he had about this woman—none of them were his.

He was Eric Fielding, the Marquess of Thorgraham. He had been born in the year 1787, and he lived at the family estate in Somerford, England. His father was the duke, and one day, he would inherit the title. It was the life he'd always known. Not this.

All around him were men who carried battle-axes and wore furs. He was speaking an ancient language and living in a home where the floor was made of earth. Nothing was the same, and he didn't want to even imagine that he was trapped within this primitive world. There had to be a way out of the nightmare.

If he thought about it too much, he would go mad. It was easier to live moment by moment, trusting that the answers would come.

Hrafn stepped in front of him. "Did you hear what I said, Arik? Leave my sister alone."

"I will not confront Leif," he acceded, "but I do intend to watch over her. If there is danger…"

"You will send for me."

Eric gave a nod. Hrafn was a strong enough fighter, even one-handed, but was it enough? "Even so, I will help you protect her, if there is the need." He wasn't certain how he could fight against men like these, full-bred warriors with the strength beyond any he'd ever seen. Yet, he believed that a strong mind and swift movement could overcome a lack of brute strength.

Hrafn sent him a doubtful look. "You need a blade." He went to his belongings and withdrew an iron dagger with a bone hilt. "Arm yourself with this, and I'll come with you."

Eric tucked the knife into his belt and followed Hrafn outside. The sun rimmed the horizon, and all around him, he saw men and women working. Some men were seated, sharpening their weapons, while on the far end of the settlement, he saw a woman carrying a jug of water. Nearby, the skin of a reindeer was stretched over a frame, and the sight of it made him uneasy.

No one treated animal hides for clothing anymore. He stopped for a moment, taking in his surroundings. This was not the Norway of 1811. It was more like the Norway from 811, over a thousand years ago.

His jaw clenched at the sight. None of this was real. It

couldn't be. But there was one way to test his theory.

Eric unsheathed the blade Hrafn had given him. The bone handle was balanced, and the edge appeared deadly. He touched his thumb to the edge and blood welled from it. The sting of pain was real, as was the blood.

Dreams usually didn't bring pain. Or blood.

He cleaned the blade and tucked it back into his belt, but inwardly, he was troubled. The people stared at him as he passed, though he was now dressed like one of them. Some murmured words of welcome, while other men stared at him in disbelief.

On the far side of the settlement, he saw a man wearing black, leaning on a carved staff. The man wore a wooden cross around his neck, and his head was shaved in a tonsure, like a monk's.

"Meddling priest," Hrafn muttered. "His name is Father Anais, and he arrived a short time ago."

Eric eyed the old man. "He appears harmless."

"He should return to Rome and take his teachings with him," Hrafn countered. He started to walk away, but Eric paused in front of the priest. He had been raised to be polite to members of the clergy.

"Good day to you, Father."

The priest lowered his head in greeting. "May the peace of Christ go with you."

Eric realized that the man was younger than he'd originally believed, perhaps in his forties. "Your travels must have brought you a long way, have they not?"

The priest appeared surprised at the question. However, Eric has his own reasons for asking.

"Why, yes, I have journeyed far over the past few years."

"And when did you leave Rome?"

The priest thought a moment. "It was in the spring. In the Year of Our Lord, eight hundred and eight."

Although Eric nodded, shielding his reaction, inwardly,

his thoughts had turned to ice. Was it possibly true? Had he traveled back in time?

If so, how could he ever return home again?

Katarina spied Leif outside his dwelling, gathering firewood. He had no thrall, and his home was smaller than hers, but that had never mattered. She didn't mind living a simple life, so long as she had a home of her own.

He had sailed here a little over a year ago. From the moment he'd arrived, he had sought out her father—almost as if he had known Lars somehow. He had been kind to her sister and had tried to befriend Hrafn. But for some reason, her brother had remained distant. It was likely because he thought no man was good enough for his sister.

Leif's broad shoulders flexed as he hefted his ax and split a log in half. His body was heavily muscled and so broad, she could not span his torso with both arms. He trained every day for fighting, and few men tried to oppose him.

She had no doubt at all that Leif would protect her from all harm…and yet, often she worried about what it would mean to share a marriage bed with him. Her instincts made her shy away from any physical affection, and she feared that the dark memories of the attack might trespass on their wedding night.

You are still a virgin, she reminded herself. It will be all right.

And yet, the thought of succumbing to his touch terrified her. She steeled herself, trying to push back the fear. As her husband, he would have the right to claim her body. Surely he would be gentle.

She clung to that hope and stepped forward to speak with him. "Hello, Leif."

He turned at her greeting, and a smile crossed his face.

"Katarina. You are a welcome surprise. I had not expected to see you this early." He nodded toward the fallen pile of wood. "Will you come and help me?" Then Leif dismissed Astrid, saying, "Your mistress is safe with me. You may wait for her over there." The thrall obeyed, seemingly eager to depart.

She did, picking up several small logs. Leif gathered the rest of the wood, and she followed him inside his house. The interior was dark and smelled of last night's meal. A few bones were scattered upon the floor, and when she stepped inside, his dog snarled at her. Though she had tried to be kind to the animal in the past, she knew better than to approach it. The hair was standing up on the dog's back, and she froze in place.

Leif only shook his head and nudged the dog outside with one leg. "Do not mind him. Build a fire, and you can join me for a morning meal."

Katarina started to say that she'd already eaten but decided that there was no harm in sitting with him while he ate. He set down the logs, stacking six of them in a neat pile before arranging the others. She added her own wood to the fire, but before she could add tinder, Leif stopped her.

"Wait a moment." He removed every piece of wood she'd brought and pointed toward his own arrangement. "There is a better way to stack them." He rearranged the first two pieces of wood, although she couldn't tell why his method was any different. Then he reminded her, "There is less smoke if you place them this way."

She didn't know why he cared so much about the way firewood was stacked, but saw no reason to voice an argument. "I did not think it would make any difference."

At that, Leif reached out to take her hand. "The smoke can be heavy, and I would not want you to ever feel uncomfortable in my home."

She supposed that was reasonable. When she had straw

and wood shavings in a small nest, she used flint to start the fire. As she leaned down to blow the ember into flames, she sensed him watching her.

Her face flushed, and when she glanced back, she saw the flash of unmistakable desire. The hair stood up on the back of her neck, and a violent memory clashed inside her. Male hands holding her down, while another tore her clothing apart. Bile rose up in the back of her throat, and her pulse quickened.

It's nothing, she told herself. Leif wants to marry you. He was not the one who hurt you that night—he saved you.

She closed her eyes and took slow, deep breaths to calm herself. But the fears did not diminish at all. Though she didn't believe Leif would ever hurt her, there was no denying that she would have to submit to him. And his large body frightened her.

"Why did you come to me, Katarina?" Leif asked in a low voice.

Katarina jerked her attention back to him, and she straightened. "There was no reason. I was out walking, and I thought I would stop to see you." She could not tell him the truth, that she had needed to clear her mind from thoughts of Arik Thorgrim.

His features softened, and Leif moved in closer. "I am glad of it." He wrapped his arms around her, and she tried to relax. She knew he only meant to show her affection. And yet, when he leaned in to kiss her neck, she felt skittish. Katarina jerked to her feet, needing a distraction. Confusion was roiling through her mind, paired with guilt. "Shall I prepare you something to eat? You must be hungry."

He paused a moment, his expression narrowed at her discomfort. "There is no reason for you to be afraid of me, Katarina."

She took a breath and steadied herself. "I know. But... there are times when memories of that night return to me."

Leif took a step closer. He reached out to stroke her hair, winding the thick strands around his wrist. His hand settled upon her nape, and he said quietly, "To overcome fear, you must face it."

Did he mean now, at this moment? Her stomach clenched at the thought, and her hand moved to the blade at her waist, without thinking.

"When I am ready," she acceded. "Not before." She straightened her spine and regarded Leif, changing the subject. "What did you want to eat for your morning meal?"

He sent her a light smile. "I am glad to see that you have found your courage." Pointing toward the corner of his dwelling, he added, "You may make oak cakes for me, if you wish."

Katarina went to measure out the oats. The task calmed her, and she was glad he hadn't pushed her. Leif knew what had happened that night, and one day, she would forget about the attack. It was over and done with.

She pounded the oats, adding rendered fat and water, preparing them in the same manner as Astrid had this morn. Though her cooking was not as good as the slave's, it was edible.

"It pleases me to have you in my home," Leif said quietly. "You will make a good wife, Katarina."

She tried to manage a smile. "I hope so." As she cooked the oat cakes, she turned to study the interior of his home.

"Leif, will we have enough supplies this winter? I do not see any grain or meat stored. At least, not much." They would need far more than this to survive the winter. It was late summer, and she had already begun drying fruits and preserving whatever she could. Her brother had hunted deer and elk, and he brought back fresh fish every day. She'd salted and dried a goodly portion of their supplies, but Leif was lacking his own stores.

"I intend to trade for more," he acknowledged. "Or I will

sail to the warmer lands over the winter, and you need only provide for yourself until my return."

Katarina frowned, for there was no assurance that he would return. She did not want to face the winter with hardly any food. "If you bring back meat, I can begin preserving it. There may be some fruit I can dry or perhaps later I could—"

Leif put up a hand. "Katarina, trust in me. I will bring back whatever is needed. Do you doubt that I can conquer our enemies and take what we need?"

"No." But the reminder that he intended to plunder and seize from others was sobering. She turned her attention to the oat cakes, turning them over to cook on the other side. Leif's gaze seemed to burn through her while she worked.

He came up behind her, his hands moving to her shoulders. The moment he did, she felt uneasiness sliding over her. He caressed her arms and drew his arms around her waist. "You need not worry about anything, Katarina," he murmured, pulling her against him. His mouth descended to her throat, and she felt her body tremble from uneasiness.

There came upon her the sharp sense that it was wrong to wed this man for the sake of protection. He ought to have a woman who would care for him—not one whose heart had once belonged to another man. And especially not one who was frightened of joining with a man.

As he kissed her neck, her uncertainties gathered and rose higher. Though she did not push him away, she questioned her own motives. It felt as if she were using him.

Leif turned her around, and his mouth came down upon hers. The kiss was gentle, coaxing more from her in a physical reminder that she would soon belong to him. Was that what she truly wanted? Katarina softened her mouth but couldn't quite bring herself to kiss him back.

He broke the kiss and stared at her. "What is troubling you?"

She could not possibly tell him the truth. Instead, she blurted out, "Arik Thorgrim has returned."

There was a barely perceptible tension in him. "I thought he was dead."

"So did I." She didn't pull away from his embrace, but he tightened his grip upon her shoulders. Most of their tribe knew that she'd once held feelings for Arik, and that he hadn't returned them. Even Leif was aware of it, though he was new to their settlement.

But that was in the past. She had learned the necessity of letting go, and she had chosen Leif as her new protector. In time, she was certain she would learn to care for him.

He stroked back a lock of her hair. "Has he done anything to threaten you, Katarina?"

She straightened and met his gaze openly. "No, of course not. His return means nothing at all."

But in spite of the words, she feared that Arik's return would change everything.

CHAPTER FOUR

Eric followed Hrafn past dozens of people, toward a large longhouse near the center of their settlement. The scent of fresh fish was redolent in the air, and several women were busy cooking at outdoor hearths while children chased each other in a game. A few dogs sniffed at his legs, before they moved away.

As he walked, he kept his gaze fixed upon the dwelling ahead, his thoughts still hazy with confusion. He rubbed at the wound on his thumb where he'd drawn blood. It held a slight ache, and his body had gone cold at the thought that this was not a dream.

But whether it was a dream or not, he had to find a way out of this place, back to his father's home. Only then would he find the answers he sought. He needed a ship, and then he could navigate to England.

He slowed his pace, studying his surroundings. Never in his life could he have conjured such a settlement within his thoughts. There were no carriages, no brick buildings or architecture of any kind. And yet, the women wore jewels and gold. They were clearly a proud folk, ready to defend their homes and their families with a sword or a battle-ax.

He caught a glimpse of Katarina leaving one of the dwellings, followed by her *thrall*, Astrid. Her long blond hair had come slightly unbraided, but her wild appearance only intrigued him. She was tall and carried herself differently from other women he'd known. Her hand rested at the weapon sheathed at her waist, and he didn't doubt she could gut any man who attempted to harm her. She glanced over in his direction, and though she acknowledged him with a nod, her eyes remained troubled.

With reluctance, he forced his attention back to Hrafn. The man's expression held a knowing look, but he said nothing.

They reached the longhouse, and Hrafn kept his voice low, saying again, "Your father has claimed your place as *jarl*. You must take it back."

Eric gave no reaction, for he had no intention of taking a leadership role in this place. What would he possibly know about reigning over this settlement? He had come with Hrafn in the hopes of negotiating for a ship to take him back to England. Though he wasn't certain how he would bargain for anything since he possessed nothing of value, all he could do was try.

He followed Hrafn inside, and the moment he entered the space, the room grew hushed. There were only men standing around, save a single female servant pouring drinks. At the far end, there was a large wooden chair, and a man with dark hair stood up and stared at him.

A numb sensation caught him in the throat, while ice flooded through his veins. For this man looked exactly like his father, Gregory. He possessed the same dark eyes, the same stern demeanor of a man determined to make his son follow the path of duty.

God in heaven, Eric thought. He must be dead. For it could not be a coincidence that his own father bore such a striking resemblance to this man.

Visions crashed over him, silencing any words he might say. His mind blurred with memories that didn't belong to him. Eric closed his eyes a moment, searching through the sea of thoughts for the right name.

Valdr. His father...and yet, not his father. Cold tightened his skin, but he forced himself to take a step forward.

A slight flicker of relief passed over the *jarl*'s face before he masked it. The man's dark hair was longer than Gregory's, tied back with a length of cord. The edges were rimmed with silver, showing his age. A beard covered his face, and he wore a dark leather tunic with leggings of a lighter color. A sword hung at his side, and he wore rings of gold on his hands and a jeweled arm band.

"You've returned," Valdr said by way of greeting. The old man took a step forward, and for a fleeting moment, Eric wasn't certain if he was meant to bow or embrace the man. He stood his ground, staring back at the leader. For a moment, he studied Valdr's features, trying to understand what had happened. Was this his own father reborn into another life? Or was he caught in purgatory, lost within the centuries?

An ache gripped his heart, and he wondered what to say. "I have," was all he could manage.

The man studied him intently, and his gaze shifted into doubts. "And what of the battle-ax that cut you down?"

There was no logical explanation. Eric had felt the phantom pain of a wound upon his spine, but it was not his. "I do not remember."

There were a thousand questions roiling within him and no answers at all. But he sensed the danger if he did not give this man a strong reason why he was alive. These people were eager to believe in divine intervention and supernatural phenomenon, and he supposed that was as good a reason as any.

"The gods willed me to live," he said, meeting the gaze of the leader, and then turning to the people surrounding him. "I thought I was dying, but I heard the voice of a woman on the wind."

At that, several men stepped backward, murmuring amongst themselves about Freya.

The *jarl* nodded his head, but gave no reaction to Eric's words. "Come with me." He beckoned for him to follow. "We will drink, and you will tell me what has happened."

He didn't know how he would manage that when he didn't know the truth himself. He remembered only fragmented moments of the shipwreck. Even so, Eric joined Valdr, still unsettled by the strong resemblance between this man and his father.

More than all else, it felt as if his life had been switched with Arik Thorgrim's. It made him feel displaced, trapped in a world he didn't know or understand. But why had it happened?

As he walked back to join Valdr, a hand brushed against his. Eric turned and saw an old woman watching him. White streaks blended within her black hair, and her ancient skin was wrinkled and gaunt. Her clothing had been fashioned from several animal skins, and she wore a cloak with black feathers sewn upon it. In one hand, she carried a brass staff.

A shudder passed over him, for she reminded him of the witches he'd read about in fairytales as a boy. Although her gaze was not malicious, there was a knowing look in her eyes that unnerved him.

But he walked past her, continuing to follow the *jarl*. Valdr led him into a small corner of the longhouse, partitioned from the rest of the gathering space. He offered Eric a goblet of ale and bade him to sit down.

Valdr paused a moment and regarded him. "I should have you killed."

They were the very last words he'd expected to hear. It took an effort to keep his reaction shielded. "And why is that?"

"You do not look like my son. There is a resemblance, but you are weak and thin."

Eric traced the rim of his goblet, knowing that he had to tread carefully. "I have been gone a long time." It was true, and no one could deny that. He understood that Valdr had brought him here to prove his identity. If he could convince the man that he was Arik Thorgrim, he would be allowed to live—or else this man would cut him down.

"Who are you?" Valdr demanded. He drained his ale and set the goblet aside, steepling his hands. There was an unreadable expression on his face, as if he anticipated lies.

"You know who I am," Eric said.

The man eyed him, as if he didn't believe it at all. "Tell me where you traveled."

Eric tried to think of the proper words to describe England and settled on, "East Anglia." He searched through the memories within his mind, but it was as if those had been lifted away. He did not know what had brought Arik Thorgrim across the sea, but he had to trust his instincts.

Valdr nodded. "You went to see your brother."

There was a hint of a question in his words, but Eric shook his head. He felt certain he had not seen Thorgrim's brother. "I never reached Magnus's settlement."

The name felt right, and Valdr seemed to relax at the mention of it. "Tell me more."

He searched his mind for the truth, but again, there was nothing there. He tried to think of anything else he could tell the older man and finally gave what he could. "A woman betrayed me. Her name was Svala."

Valdr's jaw tightened at the mention of her. "Go on."

But there was nothing to say about the woman. He could not even imagine her in memory—everything was gone, as if he had willed her to disappear. The only face that remained was Katarina's.

Instead, he told Valdr of Björn, who had struck him down. Then he recounted the blood moon he had seen and the shipwreck. The story came spilling out of him, though he knew it made little sense. And yet, the longer he spoke, the more Valdr appeared to believe it.

"You crossed back from Valhalla. No man can return from there and be unchanged." His gaze passed over Eric's form as if it had been justified it in that way.

More and more, Eric was becoming convinced that he was somehow caught within a Viking world. This language, the gods they had spoken of—even their clothing and customs were ancient. The thought was impossible...and yet, with each moment that passed, he was starting to believe it.

Valdr unsheathed the sword at his side and held it balanced between his palms. "I do not think you can fight with this anymore. The gods took your strength as a sacrifice when they returned you to us."

Eric did not deny it. Although he was strong enough among his peers and quite good at riding, he could not hope to fight against men built like barbarians. "I have no need to fight our own men."

"And what of our enemies?"

Eric understood that this was a test meant to determine his loyalties. "If any enemies attack my friends, I will defend them." Although, he rather wished he had a pistol, considering it was far more effective than a sword. Gunpowder trumped brute strength every time.

"You have responsibilities here," Valdr continued. "And yet, you turned your back on your people, seeking adventure for your own gain. You do not deserve to be *jarl*."

The words were an echo of censure his own father might have spoken, except that he was meant to be the duke. "I never wanted to be *jarl*."

"You were chosen. And then you abandoned everyone, forcing me to protect our people." Valdr's voice lowered, and he added, "You were meant to take this place, my son. More so than your brother."

A sudden emptiness caught hold of him, for in his

previous life, he had never had any siblings. After Eric's mother had died, the duke had been reluctant to wed again. He'd never truly understood why his father refused to sire another heir. Often, he'd wished that Gregory would fulfill that expectation, so the burden could be lifted from his own shoulders. But his father had never remarried.

"I do not intend to stay here," he told the *jarl.* "I will return to East Anglia." He had to visit his homeland to discover what had happened to his family. If he found Viking or ancient settlements there, then he would know for certain that he had gone back in time.

Valdr's face turned thunderous. "You will not leave Rogaland. I forbid it."

The words were a gauntlet thrown in his face. Eric was incredulous that the man would treat him like a petulant child. It reminded him of Gregory's insistence that he embrace his duties as a future duke—when he'd never wanted that life.

"Do you?" he asked quietly. As far as he was concerned, the *jarl* could do nothing to stop him from leaving. And with that, Eric walked out.

He strode across the longhouse, past the old woman who tried to stop him. He continued and had nearly reached the doorway when he heard her voice from behind him. "I know from whence you came."

The old woman's words stopped him cold. For they were spoken in English.

When he spun around, she only gave him a kindly smile and said, "I am *Móðir* Gerda, the *volva* of this tribe. Come to me this night, and we will walk beneath the moon. I will tell you what you wish to know."

Katarina carried a basket over her arm and began walking toward the forest. Her mind was heavy with thoughts of Leif and his lack of supplies. She could not simply stand aside and assume that he would provide enough. And if that meant gathering more, she would do it. She set snares daily, and this time, she intended to preserve the meat for the winter.

Though she didn't relish the idea of going alone into the woods, neither did she want to be a burden upon her brother. Other women gathered food each day, carrying only a blade for protection. So could she. She pushed back her apprehension and forced herself to walk.

Before she crossed the meadow, she saw Arik striding toward her. She slowed her pace so he could catch up. "You should not be here without an escort."

Katarina agreed with him, but did not want to appear a coward. She touched the blade at her waist. "I have a weapon. There is no need to fear for my sake."

"No woman should walk alone. A stranger could come into these woods and attack you unawares. I will not leave you defenseless." He moved to her side to prove his point.

"And you will protect me?" she teased, eying him. "Without a weapon? Or would you borrow my blade?"

His gaze grew serious. "I would use whatever was necessary. My fists, stones—even your blade, if needed."

She believed him. Although he had lost a great deal of strength, there was a quiet certainty within him that brought her reassurance. "All right."

He began walking alongside her and added, "I also wanted to speak with you."

So that was the true reason he'd come. She shrugged and continued walking. "What is it?"

He followed her into the forest, along the narrow trail. The afternoon sun rose high above them, casting shadows over the narrow saplings. "I need to return to East Anglia."

Katarina paused, startled that he would want to go so soon. "You only just arrived home. Why would you want to go back?" She wondered if his brother was in trouble, or if there was another reason…like a wife he had left behind.

"I have my own reasons." His voice was calm, giving away nothing. "But I wanted to ask you how I can get a ship."

She wasn't about to be deterred from her curiosity. "Did you leave a family there? Is that the reason?"

He sent her an incredulous look. "I hardly had time for that, Katarina."

"You were gone for over a year," she reminded him. "And after you survived a shipwreck, all you want to do is return to East Anglia? What else should I think?"

He stopped walking and rested his hand against a tree trunk. His gaze turned pensive. "My ship was lost at sea. I have to have another."

He was hiding his true reasons. "Arik, if you found happiness with Svala and are going back to her, so be it. I wish you well." She hated the edge of jealousy that hung within her voice. There was no reason to be envious, for she had a man of her own now. Let Arik Thorgrim do whatever he wished.

"Not at all." He startled her when he moved forward and took her hand. "I know that you were upset when I left. But my reasons for leaving Rogaland now have nothing to do with another woman."

Her thoughts scattered at the pressure of his palm on hers. Why did he have such an effect upon her? A year was more than enough time to forget her infatuation. And yet, she could not deny that this man unraveled her good sense.

Katarina forced a smile and answered, "As you say."

If he wanted to leave again, it mattered not to her. She pulled back her hand, needing to regain her concentration.

Just because Arik Thorgrim had accompanied her did not mean anything at all.

"Your father might help you with a ship—" she started to say, but then thought better of it. "No. He will not allow you to leave, since you only just returned. He will want you to stay for some time."

"I know he does." Arik's voice was cool and unsympathetic. "But he is not in command of my life. Let him be *jarl*, if that is what he wants."

"He wants you to lead us." Katarina was well aware of Valdr's frustration. Whether or not Arik wanted to take that responsibility, there was no one better suited. The other men lacked leadership.

"I cannot be the leader, because I intend to return to East Anglia. I need to learn what became of my land," he insisted.

There was an intensity in his voice that went beyond the desire to return. She tried to remain impassive, but her curiosity was piqued.

"It may be several weeks before anyone leaves Rogaland," she said carefully. "None of the men who accompanied you to East Anglia have returned, save you and one other. Valdr cannot afford to leave our settlement unprotected."

"Only one?" He frowned at her statement.

"Grafr arrived back a few weeks ago. He was the one who told us that you were struck down." The man had been the only survivor, so they'd believed.

"I do not remember him," Arik admitted.

"He was not part of our tribe for very long." She didn't tell him that Grafr had hardly spoken to anyone since his return. The man had retreated into himself, becoming more isolated. "He went on another journey, and we have not heard from him in some time."

Arik walked behind her into the forest, and she stopped a moment. It struck her suddenly that she was alone with a man whom she had not seen in over a year. She should have been wary, and yet, she found his presence comforting.

"You need not come with me if you have other duties," she said. "I know it has been a long time since you have seen your family."

"I would not feel right leaving a woman alone," he said. "There are too many dangers that could befall you."

Her hand moved to the blade at her waist. "I can defend myself, Thorgrim." She had no intention of being any man's victim.

"So you can." He gave her a slight smile, and the knowing look in his eyes made her skin prickle with awareness. Why did he have such an effect upon her? It seemed that, no matter her desire to let go of the past, this man still had a hold upon her heart.

Fool, she warned herself. Arik Thorgrim intended to leave again, and the last thing she needed was to let her heart yearn for him.

"You don't seem to want me here," he said quietly.

"No." She saw no reason to lie about it. "It would be better if you left me alone."

"Why?"

She thought of lying, of insisting that she needed no protection. But it was clear that he would not abandon her. Instead, she decided to tell him the truth. Lifting her eyes to his, she confessed, "When I was young, you were the man I always wanted to marry. And after you left with Svala, it broke my heart. I grieved when they told me you were dead. Every time I see you, I remember how that felt." She squared her shoulders and continued. "I would rather not feel that way again. I have a man now who wants to marry me, and it is past the time I should have a household and family of my own."

With that, she turned her attention back to gathering berries. She didn't want to see his reaction or hear any words of sympathy. There were a few early blackberries on a thorny underbrush, and she bent to pick some of them.

Her cheeks were burning, but she was glad she had revealed the truth to him. Now he would leave her alone, and it would make it easier to keep him at a distance.

But then Arik reached over to pick some of the blackberries, and his hand brushed against hers. The moment he touched her, she felt a jolt through her body. Her imagination conjured up the vision of his hands sliding through her hair while he claimed a kiss.

By the goddess, why could she not ignore these feelings? She felt as if Freya had cast a spell over her, one that drew her closer to this man.

"What made you choose Leif?" he asked, eating the berries.

She should have anticipated the question. But instead of inventing an answer about how she had fallen in love with him, she gave Arik the truth. "He makes me feel safe. I wanted to have a man who could protect me from anyone."

"And have you decided to wed him?" The look in his eyes appeared wary, as if he did not agree with her decision.

"I think so." Although Leif had his own particular habits, he had never once harmed her. She believed he was a good protector, and when she was ready, she would agree to the match.

Most women would smile at the idea of marriage, but to her, it was only an arrangement. Her brother, Hrafn, was strong, even with one arm—but she would never admit to him that she doubted his ability to defend her. It would only wound his pride.

"Then I hope you find happiness with him," Arik said. He moved beside her, but instead of feeling glad of his companionship, Katarina wanted to shy away. His nearness affected her in a way she didn't want to admit.

She continued walking along the path, increasing her

pace. Right now, she wanted to check the snares and get back to the settlement. Anything to avoid the awkward sense that this man *was* interested in her. And she could not allow herself to fall beneath his spell once again.

A gleam of silver caught her eye, and when Arik saw her stopping, he bent down to pick up the fallen coin. For a moment, he studied the markings. "What is this?"

"A silver coin." She brightened at the sight of it. "It is a sign that good fortune will come to you. Or perhaps you can use it to wager for a new ship."

He didn't respond to her, but kept his grip upon the coin. Strangely, he appeared transfixed by the silver, tracing the beaten edge. "Where do you suppose this came from?"

"It looks like it came from Mercia." She had not seen the likes of it before. "Perhaps you dropped it from your belongings without realizing it."

"Any coins I had with me are now at the bottom of the sea."

His tone was grim, and she tried to divert his mood. "Tonight, perhaps you'll wager it and win more silver for a ship.

"It's not much of a start," he replied. "A single coin will hardly buy a ship."

"No, but with several hundred pieces of silver, you could buy passage." She closed his fingers around the coin and offered a slight smile. "There is always gambling among the men."

"I do not remember how," he admitted.

"Do not be foolish. You were the best of all the men at wagering. Dice especially." How could he have forgotten it so soon? It was one of the reasons why the men had chosen him as the new *jarl*—because they respected his fighting and gambling skills.

"I have nothing to wager, except this coin," he pointed out.

"But they do not know that." The more she thought of it, the more she believed that this was his best choice. He could wager for silver and when he had enough, he could buy passage on a ship.

He grew pensive a moment. "The sort of wagering I am accustomed to is not the same as yours. We used cards not dice."

She had no idea what he was talking about. "What are cards?"

His gaze met hers, as if trying to discern something. "Nothing. Just a game they play in East Anglia."

"You could teach everyone this new game," she suggested, "while you tell us of your travels."

He shook his head. "I do not think it would work, Katarina. The pieces would be too difficult to make."

"You could make them during the wintertime. What else is there to do?"

Arik acknowledged her remark with a mischievous smile. "I suppose there are a few games I could teach you."

She choked, coughing as a distraction from the wild thoughts of bare flesh that entered her mind. Then he started to laugh. "Not *those* kinds of games, Katarina."

Her face flushed crimson. "I was not thinking of that at all."

"Liar."

His teasing tone made her wince, burying her face in her hands. "Go away and leave me alone, Thorgrim. I have had my fill of your teasing." She rested her palm against an oak tree. Dappled sunlight filtered through the leaves, casting shadows over his face.

"Why did you come to the forest?" he asked. "What was it you needed out here?"

"I came to check my snares." The change in conversation was a good means of diverting her attention. "If you want to wait here, I'll go and look."

But just as before, he ignored her and followed. She moved through the woods until she reached a small briar patch. Beneath it, she saw a hare struggling within the snare.

"Do you need help?"

She shook her head, quickly ending the animal's pain. As she took her knife to clean it, she murmured a blessing, thanking the gods for the gift of his life. If she continued to have luck with her snares, she might preserve the meat for the winter ahead.

The thought should have reassured her, but instead, she could not push back the worry. Leif had done nothing to prepare for the forthcoming snows, and it made her anxious.

Katarina placed the carcass in her basket and then inspected four other snares. Only one had prey within it, and she gathered the second hare and cleaned it with the first.

"Will you prepare them for your supper tonight?" he asked.

"I will cook one and preserve the other," she said. It seemed to be the best use of the meat. "We will have a good meal from these. Perhaps a stew, if I can find wild carrots and onions." She led him down the pathway and stopped to kneel down, gathering the herbs she needed.

For a while, she worked in silence. But when she reached for a plant, a shadow crossed over her. Arik stood guard, and she knew he would not let anything happen to her. And yet, the dark memories trespassed, reminding her of the night she'd been attacked. The shadows of the wood seemed to close in on her, and her fear reawakened. Katarina felt it rising inside, ready to spill over. Her breathing quickened, and her heart raced faster.

"Leif will not like it, that you are guarding me. You should go." She wanted Arik to leave so she could gather her senses and calm herself.

"I have done nothing to warrant his jealousy. And if you want to return, I will walk back with you. It's safer."

Katarina said nothing, but remained on her knees while the panic swelled inside. *Breathe,* she told herself. But she could do nothing to stop the terrors from returning. She had pushed them back for so many months and believed the nightmares were finally behind her. Instead, they had flared to life once more.

She pressed her hands against the soft earth, breathing in the primordial aroma of forest and moss. When Arik reached down and touched her shoulder, she flinched, letting out an instinctive gasp.

Immediately, he moved his hand and grew quiet. The flood of embarrassment pooled inside her, and she wished she had not reacted thusly.

"I am sorry," she said. "You startled me when you touched my shoulder."

When he made no reply, she wondered if he had gone. She waited a moment and finally opened her eyes, turning back to look at him. When she did, his face held the iron cast of anger.

"Tell me what he did to you, Katarina."

Night descended, and Eric trudged toward the shoreline. An amber moon rose above the horizon, no longer tinted red. It reflected upon waves of gold, and the wind slid over him like an invisible caress.

Katarina had refused to tell him anything, but her reaction spoke of a woman who had been attacked. It explained many things—her uneasiness around him and the way her hand went to her blade any time she was caught unaware.

Something had happened to her. And though it was none of his affair, he was certain that her marriage to Leif was a direct response to it. But though he'd questioned whether the Viking had harmed her, Katarina had vehemently denied it.

Eric had stopped pressuring Katarina for answers and had brought her home again. Although he was meant to return to his father's house, he'd remembered the old *volva's* bidding. Because of it, he had come to the shoreline for the answers he sought.

Though she was likely a superstitious woman who knew nothing, he was more and more convinced that he had switched places in time with someone else. It was not simply a reweaving of the years—he'd stolen another man's life. The silver coin was ancient, with a hammered image upon it. He believed he'd seen samples such as this in the British Museum. Yet, this coin hardly seemed old at all. It was physical evidence that he was no longer in the nineteenth century.

That, coupled with the priest's claim that it was the ninth century, made it all the more plausible that he had traveled through time.

The old crone was standing near the water's edge, her hands outstretched. Her hair had fallen back, and the golden moonlight gleamed on her face. For a moment, he was leery of approaching. Yet, the *volva* had vowed that she would tell him what he wanted to know.

She might tell you nothing but lies.

That was true enough. And yet, she had spoken English to him, when no one else could. When he looked into her milky gray eyes, he'd sensed that she understood what had happened. At this moment, he was willing to listen to anyone. The idea of being trapped in Viking-era Norway was a prison he had no desire to embrace.

With reluctance, he walked over the rocky ground until he stood just behind the old woman. "You have journeyed far," she said quietly, in the Old Norse language. "Across a thousand years."

He gave her no indication that she was right, but simply looked into her eyes. She was well aware of the truth she spoke.

"The moon will pass through its phases once, and that is all the time you have remaining. Use it well."

Her prediction unnerved him. One month of life—was that all he had? A chill crept over his skin, the hair rising up. He didn't want to believe it—and yet, she had known that he was not from this time period.

Or was she speaking of one month in purgatory? Was this a test before he would pass on to eternal life?

"Am I already dead?" he asked.

"Not yet. You wanted more time, and this, you were given. But it will not last."

He didn't understand what she meant. The time he'd wanted was a second chance to return home, to apologize to his father for the grief he had caused. And though he would never become the Duke of Somerford, neither did he want to die before seeing his father again.

Eric took a step closer and regarded the old woman. "Do you know why was I brought to this place?"

The *volva's* face turned solemn. "To change what was never meant to be. And to bring back what was lost."

The words meant nothing at all to him. But when he questioned her further, she merely said, "You will never set foot upon East Anglia again during this lifetime. Abandon your quest to sail away, and see the truth before you die." With that, she began walking back to the settlement.

"Wait," he called out. "How did you know English?" The language did not exist in ninth century Norway—or in any part of the world. Was it possible that the *volva* had traveled through time as well?

But she did not turn back, nor did she give him the answers he wanted. Cursing to himself, Eric picked up a stone and hurled it into the sea. He barely heard the slosh of water amid the waves washing over the shore.

His thoughts were in turmoil, and right now, exhaustion was roaring through him. He wanted a warm hearth and a place to sleep where there would be no questions.

He gazed up at the moon, knowing exactly where he would go.

CHAPTER FIVE

A soft knock sounded at the door, and Katarina saw Arik standing there. In one hand, he carried a handful of yarrow. She blinked, not knowing what it was he wanted. "Hello, Arik."

He offered the flowers to her, and in spite of the strange offering, she smiled.

"I thought you might enjoy these." He held them out to her, and his hand brushed against hers when she accepted the yarrow.

With a slight laugh, she admitted, "I do not know what you want me to do. Am I meant to dry the herbs or make a tea?"

He entered her house and shrugged. "Put them in water and enjoy them. They were the only flowers I could find."

She hesitated a moment, for Arik had never done anything like this in all the years she'd known him. He was the sort of man to slaughter his enemies, not bring a woman gifts. She couldn't help but blurt out, "Why would you do this?"

He glanced over at the hearth. "Because I am hoping you will invite me to stay for a meal. I would rather not go to Valdr's house at the moment."

She relaxed at that, realizing that the flowers were a

bribe, nothing more. The white yarrow blossoms *were* pretty, in a wild way. She was simply unaccustomed to a man bringing her a gift. "Has he been difficult?"

"He wants me to claim my place as *jarl.*" The tension in his tone suggested that he didn't want this at all.

Katarina motioned for him to sit down. "Hrafn will be returning soon. We were going to join the others at the feasting tonight. There will be games and ale to celebrate your return."

But Arik didn't seem at all glad to hear this. He muttered a curse in a language she didn't understand. "I should have guessed as much." She set the yarrow down on a low table, and he regarded her with a narrowed look. "Truthfully, I would prefer to remain here."

"You cannot avoid him forever. And if there were not a feast tonight, I would invite you to join Hrafn and me. As it is, we have no choice."

Arik crossed the small space and picked up the bundle. She wasn't quite certain what he was doing, but he found a wooden cup and filled it with water from a bucket. Then he set the yarrow inside it and placed it upon the table. "I suppose you are right."

Katarina sat down, studying the flowers with amusement. For a moment, she felt like a foolish young girl, and she saw his answering smile. "No one has ever brought me flowers before."

"Not even Leif?" He seemed surprised by her admission.

"No. He has never given me anything." She didn't know what else to say but simply shrugged. "He is a warrior and does not concern himself with such things." Yet she sensed Arik's disapproval.

"Where I come—" He stopped himself a moment and said, "That is, when I visited East Anglia, their customs are very different. If a man wishes to marry a woman, he must bring her gifts and spend time with her each day."

At that, Katarina began to laugh. "And so it is the same, here. You know this to be true. It is only that Leif spends his time fighting and training."

"And you do not think he should spend his time with you?" At that, his voice grew low, making her conscious of the differences between the two men. When she was younger, she had worshipped Arik Thorgrim, praying that he would grant her a look or a smile. He had shattered those dreams when he'd sailed away with Svala.

Now, his presence was undermining the careful life she had rebuilt. No, Arik hadn't come here with any desire to gain her affection or to steal her away from Leif. He had brought the crushed weeds because he'd hoped to join them for a meal. Yet her foolish heart seemed to have forgotten that Arik had never wanted anything, save friendship from her.

She started to stand up, but he caught her wrist. The heat of his hand upon her skin made her flush. She froze, unable to grasp the thoughts that flitted through her mind.

"Katarina, do not doubt your worth as a woman. You could have any man from this tribe, if you wanted him."

Except you, she thought. But she managed to cast off her nerves and gather her senses. "It is kind of you to say so."

"Do not settle for a man who does not treat you well."

She understood what he meant, but her desire for protection and vengeance meant that she needed a man like Leif at her side. She merely nodded.

Soon enough, she heard footsteps approaching. Hrafn entered their home, and eyed the pair of them. Katarina thought quickly and said, "Arik wanted to join us when we attend the feasting tonight."

He released her wrist and stood, greeting her brother. Hrafn returned it, and then nodded toward the flowers. "Why is there a bundle of yarrow inside my cup?"

Arik winked at her and answered, "Katarina was steeping a tea for you."

She recognized his teasing and smiled. "Are you ready to attend the feast?"

Hrafn's gaze shifted from the flowers to her, and she tried to behave as if the gift meant nothing at all. Instead, she feared that her brother had seen too much.

"Let us go." Her brother allowed Arik to leave first, but before she could follow, he reached out and squeezed her hand in silent warning.

Katarina tightened her palm in answer. She knew, too well, not to let herself believe in dreams that would never be.

A large group of men and women gathered in the center of the settlement. Several outdoor fires flickered in the darkness, and the atmosphere was one of drunken celebration.

Eric moved to the outskirts of the crowd. Someone lifted a roasted fowl from one of the fires, and it was passed around the people. His stomach rumbled at the sight of the meat, but he remained in place. On the far side, he saw men drinking ale and gambling with dice. A few others were involved in wrestling matches, openly fighting, and no one seemed to care.

Someone grabbed his wrist, handed him a cup of ale, and cheered. "The *jarl* has returned!"

He had no idea what to say, but a nod and a smile seemed to be the best response. He was not the leader of these people, but it seemed that they wanted him to be. Men clapped him on the back, greeting him by name. One of the larger Vikings punched his shoulder, nearly knocking him over. Grimly, Eric realized again that he was at a severe physical disadvantage. These men were hardened warriors, and he lacked the strength to retaliate. If he did remain in this place, he would have to train among them. The thought was strangely appealing. All his life, he'd been trapped in the genteel life of a future duke. And now, he'd been dropped into a world of barbaric warriors. He wondered if it was possible to earn their respect.

You cannot stay, his conscience reminded him. And yes, that was true, but he rather wondered what it would be like. There were days when he'd longed to stab something, after spending hours reading ledgers. A smile played at his mouth, just imagining it.

He studied the people around him and realized that there were many similarities to the people of his time. There were mothers trying to calm overexcited children, young boys chasing one another and wrestling, and shy women standing off to the side. One brazen women with a large bosom and long hair that curled past her hips sent him a brilliant smile— revealing the loss of both her front teeth.

Eric repressed a shudder and crossed through the crowd, finishing his ale while he searched the sea of faces. He was looking for Katarina. After her earlier fears, he wanted to know who had threatened her—and he could only learn that by watching.

Another cup of ale was pressed into his hand. He took a sip before he finally saw Katarina seated off to the side. A giant of a man stood behind her, likely Leif. The moment the man saw Eric, his expression hardened. He put both hands upon Katarina's shoulders in a blatant show of possession. The man's message was crystal clear.

He wasn't surprised, but Katarina appeared uncomfortable. And that didn't sit well with him. Although she'd said that Leif had never harmed her, Katarina did not appear glad to see him.

Eric finished another round of ale and Hrafn greeted him. "Come and join us, Thorgrim. The men want to hear about the shipwreck."

He followed Hrafn to one of the outdoor fires. A young

girl offered him a roasted capon breast, and he took it, biting into the juicy meat. The capon was flavored with salt and herbs, and he hadn't tasted anything so good in weeks. It didn't seem to matter that he lacked a plate or silver to eat with. He was so hungry, it was a simple matter to fall into atrocious table manners.

Eric sat down with the men, listening to their stories. His mind drifted a few moments, and he caught flashes of memory that belonged to Arik Thorgrim. He saw visions of these men as adolescents, and he recalled fighting with them. He also remembered Katarina standing nearby to watch. She had watched him with fascination, smiling in hopes of gaining his attention.

But now, when he looked at her, he saw a woman whose dreams had been broken. He didn't like that at all.

"Tell us what happened when your ship sank," one of the men bade him.

He began telling his own tale, but all the while, he continued to watch over Katarina. Though Leif seemed to be protective of her, she did not join the other women or share in the celebration. It appeared as if she was hiding within his shadow, except for the moments when she fetched him a cup of ale or gave him food.

"The moon was the color of blood," he told them, continuing to weave the story. Silence descended over the men, and a few of the children came closer to listen. One shivered against his mother when Eric mentioned the voice he had heard. But it was Katarina who captured his attention now. She was still sitting near Leif, but her eyes were locked upon his. The night wind blew strands of her long blond hair back from her face. She wore a silver circlet across her forehead, and the fire cast a glow upon her skin.

He hardly heard a word of his own storytelling. All he could perceive was her face staring at him.

If she had been a lady within a ballroom, he would have asked her to dance. He might have spoken with her parents or even paid a call upon her.

But not in a place like this. Here, there was a more visceral side to life. Leif's hands were upon her shoulders, staking a physical claim though vows had not yet bound them. It shouldn't matter to Eric…and yet it did.

The *volva* rose from her place when he had finished his tale and spoke. "Arik Thorgrim was chosen to return from Valhalla. The gods healed him of his wounds."

There was an intake of surprise from the crowd of people. One little girl's mouth dropped open, and she began whispering to her mother, asking if he was a spirit.

But when he turned back to the *volva,* the old woman's expression was deadly serious. *You have one moon remaining,* her gaze seemed to say. For what purpose? One month to search for his father's estate in England? Or one month to dwell among these people?

She was probably a superstitious woman who cast spells with frog legs and spider webs, he told himself. What did she know about how much time was remaining?

He glanced up at the moon, and a cold chill pressed over him. There was no denying the supernatural forces that had brought him here, nor the fact that he was speaking an ancient language as if he were born to it.

It's not real.

But though he wanted to close his eyes and ignore the truth, he could no longer deny it. Eric drained another cup of mead, wanting the sensation of forgetfulness. He started to cross through the people toward Katarina but was stopped by one of the Vikings.

The man was tall with a shaved head, and it appeared that runes had been tattooed upon his arm. He wore a fur cloak over his tunic and leggings, and his strength was undeniable. To Eric, he demanded, "Do you have the luck of the gods,

Thorgrim?" He pulled out a leather sack from his belt and poured out several bronze figures into his palm.

"I might." He didn't turn his gaze away, wondering what sort of a test this was. Then he held out his palm, wanting to see the bronze figures more closely. When he studied them, he saw that the figures were of crouching naked men and women. The bronze carvings revealed six drilled holes upon the back of the male figure, and two dots on each side. He suspected that they were weighted in a certain way.

When he turned them over, he saw that the bronze female figure was grasping her ankles, spread apart to reveal her nude form.

What a scandal these dice would cause, if they were used in a gaming hell, Eric thought dryly. To the bald man, he said, "I will watch you play against another man and then wager in the next round."

There was no doubt in his mind that it would not be a fair game, particularly given that this man wore several gold rings and a silver torque. By watching a round, he hoped to learn how the dice were weighted and the odds of each roll. He noticed that the female form tended to land on the side with three holes. But the Viking had a unique way of twisting his wrist, flipping the dice to roll a six. He won each time he wagered, and his pile of coins grew larger. At that point, Leif came forward and offered to play against the man.

"Sigarr clenches his fist before he rolls a six," a female voice murmured from behind him. Katarina had slipped into the shadows, but he didn't turn around.

"Does he?" Eric stepped away, and Katarina concealed herself behind one of the drying animal skins. "Why did you come to tell me this?"

"Because you will need an advantage to beat him." In a low voice she added, "He keeps his left hand relaxed when he rolls a three."

He moved in beside her and saw that she had pulled her

cloak over her hair. "What would Leif say if he saw you hiding back here with me?"

She lowered her gaze. "I told him I was returning to my brother's house for the night. I wanted him to accompany me, but he was too busy trying to beat Sigarr."

Eric watched for a while and saw that she was right. "Why did you not tell him what you told me? Don't you want him to win?"

"He does not win often. You likely won't, either. But at least you'll know what Sigarr's habits are."

His eyes narrowed in a questioning look. It struck him as unusual that she would seek him out to tell him this. "Are you trying to be rid of me so quickly?"

"I was only trying to help," Katarina admitted softly.

He realized, then, that she had unspoken reasons for helping him. It was possible that she still had lingering feelings from the past and was trying to do him a kindness. Eric reached for her hand and squeezed it gently. "Thank you for telling me, Katarina."

The moment he touched her hand, he grew more aware of this woman. Her slender body was enfolded in a cloak as if she wanted to hide from any bystanders. Although they had done nothing more than talk, he sensed that something was troubling her.

Her face grew flushed, and she pressed both hands to her cheeks. "You should go back. Valdr will be searching for you."

"I will take you to your brother's house, if you have no escort." He wasn't about to let her go alone.

"It's all right. I can walk alone." But the words belied her demeanor. Her gaze moved across the space, as if searching for an invisible threat.

"I am not about to let a woman go back on her own when drunken men are roaming about."

She straightened a little. "I can defend myself, Thorgrim."

To prove her point, she rested her hand upon her blade.

"Can you?" Eric kept his tone calm, but he remained kneeling beside her. "But if I am with you, there is no need."

"Leif will be angry if he sees you with me," she pointed out.

"Then he should leave his game and escort you himself." He had little sympathy for a man who would leave a woman unprotected.

Katarina let out a hesitant sigh as if she were still wary of Leif's jealousy. "I suppose I could stay a little longer. I will watch your game instead." She emerged from her hiding place and walked ahead of him. Eric remained behind her, resting his hand upon the hilt of the blade Hrafn had given him.

When they reached the fires, Leif's gaze narrowed at the sight of Katarina. She moved to his side and spoke softly to him. His features relaxed, and he pulled her onto his lap. Although Leif had offered to marry Katarina, there was something about the man that made Eric question his intentions.

"Join us," Sigarr ordered. "Now it is your turn."

Eric debated whether or not to take part, but in the end decided that he had little to lose, having only one silver coin. They gave him another cup of ale, and he sat across from Sigarr.

"How much are we wagering?" he asked the man.

"Four pieces of silver for the first round. Then it will double with each roll of the dice."

He didn't have four pieces of silver, but he supposed he could conceal that. In gaming hells, it was common for card sharps to lure a player by allowing them to win the first few rounds. He suspected Sigarr might do the same. "All right."

Another cup of ale was pressed into his hand. Eric pretended to drink, but didn't swallow. If Katarina was right, that he could win passage aboard a ship—or even a ship of his own—he would need his wits.

"I will call out a number before I roll the dice," Sigarr explained. "If one of the dice lands on that number, I win. If not, you win."

Sigarr reached for the dice and held them a moment. Then he called out, "Four." He rolled the dice and his left hand was relaxed. The dice landed upon a three and a five. "You win." Sigarr handed him four pieces of silver. "Now it is your turn. If you guess correctly, I will give you eight pieces of silver. If not, you give them to me."

It was still a risk, for he had only five pieces. Yet, he had no doubt the game was rigged. The question was whether or not Eric could manage to manipulate the dice correctly. He lifted the weighted dice and tried to get a feel for them. "Six," he said, before he flicked his wrist. The dice rolled hard, but one did land on a six. He held out his hand, and Sigarr gave him eight coins.

Before the next wager, Eric said, "I propose a different game. I will try to guess the number you roll. And you will do the same for me."

Sigarr frowned, considering it. After a moment, he seemed to agree with the idea. "But if you guess wrong, you must pay sixteen pieces of silver."

Eric nodded, and the man seemed intrigued. With a smile, he predicted, "Prepare to give me more silver, Arik Thorgrim. What number will I roll?"

Eric glanced at Katarina, who was still seated upon Leif's lap. She pointed to her left hand in a silent reminder. But then the man began to nuzzle at her throat, his hands wandering. It clearly made her uncomfortable in such a public place, but she said nothing to stop him.

She isn't yours, his brain reminded him. *And he isn't hurting her.*

Eric glanced at Sigarr's relaxed left hand and said, "I will guess just before you release the dice."

The man agreed with a nod, and just as he flicked his

wrist, Eric said, "Three." As he'd predicted, the dice came up as a three. His opponent appeared annoyed, but he gave over the silver. Leif lifted Katarina off his lap and patted her behind, ordering, "Bring us more ale."

Eric didn't at all like the way the man was treating her, like a maidservant. "I want to play against Leif now," he said to Sigarr. Perhaps it was a foolish idea and he might very well provoke a fight. But he wanted a chance to gain the measure of this Viking, to know whether he posed any harm.

Leif was drunk enough to agree. He went and sat across from him, draining the cup of ale Katarina brought. "I would welcome a game so I can take the rest of your silver."

"Or I take yours," Eric countered. "We will start with four pieces of silver, just as before." He glanced up at Katarina and saw the worried expression on her face. It was clear that she didn't want him engaged in this gambling match.

Leif rolled the dice and when it landed on the three, Eric gave him four pieces. He tried to do the same, but this time, the die didn't land on a three. It became clear that Leif had his own strategy, and it was working well.

Instead of worrying about the coins he'd lost, Eric continued to watch the man's body language for patterns. In time, he discovered how to read Leif, and he won a single round of thirty-two pieces of silver. Then another.

After the third win, Leif's fists curled, and rage lined his face. Katarina appeared uneasy, and she had slipped back into the shadows. It was time to end this with one final round before a fight broke out.

"I propose another wager with different stakes," Eric said. "This will be the last roll of the dice." Though he was well aware that he could lose everything, his winnings meant nothing at all. The greater challenge was to win passage back to England.

Leif had a smug expression on his face, for he had won

most of Eric's silver. "You will have nothing left, Thorgrim."

"My ship sank during the storm. I want another."

At that, Leif grew sullen. "The only ship I own is for fishing, not long journeys. You could never go a-viking in it."

"One roll of the dice. If I win, I get the use of your ship for my voyage. I will return it to you when I come back to Rogaland. If you win, you take all my silver."

But Leif was already shaking his head. "My ship is worth more than the silver."

"Then do not take the wager." As it stood, they each had half of the winnings.

The Viking stared at him, weighing the choice. "More ale," he growled to Katarina. She moved back from the shadows to obey his command. After she filled Leif's cup, he drained the ale.

"We both roll one die at the same time," Leif said. "For the same number. Whoever gets that number keeps the ship and all the silver."

It was a game of high stakes, but one that was necessary. "So be it. But Sigarr should call the number." It was the best way to keep the wager fair.

A small crowd had gathered around to watch, and when he looked up, Katarina was gone. His sense of uneasiness heightened, for he didn't know if she had left of her own accord or whether she had been taken against her will.

Sigarr was called in to judge the outcome. "To win, you must roll a one."

Eric gripped the bronze die in his palm, and he found the edge with the one. He didn't know whether he could manage to roll the die correctly, but he had far less to lose than Leif. None of the silver had been his to begin with. With a flick of his wrist, he released the die at the same time as Leif.

The bronze figure rolled over and over, coming to rest upon a corner. He saw that Leif had already rolled a six, and was reaching for the die to roll again...when Eric's die tipped and fell upon a one.

The roar of the men was deafening, amid Leif's protests. Eric took his winnings and said, "I will collect your ship in the morning."

Before he could take another step, the Viking released a battle cry and came lunging toward him. Raw instinct made him sidestep, and Leif tripped, sprawling face-first onto the ground. Eric's instincts sharpened, and he was well aware of everyone watching. If he lost this fight, he would mark himself as a target.

The man staggered to his feet, but Eric never let Leif catch his balance. He drove his fist against his opponent's ear, and the man howled in pain, dropping to his knees. One more blow to his head rendered him unconscious.

Eric didn't doubt that he could easily have lost the fight, had Leif not been drinking heavily. The man's physical size and strength was a strong reminder of just how dangerous this world was.

Several of the men congratulated him, and at the edge of the crowd, he spied Valdr watching. The *jarl* eyed him with a suspicious look before he turned his back, returning to his longhouse.

Eric knew he was meant to follow the man, but he doubted if it was safe there. Leif was furious about his losses and might try to retaliate when he regained consciousness.

Katarina emerged from the shadows and went to kneel beside her intended. The sight of her tending Leif made Eric tense. The Viking would be furious when he awakened, and he didn't want her to bear the brunt of the man's temper.

Hrafn was standing nearby, but he was not smiling. "You shouldn't have made an enemy out of Leif."

"It was a game, nothing more. He had the chance to end

the match." But he knew Hrafn was right. The sooner he left this settlement, the better.

"You'll be dead by morning."

"The man is too drunk to walk."

"But not too drunk to sever your head from your body while you sleep." Hrafn shook his head. "You'd better go before he awakens."

Katarina looked up from Leif's fallen form and nodded. "You should." Her expression held apprehension, as if she were afraid. Eric didn't like that at all.

To Hrafn, he ordered, "Take Katarina home and guard her closely. If she goes to Leif, he may take out his anger on her."

It seemed that Hrafn was in agreement. "Arik is right. Stay away from Leif this night, Katarina."

She hesitated, and Eric pressed further. "Go with your brother and bar the door." He sent Hrafn a warning look, and the man nodded in agreement.

At that moment, Leif let out a groan. Eric saw the fear that passed over Katarina's face, and he walked away, pretending he was returning to his father's house. Instead, he slipped behind one of the longhouses, watching over her.

Hrafn spoke to his sister, but before he could take her outside, Leif sat up. His expression held a blend of pain and fury, and his gaze searched the grounds. Katarina leaned in and touched the side of his head gently.

In response, Leif seized her hair, twisting it around his wrist as he tilted her face back and kissed her hard. It was a kiss of possession, not one meant to kindle desire.

Eric clenched his fists, wanting to cross the space and take the man apart. The sudden burst of jealousy made no sense at all, for Katarina was not his—she had chosen Leif.

And yet...she wasn't kissing him back. Both of her hands were poised upon the man's chest, and it looked as if she was trying to push him away.

Hrafn started to intervene, but the Viking broke off the kiss and unsheathed his blade.

"Leif, please." Katarina stepped between the two men. He was drunk beyond reason, and she didn't want him to take it out on Hrafn. "I will walk back to your house with you."

Her words seemed to have an effect, because Leif sheathed the blade and stepped back. "Yes. You should come with me." He took her hand, and Katarina leaned against him, hoping he would sheathe the blade and end the threat toward her brother.

Though it was a risk accompanying him to his house, she saw no choice. The best way to soften his anger was with obedience. If she did exactly what he wanted, tending to him and getting him to rest, he might sleep off the effects of the ale. But if her brother intervened, Leif was drunk enough to start a fight.

Hrafn didn't seem to care. "Leave Katarina alone."

His interference only enraged Leif. He shoved her aside and confronted Hrafn with the blade. "She is going to be my wife." He took a step closer, wielding the blade in an open threat.

"She has not yet agreed. And I can refuse to allow the marriage," Hrafn warned.

"Can you?" A thin smile stretched over Leif's face, chilling Katarina. She had never heard him speak in this way before. It was as if a mask had been lifted away, and the person behind it was not at all the same man.

"Katarina, you are going nowhere with him." Hrafn reached to take her by the hand, but Leif let out a battle cry and lunged at her brother.

He knocked Hrafn to the ground, and she cried out, "Stop it! Both of you." If her brother engaged in this fight, he would lose. Though Hrafn was a strong man, he could not hope to outmatch Leif.

To make matters worse, she saw Arik approaching from the opposite side. It seemed that he had not returned to his father's house after all. Hrafn appeared to exchange a silent message with Thorgrim, and abruptly, he lifted his arm in false surrender. She had no doubt at all that Arik would follow them, whether she wanted him to or not.

She stepped between the men, shielding herself before Leif could lash out against Hrafn. "Please. For my sake, end this."

Leif stared hard at her. "So be it." He pushed her away and struck her brother down, his fist crunching against Hrafn's nose. Over and over, he hit him, and a scream tore from her mouth. Through a blur of terror, she cried out for him to stop. He was going to kill her brother unless someone intervened.

She unsheathed her blade in a panic, her hands shaking. "Let him go, Leif."

His fists stilled, and a slow smile spread over his face. He left her brother upon the ground and took a step toward her. Now *she* had become his target, and the thought chilled her blood. Leif darted toward her and seized her wrist, forcing her to drop the weapon. Then he lifted her over his shoulder. "I like a woman with spirit."

His words infuriated her, and Katarina fought to free herself from his grasp. "I will never marry you. Not after this." How could she have even considered it? The man was aggressive and controlling, not a protector.

From her vantage point, she could see Arik approaching with stealth. And though she wanted to believe that he could save her, she didn't know if he had the strength. Leif strode swiftly across the settlement, keeping an iron grip upon her.

"Oh, but you will wed me, Katarina. Because you want your brother to stay alive." He held her by the waist and lowered her body as he bit her lip. "Do you know how easy it is to kill a one-armed man? I could have killed him right now, if I'd wanted to."

She stopped fighting him, fear icing through her, His lips curved in a dark smile. "You will obey me in all things and become the wife I want you to be. And Hrafn will live." His hands moved over her bottom and he rubbed his erection against her. "Do you feel how much I want you, Katarina?"

Terror lanced through her mind, and she struggled to break free of him. "I don't want you." And now she was beginning to understand that she'd never wanted this man. Somewhere deep inside, she'd sensed that he had a dangerous side.

"Within a few more days, you will be my bride. Tonight, I will teach you how to please me." He pressed her up against the wall outside his dwelling, and panic swelled within her. He was half-crazed with drunken lust, and if she didn't get away from him, he was going to lift her skirts right here. The thought made her bite her lip so hard, she tasted blood. No.

But if she fought him, he would enjoy subduing her. It was not the way to stop him. She had to yield and feign surrender.

"Leif," she murmured. "Slow down. You're frightening me."

He wasn't listening at all. His hand moved to her gown and he gripped her breast through the wool, massaging it roughly. "I could take you now, Katarina. And you will know what it means to be my wife. I will be inside you every night, claiming you."

Nausea caught her in her stomach, and she pleaded. "No, Leif, please. Not in this way. Let me go home."

He only laughed and tightened his hands around her wrists. "And where will you run to, little bird? You belong to me."

Where was Arik? She had seen him follow her, but he'd done nothing to help thus far. Her fear intensified when she realized he might not be able to stop Leif. She'd chosen this man because he was the strongest, and now she regretted that decision.

Leif twisted her arm behind her back, pushing her into the darkness of his house. In spite of her earlier decision to try to reason with him, her fighting instincts overrode all else. She kicked at him and cried out for help.

He let out a laugh. "Struggle all you want, Katarina. I'm going to enjoy taking your innocence. Especially if you fight back."

The air within the space seemed to disappear, and her throat choked up in an effort to breathe. Fear flared inside her, and she moved toward the door in desperation. He caught her waist, laughing as he struggled.

"Leif, please don't." She was sobbing now, so afraid of reliving the nightmare of before. She couldn't bear this. Not now.

The door flew open and Arik Thorgrim moved in. "Let her go." In his hand he carried a battle-ax.

Leif started to laugh. "Were you expecting to harm me with that weapon, Thorgrim? You lack the strength to wield it."

Katarina tried to pull her way free, but Leif only twisted her hair, pulling it hard. She was trembling from the knowledge that she could not escape. Even if this was Arik Thorgrim, returned from the afterworld, Odin had claimed his strength as sacrifice. He could not hope to fight a man like Leif.

"Let her go," Arik repeated quietly. "Then we can talk about it outside."

There was a sudden change in Leif's demeanor. "Were you wanting her for yourself, Thorgrim? Is that why you interrupted us?" He reached for his own battle-ax, and the moment he did, he loosened his grip on her hair. Katarina scrambled backward and seized a wooden stool as a shield. Though it might do her little good, it made her feel better to have some means of defending herself.

Arik started toward the door, but Leif growled, "You are not going outside, Thorgrim. I'm going to sever your head from your body."

"Please," Katarina said quietly. "Let us both go, and—"

The warrior spun and stared at her with hatred. His eyes were glazed and he stumbled slightly. "Why did he come for you, Katarina?"

"To guard me," she answered. *From you.* And she was deeply grateful for it. There was no doubt in her mind that if Arik had not come after her, Leif would have raped her.

Arik's stare met hers, and she saw him nod toward the door. She needed to leave as soon as possible. "Go outside, Katarina." He moved toward the table and placed the oil lamp upon it. The gesture seemed to confuse Leif, and she used that moment to drop the wooden stool, fleeing outside.

The night air was frigid, but it was her heart that had gone cold. She was terrified that Thorgrim would die. If she turned her back on him, she feared it would happen. Leif was unbearably strong. She couldn't believe she had been soft-headed enough to think that he would never harm her.

She hurried back to where Hrafn had fallen. She needed to know how badly her brother had been hurt, and someone had to help Arik Thorgrim.

Even if she found a warrior willing to come, he might not be strong enough to save Arik. The thought bothered her deeply, for he had risked his own life for her sake.

And yet, it might already be too late.

Eric moved toward the open door, thankful that Katarina had escaped. Seeing this man trying to hurt her had provoked a primal side to him. Never had he felt such fury, seeing a man attack an innocent maiden. Rage filled his veins, boiling his blood. If he'd had a pistol, he would have shot Leif without a second thought. The man didn't deserve to breathe.

But there were no pistols, no advanced weapons to bring down this enemy. All he had were his wits. And somehow that would have to be enough to defeat this Goliath.

Leif swung the battle-ax downward in a violent blow that could have cleaved Eric's body in two, had he not moved. He should have been petrified at the sight of this berserker.

Instead, he held out his own ax. At least he had the advantage of being mostly sober, unlike the Viking.

You've gone half-potted, his brain warned. *Why would you think you can fight a man of this size? Leave now while your head is still attached.* He knew that was the logical course of action—but a darker side of him was warming to the fight.

This man had tried to attack Katarina, and that could not go unpunished. He wasn't a coward who would run away in fear or shy away from a fight. Right now, he wanted to avenge her honor.

Eric took a step closer to the table. The oil within the lamp was flammable, and if he used fire as a distraction, it might end the fight.

Leif tightened his grip upon the ax. "I'm going to kill you, Thorgrim."

Not if he could stop him. But Eric knew better than to attack the man with a battle-ax. His weapon was a distraction, a means of buying time while he determined how best to use the fire. There was no doubt that if Leif managed to seize him, the Viking would snap his neck.

Eric's gaze shifted back to the lamp oil and a piece of wood burning in the hearth. It might be possible to seize the wood and ignite Leif with the oil. He kept the ax held high, while Leif stared at him with amusement. It occurred to him that there were only two means of winning this fight. Either with a physical maiming, or he had to invoke fear within the Viking.

His mind tried to recall knowledge of Norse mythology. Superstitions and the threat of magic were all he had.

"I have been to Valhalla," he told Leif. "And I have seen the face of Odin." But the proclamation sounded forced and had little effect upon his enemy.

"You were sent back because you were unworthy to dwell with the gods," Leif taunted.

"No." He thought quickly, searching for a means of protecting Katarina and himself. "Because Katarina is a chosen maiden of Freya," he finished. "She cannot belong to you."

Leif snarled, "And who will stop me? You lack the strength, Thorgrim. It was taken from you."

"Strength, perhaps. But not wisdom." Again, he commanded, "You will end your betrothal to Katarina and let her go."

"Think you I will allow you to claim her?" Leif stared down at him, trying to use his height as intimidation.

"I will keep her safe," Eric answered quietly. "By any means necessary."

At that, Leif's gaze shifted to the open doorway. Katarina had returned, and behind her stood Valdr and her brother Hrafn. He was glad to see that the man was able to stand, though blood matted his hair and face.

Valdr moved inside and stood near the hearth between them. The old *jarl* appeared furious, and he faced Leif. "If there is a disagreement, let it be brought among the leaders to be resolved. You may not slay my son because you've drunk too much ale."

"He intends to take Katarina from me," Leif remarked.

A change came over the young woman, and she lifted her chin. "I am ending my betrothal to Leif. He tried to force me against my will, and Arik saved me from that."

Her brother's face turned thunderous at the confession, but before Hrafn could intervene, Leif lifted his ax. Eric seized the fallen stool to use as a shield. Just as Leif swung the blade, he braced himself against the impact. The iron blade caught within the wood, and Eric jerked it hard, pulling the weapon from Leif's grasp. Without hesitation, he reached for the lamp and tossed the oil on Leif. For a moment, the man appeared surprised as the liquid dripped down his tunic. Then Eric seized the burning stick from the hearth and ignited the fuel.

The fire took hold and spread across his enemy's torso. Leif let out a roar, thrashing as he ran from the house. He threw himself against the ground to put out the fire, but before he could rise, Eric used the wooden stool to knock him unconscious. It was unlikely that the fire had done any damage, given the man's layers of clothing, but he had proved his point. He could indeed win a fight against a man physically stronger than himself.

Hrafn's expression held approval, and he nodded. "I am taking my sister home."

"No." Eric set down the stool and returned for the fallen blade, which he sheathed in his belt. Then he reached for Katarina's hand. "She would not be safe in your house after what happened with Leif. She comes with me to Valdr's longhouse."

The older man gave a single nod, indicating his approval—but Katarina was harder to convince. "I will not go—" she started to protest, but in this, Eric would not yield. She would not be safe anywhere else—especially after Hrafn had been weakened by his injuries.

"Make a place for her," he told Valdr, "and I will bring her there soon." To Hrafn, he warned, "Be prepared if Leif tries to attack your longhouse after he awakens. You may stay with us, if that is your wish."

"And what of my sister on the morrow?" He studied Eric as if he didn't believe him capable of protecting her.

"Leif will not touch her again."

Valdr eyed him, and said, "Bring her with you, and we will make a decision about her fate soon enough." With that, he turned back and left.

After he had gone, Katarina's expression held wariness. "Am I not to have any say in my own future?"

Her brother took her hand. "Go with them for your protection tonight. You will be safer there than with me."

She looked as if she wanted to argue, but Hrafn held up the stump of his arm. "Heed my words, Katarina." Her face softened at the silent reminder of his weakness, and her shoulders lowered with acceptance. Then, she tightened her lips and gave a single nod. "Only for this night, then."

Yet when Hrafn caught his gaze, he suspected that her brother intended it to be for several nights. Eric had chosen to interfere, and now it meant Katarina was under his protection. It wasn't clear what the implications would be, but he had no qualms about keeping her safe.

Before she could say another word, Eric moved beside her to escort her toward Valdr's house. "We must talk alone."

"I would rather return home to my brother."

"It is not a choice, and you know this." He continued walking with her until they reached the *jarl*'s longhouse. He took Katarina by the hand and led her to a small lean-to where one of the horses was standing.

When they were alone, he released her and studied her face. Her cheeks were flushed, but worse was the fear in her eyes. She was a breath away from weeping but was trying to remain strong.

"He will not hurt you again," he swore. "No man will."

Eric knew that Katarina was not his responsibility, and

her brother was meant to protect her. But he could not shake the feeling that his fate was intertwined with hers.

If you turn your back on her, Leif will claim her. Neither Hrafn nor Valdr can stop him.

And you can? his incredulous mind countered. *She is not yours and never will be.*

He tried to imagine what would happen, if she had been a part of the Regency ton. If word got out about the attack, she would be forced to wed Leif. Or forced to wed Eric, since he'd dared to save her. The London gossips would believe Katarina's reputation was irreparably damaged, through no fault of her own.

Someone has to save her, he reasoned. And why not him?

Because you don't belong here. You cannot stay. He knew that—truly, he did. And yet, the thought of leaving Katarina to the undeniable nightmare that awaited her seemed unthinkable. There was no choice but to grant her his protection, just as he would any maiden from his own century.

Her hands were trembling, but she clenched them together, steadying herself. "Thank you for saving me. I...never saw Leif behave that way before."

Eric acknowledged her gratitude with a nod. "You will be safe now, I promise." But he could tell she still didn't believe him. He studied her and asked, "Do you want to come with me, away from this place?"

Her eyes widened slightly, as if she hadn't even considered it. "What do you mean?"

"As I told you before, I intend to travel by ship back to East Anglia," he told her. "You could leave the settlement with your brother."

There was a slight glimpse of hope before her mood dimmed. "I would, but—" She lowered her head. "This is our home. Hrafn won't want to leave, and I cannot travel as a maiden alone."

He understood that. But there *was* a means of protecting her, one that would keep other men away. For a moment, he weighed the decision in his mind. Was it right to bind himself to this woman when he knew not if he could remain here?

The alternative, to leave her unguarded, filled him with far more guilt. It wasn't right, and when he considered the consequences, there were no regrets. She had become a friend, and he would not turn away when she was in need.

"You need not travel as a maiden alone," Eric reassured her. He took a step closer and reached for her hand. Her fingers were cold, and her blue eyes were filled with fear. "You could travel as my wife."

She appeared shocked at his suggestion. But Eric knew full well that his time here would be fleeting. Any marriage between them would be temporary. Then, too, if she bore the protection of Valdr's house, she would be safe from harm. When he was gone, she would have her freedom to do as she chose.

"What is your answer?"

CHAPTER SIX

Katarina could hardly believe what he'd suggested. As his wife? How could he even consider such a thing? Arik was still holding her hand, his thumb pressing circles upon her palm. It unnerved her feeling his touch upon her skin. And what if he wanted to share her bed? Surely he would claim a husband's rights.

As a young girl, she had once dreamed of being Arik Thorgrim's wife. But not like this. She didn't want to be the object of his pity. A twisted knot of worry ached inside her stomach as she tried to imagine a marriage between them.

"Why?" she blurted out. "What purpose is there in a marriage between us?"

"Because Leif will not let you go," he said. "He would kill your brother and any man who stood in his way."

Her heart was beating faster, standing so near to him. Arik *had* proven himself able to defend her, even if his method was not one she had seen before. And right now, the look in his eyes was of a man bound to keep her safe.

"You do not want me as your wife," she forced herself to say.

"I had not planned on taking a wife, this is true," he said. "But neither will I leave you behind at Leif's mercy."

"You speak as if I cannot defend myself," she accused. Her words were laced with bitterness, for she knew the truth of them.

"Would you rather marry Leif?" His voice turned gentle then, as if allowing her the choice.

"N-no." She hated the weakness in her voice, and the fear invoked by this night. "I do not want to marry anyone right now."

"It need not be a true marriage," he told her. "I could protect you by name but leave you untouched."

She had been holding back her feelings and fears for so long, the kindness made her crumble. A rush of tears came to her eyes, and she could not stop herself from weeping. She loathed herself for behaving like such a foolish woman, but it was the first moment she'd had to react to Leif's attack.

Arik pulled her into a warm embrace but did nothing more than hold her. "You are safe now," he promised. "I will take care of you."

She didn't know why he had offered to marry her, but he was right. She could not stay in Rogaland—not with Leif. He would only continue to pursue her.

After a time, her tears slowed, but Arik kept his hand upon the back of her neck. His touch was gentle and soothing. And though she was afraid to consider an arrangement like this, she saw no alternative.

Gathering her courage, she drew back and regarded him. "I will wed you. But only if you do not force me to share your bed."

"You will sleep beside me at night," he clarified, "but I will not touch you unless you ask it of me."

It was the best she could hope for. Katarina took a breath and nodded. "In the morning, then."

Arik was staring at her, but the look in his eyes was not threatening—only thoughtful. "I always knew I would have an arranged marriage," he remarked. "But I never expected it to be quite like this." A faint smile pulled at the corners of his mouth.

"Neither did I." She refrained from mentioning that she had always wanted him as a husband—at least before she'd been attacked. It was strange to think that it had finally happened in a way she'd never imagined.

"There is something I *would* like," he admitted. "If you are willing to seal our agreement."

She waited for him to continue, and this time, he rested his palm against her cheek. His thumb nudged her mouth, and she understood then. He wanted to kiss her.

Every instinct warned her to pull away, but she could hardly breathe, much less move. She held herself motionless, terrified of what would happen now. The only kisses she had ever had were Leif's possessive ones, or a few stolen kisses when she was younger. Never had she kissed this man, though she had dreamed of it.

He leaned in to her face, giving her every chance to pull back. Her heart was racing as his nose touched hers and he took her mouth.

The kiss was soft, an invitation instead of an act of possession. His mouth was teasing, stroking hers as he nipped at her lips. Katarina felt herself dissolving beneath the kiss, his mouth unraveling her senses. He took several kisses, savoring her mouth in a way that warmed every inch of her flesh. She wanted to go deeper, to fall beneath his spell and surrender.

But then he pulled back. His brown eyes had grown hooded, and she suddenly realized that he *did* want her. Very badly.

What startled her the most was the knowledge that she was not unaffected by the kiss at all. And marrying this man might well lead to far more than she'd anticipated.

Katarina's blue eyes held confusion, and her lips were swollen from where he'd kissed her. Eric cursed himself for giving in to impulse. What had he been thinking? At first, he had intended only for it to be a kiss sealing their bargain. But the moment he'd tasted her, he'd been drawn deeper. It was as if invisible bonds had brought them together making it impossible to stop kissing her. He'd wanted to tangle his hands into her hair, stripping away her clothing until her bare skin was beneath his.

A marriage in name only? Such a thing might well be impossible.

"Go inside, and I will speak with Valdr about the arrangements," he told her. When he took her hand, her palm was cool within his, as if he'd made her nervous. Her face appeared flushed with embarrassment and perhaps a trace of fear. For all that Katarina was a Viking woman, she was not bold and aggressive, as he'd anticipated. Instead, there was a vulnerability about her.

He opened the door for her and thought back to the moment when she'd held a knife to his throat. It had been an act of fear, one with no true threat beneath it. She wouldn't have killed him at all.

Nothing had infuriated him more than when he'd seen Leif try to hurt her. It made him eager to train, to be a better fighter so he could protect Katarina. But first, he had to take her away from Leif. And for that, he needed a ship.

When they were inside, Valdr was waiting, along with a female servant. The old *jarl* regarded Katarina and said, "Go with Yrsa. She will give you a place to sleep."

Eric waited until she had gone behind a partition with the female servant, and then he regarded Valdr. "We need to speak alone."

The *jarl* led him to the far end of the longhouse and brought over a chair for him. "I have already said that you cannot leave Rogaland. You must take your place here."

He'd known the old man would say that. And yet, it was not possible. It was better to try a different tack.

"My strength is not what it was," he said quietly. "I need to train."

At that, some of the tension within Valdr dissipated. "You do."

"And I cannot do that here, where men will judge me by my weakness." He watched the *jarl* carefully, noting that thus far, the man was responding to reason. "I also will not leave Katarina unprotected. I intend to give her my protection and wed her myself."

He waited for the old *jarl* to protest or give reasons why Katarina was not a suitable bride. Instead, the old man stood and poured wine into two silver goblets. "For the first time in your life, you are making wise decisions." He offered Eric the wine, and he accepted it.

It surprised him that Valdr encouraged this marriage. Why? Had he wanted Thorgrim to wed Katarina in the past? Or did he have other reasons? None of it mattered, Eric supposed, for he intended to keep this woman safe. If he left Katarina behind, Leif would threaten her again.

"Tomorrow," Eric told Valdr. "I will marry her then, and afterward I will sail to a place where I can train and regain my strength." He watched the older man carefully, being careful not to reveal his intentions. The truth was, the moment he had a ship, he intended to sail for East Anglia.

Valdr thought a moment, and then added, "I will journey with you and oversee your training. We will travel to the north, where we will stay with my brother."

He started to argue, but caught the look in the old man's expression. *He knows.* And perhaps it was better to outwit the fox by playing his game—for now.

"Send word to her brother, Hrafn, about the wedding in the morning," he told Valdr. "He will want to be there."

With that, he took his leave from the *jarl* and walked over to the partition where Katarina was staying. She was seated upon a pile of furs, her attention fixed upon the ground.

"May I come and speak with you?" he asked.

"Yes." Her voice was quiet, and he stepped behind the hide covering and saw that she had removed her apron overdress and was wearing only a linen undertunic.

He hadn't realized she would be in such a state of undress and started to apologize. "I did not mean to intrude."

"What did you want to talk about?" She kept her back to him, her shoulders lowered. He knew he should remain where he was, but the dim oil lamp cast shadows over her nape. When he drew closer, he realized that her skin was marked and bruised from where Leif had seized her neck. It infuriated him that the Viking had done this to her, and he vowed that Leif would never again lay a hand upon Katarina.

"I have told Valdr that I will wed you in the morning. Then we will leave this settlement for a time."

She gave no indication that she'd heard him, no response at all. Her silence made him wonder if she had changed her mind.

"Is that acceptable to you?" he prompted.

When she did not speak, he suspected that something else was wrong. Slowly, he walked to the other side, and she kept her face turned from him.

"What do you want, Katarina?" Gently, he touched her chin and lifted it so she would meet his gaze.

"It does not matter what I want." Her voice came out flat, emotionless. "On the morrow, I will belong to you, and I will go where you tell me to." She was behaving as if she were property with no freedom of her own. Was that truly the way she felt?

"You are not a slave in this." He took her hand and gently pulled her to a standing position. "But you must know that it is not safe for you to remain here. Leif will not give up."

She nodded. Yet there was no sense of relief in her eyes, only wariness.

"Tell me what troubles you." He held her hand, squeezing it gently.

Her blue eyes finally met his, and he saw the fear in them. Whatever had happened, she had not relinquished the nightmare of the past few hours.

"I want to feel safe again," she whispered. "And I do not know if it's possible."

He kept her hands in his, regarding her with all seriousness. "For as long as I am with you, I will not allow Leif, or any man, to harm you." He couldn't know how much time he had remaining, but he intended to keep that promise.

It would mean training harder than he'd ever imagined, but he could not stand by and let her become a victim. When Leif had attacked her yesterday, he'd wanted to slaughter the man. Never had such violent instincts risen up within him, but he would have done anything necessary to save Katarina.

He could see that she was terrified of what lay ahead. Though he didn't know what had happened to her in the past, she'd been shaken by it. His offer of marriage had not brought reassurance at all, and he needed to gain her trust.

The old *volva's* words came back to him, that he should change what was never meant to be. And bring back what was lost.

Was she speaking of Katarina's marriage to Leif? He doubted if that was ever meant to be. But what was he supposed to bring back?

More and more, it seemed that Fate was guiding him in a different direction. Despite his desire to journey to East Anglia, it seemed that the pathway remained closed to him. He *had* been given a second chance. He wondered if the old seer was right that he could only remain alive through the phases of this moon. But marrying Katarina—even if only for a short time—felt like the right decision.

He was an English marquess, not a Viking. Despite knowing nothing of their ways, he did know how to court a woman slowly, building friendship first. Eric took Katarina's hand and kissed it softly. The gesture was meant to comfort her, and when he released her fingers, he saw the confusion in her blue eyes.

"Get some rest," he said. "We will marry in the morning. And I swear, you will be safe again."

The vow went deeper than words. He would never let any woman be harmed, if he was there. He might not have the brute strength of these men, but he would train until he could stand against any Viking—even Leif.

Her cheeks flushed, and she nodded. "I hope so."

The morning dawned, but Katarina hadn't slept at all. Her mind was churning with thoughts of this unknown day when she would take Arik as her husband. As a girl, she had dreamed of a day like this—and yet, it seemed unreal. Everything had changed so fast, and she didn't doubt that Leif would try to interfere if he learned what was happening.

Arik was only making this arrangement so she would be protected. And although she was grateful to him, she worried about him keeping his word. He might have said that he would not demand a true marriage from her, but she didn't believe that. In return for his protection, he would expect her to offer the comforts of her body. All men wanted that from a wife.

Her mother had raised her to know her marital duty. She simply didn't know if she could get through it without pain and humiliation. *Freya, give me strength for this,* she prayed.

When he had kissed her yesterday, his mouth had evoked a strong response. Tremors had flooded over her body, making her feel a yearning she hadn't expected. It was as if her flesh was confused about desire and fear.

She was starting to believe that this truly could be Arik Thorgrim, brought back from death. Though his strength had been taken from him, she still held feelings toward this man. The years of wanting him had flooded back, and she could not deny her heart's wish.

Yet, she didn't understand why he had offered to wed her. He could have granted her his protection without marriage. Valdr would have kept her safe for a time, if she had asked it of him—though she doubted if Hrafn would have permitted it. Her proud brother would have insisted he could protect her, and eventually, he would have challenged Leif. A cold fear caught in her stomach, for she didn't want Hrafn to die.

No, Valdr could not have kept her safe for very long. Perhaps Arik had sensed this. He and Hrafn had been friends for some time, and he knew her brother would only step back if someone else was her protector. Was that why he'd suggested that they marry?

Her mind drifted back to the kiss he'd offered. From the moment his mouth had touched hers, she'd felt a sudden connection with this man. It was more than the years she'd longed for him. For the first time, it had felt as if *he* wanted her, too.

There were no clear answers, but her foolish heart was glad that she would be his wife. And in time, he might help her overcome her fears of joining with a man.

Yrsa helped her to dress, and then two other women arrived to accompany her to the bath house. Ana, her mother's best friend, accompanied the *volva, Móðir* Gerda. Katarina wished, somehow, that her own mother could have been here, but Kolla had died five years ago. With no sisters or female relatives to join her in the preparations, a sense of loneliness came over her.

Before she could leave with the women, Arik approached and interrupted them. "Good morn to you, Katarina."

She murmured a greeting and reminded him, "You are not meant to see me yet."

A kind smile came over his face, and he eyed the women. "Wait for your lady outside, and I will send her to you when we have finished speaking."

Apprehension swept through her, and she wondered if he had changed his mind. What if he had decided not to wed her anymore?

But when they were alone, Arik studied her and drew his hand over her hair. Yrsa had unbraided it for her, and it fell in long waves past her hips. No longer was she wearing the silver *crozen* around her head, for she would not be a maiden after the marriage took place. "You are beautiful, Katarina."

Every muscle within her tensed as she waited for him to kiss her. His thumbs brushed over the bruises on her throat, and his expression darkened. "No one will ever hurt you again."

She hesitated but asked the question burning in her mind, "Why did you decide to wed me?"

He let his hand fall away. "Valdr approved of the match."

"I did not ask about Valdr. I asked about you." She deliberately cast the words back at him, needing to understand his expectations. In the past, he had not wanted her—that had been clear enough. So why had he changed his mind now?

Arik sent her a slight smile. "It seemed like the right thing to do."

Strangely, his honesty was reassuring. Though it did seem like the best choice, under the circumstances. Her only concern was what benefit there was to him—especially when she could not offer a strong family alliance.

He leaned in and murmured, "I should go and let you finish your preparations. Hrafn is meeting with us to change the betrothal agreement and negotiate your bride price with my father. He will also travel with us to my uncle's settlement." His hand moved against her hair in a light caress. "When you return, we will finish the ceremony, and your brother will be one of the witnesses."

Katarina nodded. But before she could depart, he caught her hand again, raising it to his lips. Such a strange gesture, to kiss her hand. But the warmth of his mouth seemed to sink within her skin, an offering of more between them. Her skin flushed at his touch.

She forced back the rise of sensation and offered, "I will be ready soon."

After he had gone, she rubbed her hand where his lips had touched her. Instead of being afraid of him, she felt the rise of unexpected anticipation. A slight smile faltered at her mouth, and she walked outside to join the other women.

Ana, Yrsa, and *Móðir* Gerda were waiting for her beside the longhouse. As they walked alongside her, the *volva* took her by the hand. The old woman tucked it in the crook of her arm, her thoughts seemingly preoccupied.

The early morning sky was a pale white creased with rose. There was a chill in the air, and Katarina was looking forward to the steam of the bath house. It might calm the storm of restless emotions rising within her.

"Go and prepare the bath house," *Móðir* Gerda ordered the women. "I will speak with the bride here."

When the women were gone, the *volva* murmured a silent prayer to the gods, touching Katarina's forehead, then her heart, and at last, her womb. The moment the old woman's hand touched her there, she flinched.

"There is no reason to be afraid," *Móðir* Gerda said. "He will not harm you."

Katarina believed that, and yet, her hands began to tremble. "I know it."

"He was sent to you by the gods," the *volva* continued.

"And though his time here is short, he will heal what was broken."

A shudder crossed through her at that. The *volva* had the gift of prophesy, and she wondered what the woman had seen in her visions. "What do you mean, his time is short?" Katarina didn't want to imagine that something would happen to him.

But *Móðir* Gerda ignored her question. "Go inside, and let them prepare you," the old woman said. "And when you wed the man chosen for you, you will be among the blessed of *Freya.*"

She tried to brave a smile but didn't feel it. The old woman opened the door for her, and clouds of steam rose within the air. The heat was a welcome respite from the cold air, and Yrsa helped her strip away her outer garments until she was naked.

Móðir Gerda spoke another blessing upon her while Yrsa helped her to bathe. The two women helped cleanse her body, and then poured cool water over her to rinse the impurities away.

Her mother's friend, Ana, sat down upon one of the wooden stools. "I am sorry that Kolla could not be here for you," she began. "But as her friend, I must ask if this marriage is your choice."

"It is," she answered. She could not imagine wedding Leif now, after he had attacked her. And though it might be foolish, she believed that there could be a good marriage with Arik. As a young girl, she had yearned for him to notice her. It might only be an arrangement, but she believed he would keep her safe.

"You know what will happen between a man and a woman," Ana said. "But there is much that you do not know." From her discarded clothing, she withdrew a small vial. "Take this."

Katarina accepted the vial and opened it. A soft herbal

scent emanated from the oil, and she sent Ana a questioning look.

"Tell your new husband to spread this oil over your body when he takes you for the first time. Especially there." She pointed to the juncture between Katarina's legs.

Her face burned with color, for she now understood what it was for. The oil would make the joining easier. A rise of tears came to her, and she lowered her head, feigning embarrassment so they would not see her fear. But the old *volva* took her hands and poured some of the oil upon Katarina's palms. "Take this and anoint yourself."

She didn't understand what *Móðir* Gerda wanted, but spread some of the oil upon her stomach. The matron shook her head and took Katarina's hands, drawing them directly to her breasts. The moment her palms touched her bare nipples, they tightened and she felt a slight ache of pleasure.

"Here," Gerda commanded. "Spread the oil over your breasts. And then in the sacred place of the goddess Freya."

Shame washed over her at the thought, but she understood that this was part of the wedding blessing. The old woman was trying to instruct her in what would happen, and the oil was undoubtedly meant to bring fertility.

She touched her own breasts with her oil-slicked hands, trying to do as she was ordered. Then she briefly touched herself intimately, intending to end the ritual before she revealed her terror.

But she realized what the old woman had done. The oil must have contained herbs to bring about arousal. Even now, her nipples were erect and incredibly sensitive. Between her legs, she ached, her body craving something she didn't understand.

The women washed her hair with more cool water and combed it back, but with every minute she endured naked in the hot steam, her body grew more aroused. She wished now that she hadn't obeyed the *volva*. *Móðir* Gerda must have known that she would resist the marriage bed, and she had given this oil as a means of drawing her back to it.

After Ana and Yrsa dressed and left the bathhouse to retrieve her wedding garment, Katarina turned to the old woman. "What did you do to me? What spell did you cast?"

A kindly smile crossed over Gerda's face. "Accept Freya's gift and the man given to you."

"But the oil…I don't—I can't—" The words spilled out of her, and she crossed her arms over her aching bare breasts. Between her legs, she felt moisture blooming, her body swollen with need.

"Your new husband will soothe you," Gerda said.

But Katarina bit her lip hard. "I cannot lie with him, *Móðir* Gerda. Not…so soon." The old woman knew nothing of her attack, but it almost seemed that she sensed the reason for Katarina's reluctance.

The *volva* shrugged. "It is your choice. But it will take many hours before the effects wear off. Why would you not want to let him pleasure you?"

"I hardly know him."

At that, the old woman laughed. "You know his soul, and he knows yours. You were meant to be together, for however short a time."

Her heart clenched at that. "You said that before, but you never answered me when I asked what you meant."

The *volva* sobered. "He was brought back from death to fulfill a purpose. To grant you a child. And when it is done, he will return from whence he came."

He's going to die, Katarina realized. And though she wanted to deny it, she feared the old woman was right. There was no means of knowing when death might befall Arik, but the thought troubled her deeply.

"Will you take him as your husband, even knowing this?" Gerda asked.

The instinct to refuse came to her lips. But she could not

voice it. It did seem that Fate had drawn her to this man, now more than ever. Despite all that had happened, he was still the man she'd wanted.

"I will take him."

When Eric saw Katarina, the women had replaced her silver circlet with an elaborate golden crown set with rock crystals. Green and red silken cords were tied to it, and her long hair fell in waves to her waist. It was still damp from her bathing.

His father had guided him to the bath house to complete the same ritual cleansing, and after it was done, Valdr had given him an ancient iron sword.

It looked as if the weapon had been forged hundreds of years earlier, and the moment he held it, he sensed a trace of power.

"This sword belonged to your *Ái*," he explained. Eric did not understand the word at first, but when the man began reciting the names of his father and the father before him, he took it to mean great-grandfather. Though he did not know the purpose of the sword, he had no qualms about following their traditions.

He wore the clothes they selected for him, and seven witnesses were named. It became clear that when the witnesses were dead, the marriage would no longer be valid in the eyes of the law. Valdr gave him a hammer to wear at his waist, and then he joined them outside where they walked in a procession toward the shoreline. Most of the tribe was waiting, but there was no sign of Leif, thankfully. The *jarl* had ordered that the man be held captive for one day and night until after the wedding.

A small longboat was tied to a wooden pier, and Arik suspected that they would later travel by boat toward the northern settlement Valdr had spoken of.

One of the men led a sow by means of a rope tied around the animal's neck. Eric wasn't certain whether the swine was meant as a bridal gift, but when they reached the edge of the rocks that jutted above the shore, he was startled to realize the animal would be sacrificed to the gods.

It was done swiftly, and a bowl was used to catch the animal's blood. The *volva* came forward with a fir twig and dipped it in the bowl, sprinkling both Katarina and him with the blood. Then she blessed the witnesses, sprinkling them, too, with blood.

A hint of amusement crossed his face as Eric imagined a lady of the ton enduring such a violent wedding. She would have lost her breakfast or fallen into a swoon. Katarina, however, remained intent upon the ceremony. He gave her the ancient sword, and she, in turn, gave him a sword from her brother.

It was a symbol of protection, he realized. A promise to guard her, one given with complete sincerity. And a trace of unrest slid within him, at the knowledge that he was unprepared to use a sword to guard this woman. He had to learn quickly, in order to keep this promise.

Valdr placed a gold ring upon the hilt, to give to Katarina. She slid the ring onto her finger and then did the same for him. Then, with the rings on their fingers, they both placed their hands upon the hilt of the sword and recited vows.

He found himself caught up in her blue eyes, noting the anxiety within them. She was deeply afraid, and undoubtedly she had not wanted this wedding. But it would protect her, and he sensed that it was the right thing to do. He had no ties to any other woman, so what did it matter? There was no need to consummate the wedding when they were alone.

After the vows had finished, he leaned in to her and kissed her mouth softly. Though he did not know if it was a Viking custom, it did not seem right to leave his bride unkissed.

Her startled smile made him glad he'd done so, and a

cheer rose up from the people. He sheathed the sword and took her hand, turning to face them.

But Katarina pulled him by the hand and began running. He had no idea why, but apparently it was another custom. She hurried with him back toward Valdr's house, but paused before the door.

"Shall I carry you over the threshold?" he guessed, and she nodded.

She was a tall woman, not at all fragile like the women he'd known. But when she was in his arms, he liked the feel of her. Carefully, he brought her inside, and set her down within the space. By law, she was his wife now.

A strange memory crossed through his mind, a vision he didn't understand. His mind conjured up a wedding custom he'd never heard of, and he could not say if it was right to obey the instinct born of another man's memories.

And yet, when he touched the hilt of the sword at his waist, Katarina gave an encouraging nod. Without hesitation, he took the sword and plunged it into one of the beams supporting the longhouse. Behind him, he heard the cheers of the wedding guests.

Katarina went to a silver ewer and poured him a cup of ale. He accepted the ale, and before he took a sip, Valdr spoke a toast. "To Odin!"

At that, Eric drank deeply. The old *volva* came up beside him and took the cup, commanding him to take the hammer from his belt. "Place it upon your wife's lap, for the blessing of children."

He obeyed, and it was then that the sexual jesting began. Katarina blushed when one of the witnesses spoke crudely about Eric's hammer and what he should do with it. He stood and faced down the man, but Katarina took his hand and led him away. The *thralls* had been cooking outside for most of the morning, and before long, the guests began to seek their own food and drink.

105

His bride was appearing more and more nervous, and it soon became clear why, when the women took her away and led her to the back of the longhouse, separated by a hide partition. A sudden unease came over him when he realized that they were expected to consummate the union now, instead of at night. The witnesses weren't going to watch, were they?

He'd thought they would spend time feasting and drinking before they departed. But it seemed as if they were expected to lie together before they joined the remaining wedding guests.

Eric found himself surrounded by Viking men who teased him with ribald jokes. He was pushed toward the hide partition where his bride was waiting. And when they drew back the curtains, he saw that she was naked with only a fur coverlet. The headpiece had been removed, and her blond hair fell across her bare shoulders.

His attention was drawn to her face, to those haunting eyes, and the mouth he had kissed only an hour before. Though she was trying valiantly to be brave, he didn't miss her fears.

She had known this would happen. And it appeared that she was trying to go along with the traditions of fulfilling her duties as a wife.

He felt the need to shield her from the view of these men, and he stepped forward, intending to draw back the curtains. Instead, two men grabbed him, and they began disrobing him.

"I can remove my own clothing," he protested, but they only laughed. He didn't care that they removed the tunic and sword belt, but when they tried to shove down his trousers, that was the last straw. He jerked his way free and stood before them. "Go and join the others at the feasting."

Thankfully, they did, and he moved forward, drawing the hide partition shut. Katarina was lying upon the bed of furs, her hands clenched upon the coverlet to shield herself. She appeared like a virgin sacrifice, and it bothered him to see her presented like an offering. She deserved more than this, and he would not harm her in any way.

He took a deep breath and sat down beside her. In a low voice, he said, "You need not be afraid of me, Katarina. I will keep the vow you asked of me. There is no need to lie together."

She closed her eyes, as if trying to gather her thoughts. "I know what I said to you. And I do not deny that joining with you is not what I want. It frightens me." Slowly, she sat up and let the furs fall away, revealing her naked body. "But I also know that in the eyes of the gods, it will not be a true marriage until it is consummated. I spoke with the *volva* and...I know what must be done. She prepared me for this."

He was staggered by the seductive image of her. Full, round breasts were tipped with coral pink nipples. Her skin was pale, but firm, with a flat stomach and a swell of hips. God Almighty, he was struck speechless by this invitation. There was no question that he desired her—any man would. But this primitive act was not something he would force upon any woman.

It was strange to think of this dilemma. What man would turn down an invitation from a beautiful woman wanting him to make love to her?

A man of honor, that was who, he thought with a sigh. And although his body was raging to claim her, it was wrong to do so.

"You are a beautiful woman," he told Katarina, "and any man would be honored to call you wife. But I would not ask this of you. Not when I agreed to a marriage in name only."

She flushed as he handed her the gown and helped her put it back on. "Is it because I am not Svala, the woman you wanted?"

He could hardly believe what he was hearing. "Svala

nearly had me killed. And I am offering you an escape from consummating the marriage because it was what you wanted. No one need know the truth, save us."

Katarina swallowed hard, and then admitted, "I would know." She closed her eyes and then let out a breath. Beside the bed, she reached for a small vial and offered it to him, saying, "The *volva* told me to give this to you, to use upon my body before you claim me. It will…help."

He took the vial, and she lay back, closing her eyes again. Then his bride spread her legs apart, and the last of the furs fell away, revealing a darker blond patch of hair covering her womanhood.

Eric opened the vial and sniffed it. There was an herbal aroma, and he realized that it was an oil of some kind. Likely to make the joining easier. God Almighty.

But he had no intention of claiming her innocence. Not this soon, when they barely knew one another. "Katarina," he said softly. "Look at me."

With great reluctance, she did. There was no doubt that she was afraid of him. And he wasn't going to behave like a barbarian, claiming her when she wasn't ready. He leaned in to speak low. "We do not have to do this, Katarina."

She rested her palm against his chest. "Yes, we do. I was wrong before, and the *volva* made me understand this. Just…get it over with. I will not fight you."

It was entirely the wrong answer. He touched her cheek and commanded, "Open your eyes."

When she did, he saw that her fear was consuming her. He stroked her hair and moved his hand down to her bare shoulder. The moment his palm touched her bare skin, she tensed.

"Did Leif hurt you, before?" he asked quietly. "Or was it someone else?"

She shook her head and tried to roll away. But he tilted her face back to look at him. "What happened to you?"

He expected her to hold her silence. But instead, Katarina let out a shuddering breath. He released her waist, allowing her to keep a distance. "I was…attacked one night. They were planning to rape me, but Leif saved me from that. I thought if I wed him, he would protect me. Instead…" Her voice trailed off, and he understood then, why she had chosen the man—and then Leif had threatened her.

She curled her body into a ball and said, "I am sorry if I am not the wife you wanted."

He didn't miss the humiliation in her voice. But that wasn't why he'd chosen to wed her. There was something about this woman that beckoned to him. He believed the old *volva* who claimed that his time here was fleeting, bound to the phases of the moon. And he was certain that Katarina's path was connected to his somehow.

"I have no regrets about marrying you," he said. "But I want there to be honesty between us. We can be friends." The only way she could overcome the dark memories was to trust in him. And trust was something earned, not given.

Katarina said nothing for a time. Then finally, she admitted, "You are the only one who knows I was attacked, besides Valdr and Leif. I never told Hrafn or anyone else what happened to me—they only know that our sister died in that same attack."

She rolled over to face him, baring her breasts once more. The sight of her body drew a painful arousal, and he thanked God that he had not removed his trousers. She was entirely too desirable.

"Shall we return to the others?" he suggested as he released her and sat up.

"Not yet." Katrina paused a moment, then caught his hand. She made no effort to cover her body from view. Then she got to her knees and drew his face to hers, kissing him. "Thank you, Arik."

The affection was swift and it caught him unaware. But

Eric found himself wanting to kiss his new wife more thoroughly, and he thought there would be no harm in it.

"May I kiss you again, Katarina?"

She hesitated, almost startled by his request. "You do not need my consent."

But still, he waited. Eventually, she gave a slight nod, and he touched her chin, drawing her mouth toward his. There was a sense of anticipation between them, and he took a moment to drink in her features. Never in his life had he been faced with a situation like this.

And yet, she was no different from a shy debutante. Her blue eyes held trepidation, along with a slight curiosity. He bent to kiss her and kept his mouth gentle.

Katarina didn't seem to know what to do, but she did not push him back or try to break away. His breath mingled with hers, and he took another kiss, nipping at her upper lip. Softly, he threaded his hands into her hair, offering a new beginning.

She was tentative, but eventually began to respond. When she kissed him back, he caressed the back of her neck. He coaxed her to open her mouth, and deepened the kiss, tilting her head slightly. "Do not be afraid," he murmured against her lips.

In response, she wound her arms around his neck, pressing her breasts to him. The touch of her skin undid him, and he kissed her harder, sliding his tongue inside her mouth. Against his chest, he felt her nipples harden, and he tightened the embrace. She touched his hair, kissing him even more, and he fell beneath her spell, wanting her with an intensity that pushed the boundaries of honor.

It was only with the greatest of control that he managed to end the kiss. His bride was staring at him, her lips swollen. Her fingers drifted up to her lips, and the look in her eyes captivated him. Her breathing had quickened, and she studied him as if uncertain what to do next.

There was a raucous cheer from outside the curtain, and he realized that the others were still waiting for them. It was possible that they were trying to watch, in order to determine whether the marriage had been consummated. If he took her back to the feasting now, they would indeed believe that the union was invalid.

But there was another way to convince the crowd, however unorthodox it might be. He regarded Katarina and asked, "How good are you at play acting?"

She frowned. "At what?"

Of course—the word would be entirely unfamiliar to her. Against her ear, he whispered, "There is a way the others would believe this marriage was indeed consummated…even if we know the truth."

She still appeared confused, so he turned from her and removed his trousers. There came another roar of approval, but he kept himself mostly hidden from her view, covering himself with the furs. Then he turned back to her, bringing the coverlet around both of them until they were cocooned together with a layer of fur between them. He waited a moment to see if she was made uncomfortable by his actions, but despite her tension, she did not try to push him away.

"Would it bother you to feign…noises, as if I were consummating this marriage?"

She sent him a disbelieving look. In a low whisper, she asked, "You mean, I am supposed to moan and behave as if we are lovers in truth?"

"If you think it would convince them." He rolled onto his side and adjusted their position until it looked as if they were joined. It was a good solution, he thought. No one would know what was happening, and he supposed it was a means of defying their traditions.

"I do not know what you want me to do," she confessed.

His answer was to gently move his hips against hers. She let out a slight gasp, and he bent to her mouth. In a teasing voice, he ventured, "You could pretend to like that."

The sudden laugh that broke forth startled him. "I am sorry," she apologized. "I was not expecting you to begin."

He bent to her ear and kissed her earlobe. "It was not my intent to make you laugh, Katarina." In a teasing voice, he added, "You wound my pride."

She only began to shake—but not with fear. No, the woman was holding back laughter. "That tickles."

"I suppose this is not quite the wedding night I had hoped for," he said. "You could say, 'Oh, yes, Arik,' or something of that kind."

Her laughter was contagious, and the tension between them seemed to dissipate. He kept his weight balanced on his arms, so as not to crush her, but his body was fully aware of this beautiful woman.

Katarina was smiling at him, and she admitted, "I did like it when you kissed me. Will you do it again?"

He knew he shouldn't agree, but he was fighting the temptation with every breath he took. "If you wish."

He leaned in, but before he could kiss her, the curtain was pulled back by drunken wedding guests. Eric glared at them. "Get out."

The men cheered and one offered, "Do you need me to show you how it's done, Thorgrim?"

"Only if you want to die," he countered. But although they drew back the curtain, he was well aware that they would not leave until they were certain the marriage had been consummated.

A strange dilemma this was. In 1811, no one cared if a man and wife lay together. But here, it held a much greater weight.

"They aren't going to leave, are they?" his bride murmured. Her cheeks were flushed with embarrassment, and he knew they would have to do something to pacify the bystanders.

"Not yet," he agreed.

"Then you should…continue our deception. Do what you must," she whispered.

He rested his weight upon his forearms and bent down to her lips. Every muscle in her body was tight as she kissed him in return. He was aware of her female scent, and when he deepened the kiss, she wound her arms around his neck, pulling him close.

"I have to move against you, so that others believe you are mine." He didn't want her to be afraid of him, particularly during this intimacy. Although there was a barrier between them, he was well aware of her curves.

"I will not deny you." She braced herself, tensing beneath him. "Do what you must."

Eric had been with a few women over the years, but although he knew what to do, he was unprepared for the rush of desire that flowed over him. This woman captivated him, and when he arched against her, his erection hardened with intense need.

Her tongue moved against his mouth, and he invaded her softness with his own tongue. The erotic kiss consumed him, but he didn't want to frighten her. He kissed her until her lips were swollen, thrusting with the furs between them. Her eyes were closed, her face tense.

"Are you all right?" he asked, against her lips. "Shall I stop?" He was well aware that his actions might bring back unwanted memories.

Her blue eyes opened, and she reached up to touch his mouth. "No. You do not have to stop." For a moment, she seemed to push back her fear, and then she ventured a soft smile. In a teasing voice, she added, "Oh, yes, Arik."

"I think you'll have to shout that louder, if you want the others to hear you," he remarked. But Katarina only smiled.

He nipped at her fingers, suddenly wanting to arouse her. Slowly, he moved his kiss to her cheek, then her chin. She shivered when he drifted lower to her throat. As he thrust against her, the furs began to part, and her high, firm breasts were exposed. Her dusky nipples were erect, the tips sensitive to the cool summer air.

Katarina's hands threaded through his hair, guiding him lower. He knew that this was not real, that it was only a ruse. And yet, reality blurred with his own desires. His mind roared at him that this was not wise. But her legs had tangled with his, and with each movement of his hips, she was arching in turn. His body was rigid and aching with lust, and he fought hard for control.

He had no right to touch this woman, especially when her feelings were for a different man—the true Arik Thorgrim. He was taking advantage of her in a way that was dishonorable and wrong.

And yet, her eyes were locked upon his in a way that twined across his senses. He felt a strong connection with Katarina that went beyond physical desire. She had been the first woman to offer him food and shelter, and he had welcomed her friendship.

But this went deeper. When he looked into her eyes, he felt as if she had pulled the threads of time to bind him to her.

"I made you a promise," he ventured. "I think this has gone far enough to satisfy them." He needed to leave her untouched, not only out of honor, but because he would never break his word.

She was trembling, but she twined her fingers in his, meeting his gaze. "Arik, is it that you do not want me?"

The vulnerability in her eyes only heightened his guilt. "I want you more than I've wanted any woman in my life. But I swore I would not touch you."

She trailed her fingers along the edge of his face. "And what if I ask you to?"

He closed his eyes, caught between desire and responsibility. The man she wanted was someone else, a

Viking warrior whose life had been switched with his. He wanted to tell her that he was a stranger, that he had no right to be with her.

"What if I want you to take away my memories of the attack?" she continued. "What if you could make me no longer afraid?"

"You deserve a better man than me, Katarina."

She moved her hips beneath his, and the unexpected motion sent a bolt of heat within him. But she clung to him, biting her lip with her own needs.

"The *volva* anointed me," she murmured. "The spices within the oil are driving me toward madness. Every part of my skin is aching for your touch."

It was something he hadn't anticipated, but now it made sense. The old seer had given her an aphrodisiac, and he suspected it was meant to relax Katarina's fears.

"I feel such a yearning," she whispered. "And the more you touch me, the more it burns within me. I need…something. And I can feel my heart pounding."

When she guided his mouth to her bare breast, he lost it. There was no way he could deny her, and when he kissed the erect tip, she gave a shuddering moan.

"Please, Arik," she whispered.

He could no longer stop himself. The simple words undid him, and he covered her breast with his mouth, teasing her with his tongue. Her body racked with tremors, and he felt her fingers digging into his hair. Katarina was a beautiful woman, and as he imagined sinking between her thighs, he kissed the other breast.

He wanted to remove her memories of being attacked, to replace them with feelings of desire.

Her breathing had transformed, her cries keening as he thrust against her. He thanked God for the layer of furs between them, for if she had been naked, he doubted if he could have stopped himself.

He sucked hard upon her nipple, and she spasmed against him, making him wonder if he could pleasure her like this. Despite his vow to leave her a maiden, he also knew that the effects of the aphrodisiac were strong. He drew his hands over her body, pushing back the furs to reveal her bare skin.

"I will let you claim me," she offered, her voice breaking from the effort.

Arik was spellbound by the softness of her skin, though a voice inside him warned that he could not stay with her. There was no knowing how he had come to pass through time, but he did not belong here. And it was not right to take her as his wife in body—not when he intended to leave.

But he could pleasure her.

He drew his hand down her stomach, over the nest of curls. He found her wet, and she let out a cry when he touched her intimately. Instead of sinking within her damp well the way he wanted to, he began to stroke her. With his thumb, he nudged at her hooded flesh, while he kissed her nipple again. Gently, he slid two fingers inside her, and after a few moments of penetrating her while he rubbed her center, she began to move in counterpoint to him.

"Arik," she breathed. "I can hardly breathe."

He slowed his pace, not wanting to overwhelm her with the sensations. It heightened his own desire, watching her moan as he drew out her arousal. Her fingers dug into his shoulders, her hips tilting as he caressed her intimately. She was instinctively arching, her body trembling as she reached toward her climax.

A ragged sigh erupted from her as he stroked, and he felt the moment she came apart. Her back arched, and she pressed herself hard against him, crying out as the release poured over her. He felt her inner muscles squeezing against his fingertips, and her pleasure sent him past the brink. His own release spurted forth, and he thrust his hand in time to his own hips moving, imagining that he was within her.

At last, she pulled him down, skin to skin. Their bodies were slicked with sweat, and anyone who looked at Katarina would see a woman well-pleasured. It was enough.

"I would not have fought you," she murmured, kissing his mouth. "You made me feel so good."

And perhaps that was so, but he knew he would only hurt this woman when he left her behind. He didn't belong here with these people.

Silently, he leaned back, helping her to sit up. Without a word, he helped her dress before he donned his own clothing.

There was nothing at all he could say.

CHAPTER SEVEN

The weight of his silence was crushing. Katarina felt as if her life had been blurred by the intimate way Arik had touched her. He had awakened the dormant piece of her heart that she'd given him so many years ago.

She hadn't lied when she'd said she would welcome his touch. His kiss had drowned out the horrifying memories, pushing them into the shadows, until she was aware of nothing but him.

Never had she imagined that he would arouse her like that. She had wanted him desperately, but he had refused to claim her.

Was it because he had been forced into this union? Had he taken her as his wife out of pity? She didn't know. But as she stood and took his hand, her body was sensitive beyond words. Although he had pleasured her, the act had felt empty when he did not join with her. She wished she could lead him back to the furs, to finish what they had begun.

But he intended to keep his promise of not touching her—that was clear enough.

When she was fully dressed, he held out his hand and led her from the partition. The men awaiting them let out a loud cheer of approval, and she felt her cheeks burning with humiliation. They believed that she had consummated the union, that they were now truly husband and wife. But it was nothing but a lie.

Suddenly her emotions felt battered, as if she were an undesirable woman. She couldn't understand the tangle of thoughts within her.

Outside, he led her toward the feasting, and someone gave her a plate loaded with food. Arik found a place for her to sit and they shared the roasted mutton, fresh fish, and boiled eggs. Her new husband seemed distracted, his gaze searching.

"What is the matter?" Katarina asked quietly.

He reached out and touched a lock of her hair, fingering the waving length. "We are traveling north at dawn—to my uncle's settlement."

She stilled, for she had wanted put the sea as a barrier between herself and Leif. He would not accept this marriage, nor would he let them go. She had no doubt at all that he was conspiring at this moment, waiting for his chance to kill Arik and claim her for himself.

A coldness swept over her, and she reached out to her new husband, seeking to allay the chill. He took her hand in his, placing his other arm around her. "Have you eaten enough to satisfy you?"

"I have." She had little desire to consume any more, and the longer they remained among the people, the more nervous she grew. At this moment, she wished they were back inside Valdr's house, surrounded by so many warriors. Leif might be a captive for one day and night, but she worried that he would challenge Arik again, catching him unawares.

Her husband was not at all weak, despite her earlier fears. Though he lacked the brute muscles of the other men of her tribe, he was intelligent and swift. He *had* defended her...and yet, she couldn't help but worry about the uncertain future.

Her husband's thumb slid over her palm in an unconscious caress, and she lifted her gaze to his. For a moment, his dark eyes regarded her with undisguised heat. She remembered his touch upon her skin, and beneath her gown, her breasts grew heavy and aroused.

Many of her kinsmen played music, and soon, the women pulled her away from Arik, forcing her to join the dancing. His face held the shadow of a smile, but he hung back, watching her as she spun with them.

The ale made her mind drift with thoughts of him. And as she danced, she saw him watching her move.

This will be a good marriage, she thought. *Freya will bless us.*

Several of the men seized Arik, dragging him toward her. He started to protest that he did not wish to dance, but they would not allow him to remain on the outskirts.

There was a slight awkwardness about him, almost as if he'd forgotten their dances. She joined hands with him, trying to coax him into spinning with her.

But he caught her waist with his left arm, drawing her to him. Against his body, she felt his arousal returning, and he caught her hair with his other hand. She stopped dancing, caught up in the fierce expression upon his face. Her lips parted in invitation, and he bent down, capturing her in a ruthless kiss.

By the gods, her husband knew how to steal the very breath from her soul. She clung to him for balance, savoring the rough kiss, responding in kind. He kissed her for a long moment, his tongue invading her mouth.

She didn't understand the wildness between them or the preternatural sense that they belonged with one another, two parts that joined to make a whole. This marriage had been an arrangement, only a means of protecting her—and yet now, it seemed like far more.

She was startled when Arik lifted her into his arms and

strode through the crowd. She never took her eyes off him, but instead of bringing her inside Valdr's house, he walked toward the coast.

"You can put me down, and I will walk with you," she offered, feeling self-conscious while he carried her. But once they reached the view of the sea, he set her down. They stood upon a hill overlooking the sand. A clouded moon shone over the dark waves, casting a hint of gold upon the water's surface.

His expression was grim, and for a long while, he didn't speak. He stared out into the water, and a chill rose over her skin.

"I don't understand why you asked me to be your wife," she confessed. "Not really." All her life she had yearned for this man, knowing that his feelings were not the same. And yet, a few moments ago, he had kissed her as if she was the only thing in the world he desired.

"I did not want to see you with a man like Leif. He would have hurt you."

It was the answer she'd expected, but his actions spoke otherwise. She pushed a little further. "But why marriage?"

Arik's hands moved around her waist. "Do you know what would have happened that night if I hadn't been there to save you?"

She fell silent, remembering the terror. But his arms came around her, pulling her against him. "You would have been helpless. And I wasn't about to stand back and let it happen."

Katarina stared out at the sea, and the wind prickled a chill over her skin. Not only because of his prediction, but because she sensed that something else was wrong. Something he wasn't telling her. There was a hint of foreboding within his voice, though she wanted to deny it.

To distract herself, she murmured, "You said we are leaving in the morning. How long will we be gone?"

"Until I've rebuilt my strength. Valdr will help me to train among my uncle's men."

She turned in his arms to face him. "Will you take your place as *jarl* of our tribe?"

His gaze locked with hers. "I don't know." He looked over at the moon and admitted, "Your wise woman told me that my time here is running out."

Móðir Gerda had said the same to her, and the prophesy frightened her. *You were meant to be together, for however short a time.*

"She could be wrong." But a part of her feared that it might be true. She studied him a moment. "There is something else, isn't there? Something you haven't told me."

He met her gaze and fell silent. It was true, then. She waited for him to speak, but he merely said, "One day, I will tell you everything that happened to me. But not yet. You wouldn't believe me if I did." He took her hand and kissed it again with reassurance. "All I can tell you is that I shouldn't have survived that shipwreck. And although I was saved for a reason, I know I cannot stay."

"Will you leave Rogaland again?"

He shook his head. "You misunderstand me. I have the feeling that I'm going to die, Katarina. I don't know when or how…but I sense it. I should not be alive at this moment."

The premonition cloaked him in death, and it unnerved her. He had crossed the boundary once before and Freya had brought him to her. Perhaps to protect her from Leif. Or perhaps there was another reason.

"Don't say that. You cannot know what will happen." But cold fear clenched her heart, for the old seer had prophesied the same fate.

"I don't know how much time I will have," he continued, "and I don't know if there is truth to the *volva's* words. But I will fight for every last day I have left."

She saw the intense determination in his brown eyes. In

his arms, she felt safe and protected, though she could not say why. She reached up and touched his face. His beard had grown in, and it felt rough beneath her fingertips. Arik's eyes grew heated, and he caught her palm, drawing it to his lips.

Her heart beat faster, but she did not turn away. "Then we should make the most of the time we have."

Eric helped the men push the wooden boat through the shallow water before climbing inside and taking his place at the oars beside Hrafn. Katarina sat at the bow of the ship, her long blond hair streaming behind her. She wore a linen gown dyed green, and her cheeks were flushed from the wind.

Just watching her made him feel the burden of guilt. He had no right to wed a beautiful woman like her, even if it was an arrangement for her protection. She ought to wed a man who could provide her with a home and children—not a man trapped between centuries. But Eric could never stand back and watch her marry a man who would ravage her and break her spirit.

He didn't belong in this era. And though the *volva's* prophesy sounded rather superstitious, he was rather inclined to believe her. A man from the year 1811 could not possibly remain in the Viking age of 811. He'd nearly had his head taken off by Leif, and no amount of rapier training could have prepared him for this.

No, the odds were that he would die—if not by Leif's hand, then by a hundred other ways. It was not natural for him to be here.

It sobered him, making him aware of just how precious every moment was. And though it was selfish, he found himself wanting to spend his last weeks with this woman.

Katarina was strong-willed, fiercer than any of the English ladies he'd known. She hadn't sobbed or faltered in the face of danger. From the moment he'd kissed her, it was as if the years of loneliness had fallen away. Although the marriage had been a means of keeping her safe, he didn't regret it for a moment.

The longer he remained in this primitive age, the more he felt the trappings of his former life slipping away. There was freedom here, a wildness that flowed through his veins. It was so different among these people, but he welcomed the challenge.

When they were a short distance away from the shoreline, Katarina moved from the bow and came to kneel beside him. Her face had gone the color of snow.

"What is it?"

She leaned in, keeping her voice low. "I saw Leif watching our boat leave. I fear what he might do." She rubbed at her arms, as if her skin was freezing.

Hrafn was listening, and Eric exchanged a glance with the man. "Will he follow us?"

Her brother shrugged. "He might. But we outnumber him."

Eric stared at the shoreline, wondering whether there was a threat. He knew Valdr had ordered the man confined during the wedding. But would he seek vengeance?

He turned back to Katarina. Despite his uneasiness, he revealed none of it to her. "I will not let him lay a hand upon you. Trust me in this."

Her blue eyes met his, but he saw the doubt within them. Even if Valdr could teach him how to fight like a Viking, he lacked their strength. But he didn't want his wife to be afraid—not when he was guarding her.

Eric edged her cheek with his knuckle, and she tried to smile. "I will try."

He answered her smile and turned his attention back to rowing while she returned to the bow of the ship. Beside him, Hrafn admitted, "You surprised me, Thorgrim. I never thought you would wed my sister. You only had eyes for Svala before your last journey."

"Not anymore."

"Treat her well, or I will gut you," Hrafn warned. But a smile tilted at the man's mouth.

They rowed alongside one another, and Eric welcomed the burn through his muscles. It felt as if he'd been trapped within a life of manners and rules. Here, strength meant everything. He vowed to train hard, to become a man equal to the warriors around him.

One of Valdr's men turned to him and smirked. "Katarina looks tired. You must have ridden her hard last night."

Without thinking, Eric shoved his oar aside. He stood and seized the Viking, slamming his fist into the man's jaw. "Do not speak of my wife in that way."

The man started laughing, rubbing his chin. All around him, the others joined in. Hrafn sent him a knowing look. "It's good that you haven't forgotten how to fight, Thorgrim."

He stopped rowing and faced the men. "I have forgotten nothing. And you would do well to remember what happened to Leif." With that, he left the oars and went to join Katarina. She was staring out at the water, but he didn't doubt that she had heard every word.

The wind caught the sails, and the men worked to harness it, pulling hard against the ropes. Katarina held on to the edge of the boat, her long blond hair streaming behind her. Tension lined her face, and her blue eyes were wary.

"We should reach the settlement by nightfall," she said quietly.

"You're still afraid, aren't you?" He rested his hand upon the small of her back, and she nodded.

"I can't help but feel that Leif will not let me go. His pride will not allow it."

"I swore I would keep you safe, and this I will do." He

pulled her to him and was rewarded when she rested her head against his shoulder. Despite her inner strength, there was a worry within her. He wanted her to trust in him, to believe that he had the same strength as these men.

"Do you like being on the water?" he asked.

She met his gaze and offered a slight smile. "I do. Hrafn sometimes took me out fishing or we would sail along the coast. I love the wind." She closed her eyes and turned toward the breeze. It shifted direction, blowing her hair directly into his mouth.

He turned his face, pushing it away, and she started to laugh. "Do not spit in my hair."

In response, he twisted his wrist around the thick length, drawing her face close. Her laughter ceased, and she suddenly appeared embarrassed. She cast her gaze downward, and a faint flush stained her cheeks.

"You have no reason to fear me, Katarina. I would not harm you."

Despite her nod, she still appeared nervous. Yet, as Eric stood beside her in the boat, letting the wind carry them through the waves, it felt right to be with her. Never had any woman fit against him in such a way, as if they were destined for one another.

The wind slashed at his face with a sudden chill, reminding him that it could not last. If he let himself get too close, she would only be torn away from him.

She reached up and touched his face. "I know you are keeping secrets from me. But I am glad we married." There was a softness in her voice, and he gave in to the urge, stealing a swift kiss.

After he pulled back, Katarina flushed. "There is something I did not tell you." She covered her face with her hands, looking back at the sea. "Something *Móðir* Gerda said to me."

He waited for her to continue, resting his hand at her

waist. She appeared embarrassed, but finally said, "She told me that you were brought back from death so that I could conceive a child. And then you would be taken from me."

He had no idea what to say to this. It had never been his intention to lie with her or risk a child being born from them. And yet, each moment spent with Katarina was a strong temptation. He wanted to join their bodies together and watch her come apart with her release.

At last, he answered, "We do not know whether any of what she has said will be true. Not every prophesy will come to pass."

His words seemed to ease her fears, and she nodded, resting her head against his shoulder. "You are right, I know." Then a moment later, she turned to face him, resting her palms upon his chest. With her voice in the barest whisper, she added, "But I should tell you, if you do want to consummate our marriage, I would not deny you. I would...be glad of your touch." The color deepened in her cheeks, and he knew it had taken all her courage to voice such honesty. If he refused her offering, it would shatter her feelings.

For now, all he could do was hold her and stroke her hair. There were no answers for why he had been sent to this place. But he suspected he would soon find them.

ONE WEEK LATER

Leif bided his time, waiting to pursue Katarina and Arik. Let the others believe that he cared nothing about his bride being stolen away from him. He had gone about each day, feigning indifference.

But he did care. No one had the right to deny him what he had waited for so long—the vengeance that was his right.

He loaded a small bundle of supplies into the small fishing vessel and stepped into the water as he shoved it away from the shoreline. The boat was hardly large enough to fit two people, but it was enough for him.

Leif pulled hard against the oars, rowing out to the open sea. The morning sky was streaked with red, and it gratified him to see the gods showing favor upon him. He would have his revenge, spilling the blood of his enemies. And Katarina was one of many.

Her father, Lars, had been the first to die. Then his youngest daughter, Ingirún.

Katarina would be next, and then her brother Hrafn. Arik Thorgrim would be last, after he witnessed their deaths.

Leif knew he could have slit Katarina's throat easily, but that wasn't what he wanted. He'd wanted to make her suffer, to watch her eyes darken with fear. It would make her death all the sweeter to watch.

It pleased him that she hadn't known he was one of the men who had attacked her sister. She believed he had been the one to save her. Her naiveté had given him the idea of a betrothal, for he'd wanted to destroy her spirit before he killed her.

It enraged him that she had been taken and claimed by Arik Thorgrim. The man had no right to interfere. Leif let his fury flow through him, harnessing the anger into raw strength as he rowed. It would take longer to reach the settlement with the smaller boat, but he would use the time to plan his strategy. Both Katarina and her brother would suffer and die. He would wipe out every living descendant of Lars.

Only then he would find satisfaction, knowing that he had avenged his family.

Chapter Eight

The summer air was cool within the settlement, and Katarina watched the men circling one another in the fighting ring. Strangely, Arik had chosen a sword instead of the battle-ax he normally favored. He gripped the weapon with familiarity, and he never took his eyes off Hrafn.

"Odin's blood, but you've gone soft." Her brother spat into the dirt as Arik stripped off his tunic. Her husband had indeed lost a great deal of strength. Instead of the large muscles, he was lean, his skin lighter in color. But he was not weak. His arms did reveal the tight curve of muscle, though it was not the same as before. What bothered her most was the lack of scars. It was a clear indication that Arik had crossed through the world of the gods, and his brush with death terrified her.

Neither of them believed he could stay. And with each day, she feared she would have to watch him die. The thought bothered her deeply. Although this marriage had been formed out of his desire to protect her, she had never fully buried her feelings for him.

His kindness and patience were like water, eroding the edges of her stony defenses. Valdr's brother had given them a small dwelling of their own near the edge of the settlement. The shelter was a space she could stride across in three steps, but she had welcomed the privacy.

Each night when they returned, Arik had talked with her while she prepared a meal for them. He kissed her and pulled her body against his at night, but he had made no move to touch her. It was possible that he was keeping his distance because of the risk of conceiving a child…but it had become a physical torment. She remembered his hands upon hers, and she had grown so used to his warm body pressed against hers, she wanted to join with him. He had touched her only once, on the day of their wedding, but she could not forget the arousal he had kindled.

Now, as she watched him train, it only brought those memories to the surface. And she realized that if she wanted her husband to make love to her, she would have to seduce him. The thought was frightening, but she wanted him.

Katarina shielded her eyes against the sun, letting her thoughts drift back to the past. She remembered how she used to watch him with the other young men, and the daydreams took her back to a memory she'd nearly forgotten.

"You're too small for Arik Thorgrim to notice you," one *of the young maidens had taunted. "You're hardly a woman at all."*

Katarina knew the maiden was right. She was shorter than all the others, with no breasts to speak of, and they teased her for it. But she had faith that one day she would grow.

She had come to watch the men fighting in the contests, and like the other maidens, she had worn her hair down around her shoulders, with a crown of flowers upon her head. Arik had joined in the competition, and she had long ago decided that he was the man she wanted. He was a few years older than her, and he was so strong and brave.

Katerina had given offerings to Freya over the past few weeks, hoping that Arik would come to love her. In the meantime, she kept her feelings to herself, knowing how unlikely it was.

A small hand caught hers, and her younger sister Ingirún was at her side. She whispered, "Don't worry, Katarina. You're going to be more beautiful than all of them. And I think Arik Thorgrim is watching you."

She squeezed her sister's hand, wishing it were true. But then, to her horror, her younger sister hurried toward the circle. What was she doing?

"Ingirún, come back!" she called out. But the young girl had walked up to Arik and was speaking to him.

Oh no. The last thing she needed was a matchmaking little sister. Her cheeks blazed with color as she followed Ingirún to the edge of the fighting. Arik was smiling at the little girl, and when he looked up at her, he winked.

Her heart pounded hard, and she wondered whether to hug her sister or berate her. "Ingirún, you cannot stay here. Give the men their...space."

But Arik crossed over to stand in front of her. He towered above her, and his eyes held merriment. "I like your sister."

Ingirún beamed at him before running back to the other girls. Katarina felt her cheeks burning, but she forced herself to face him. "I don't think I want to know what she said to you. She knows she shouldn't be here."

"She told me that the other maidens were mocking you because you are small." He reached out and plucked one of the flowers from her crown. "And she offered to pay me in gold if I showed you my favor."

Katarina wanted to groan with frustration. "I cannot believe she offered such a thing. I am so sorry she interrupted you."

He took the flower, twirling it in his fingertips before he tucked it inside his tunic. Then he rested his hand upon her cheek for a moment. "This may give them something to talk about. And tell your sister I do not require her gold." He leaned down and kissed her forehead.

The gesture startled her, and she felt the trace of heat from his lips. She stood frozen in place while he went to join the others.

It hadn't meant anything, really. Only a kindness that was meant to prove the others wrong. And because of that first kiss, she had held Arik Thorgrim in her most secret desires until the day he had sailed away without her.

"You're going to be killed," Valdr predicted.

The leader's voice broke through Katarina's daydream, and she turned her attention back to the fighting men. "A one-armed man is defeating you. How can you become the *jarl* now?"

"I am not the *jarl*," Arik countered. "I never wanted to be." He swung his sword hard, and her brother darted out of the way. Over and over, they struck out, and a line of blood appeared across Arik's chest when Hrafn's blade skimmed him.

She winced, though it was a minor wound. The other men appeared uncomfortable at the fight, and several left. In her husband's expression, she saw the frustration and determination.

"Get some water, Thorgrim," Hrafn said at last, sheathing his weapon. Her brother exchanged a glance with Valdr, and she didn't miss his dissatisfaction. Arik had been the strongest fighter of all the men. And now, his movements were tentative, as if he'd hardly fought with weapons before.

He strode across the open space, and Katarina filled a wooden cup with water, bringing it to him.

"Here," she offered. He took it and drained the cup,

hardly meeting her gaze. She didn't quite know what to say to him. "Is there anything else you need?"

"I need strength I don't have. And more time." His dark eyes held annoyance, but she reached out to touch his shoulder.

"It will come."

He stared at her, capturing her gaze. She suddenly grew aware of how her touch affected him, and she drew her fingertips down his bare skin. He inhaled sharply and said, "Do not touch me here, Katarina. It is too much of a distraction."

She felt her breathing grow unsteady, and she murmured, "Later, then."

It was as if she'd struck a spark onto tinder. His eyes turned heated, and she sensed the desire within them. Although she should have been afraid, she had made her decision. Tonight, she would touch her husband and try to coax him into consummating the marriage. She did not believe the *volva's* words, that he would leave her once they conceived a child. No, a child would only bring them closer together.

"I will wait for you," she said.

But when she turned to walk away, she was well aware of him watching her.

Every muscle in Eric's body was screaming. He'd spent most of the day training with Hrafn, both with swords and later with a weapon he'd used only once before—the battle-ax. And all the while, Valdr had been watching. The man was a vivid reminder of his own father. And it felt as if he were leading a parallel life, one where Fate was demanding that he become the leader of these men.

Years ago, he had led a life of ledgers and Parliament,

before he'd left it all behind to travel the Continent. He'd been seeking his freedom, knowing he wasn't suited to become a duke. That life had suffocated him, and he'd turned his back on his father to escape it.

And now, he was faced with the prospect of becoming their *jarl,* essentially the same rank. His instinct was to deny the responsibility, but if he did so, it was repeating his previous choices. Was that why he was sent here? For another chance to alter his fate?

He could not deny the resemblance between Gregory and Valdr, nor the duties ahead of him. But if he did agree to be their *jarl,* what then? He lacked any knowledge necessary to lead a band of Vikings.

No, there had to be another reason. He was only too aware that he was living another man's life. Pride kept him from admitting any weakness, though he knew his meager strength paled before these men.

But strangely, he'd felt more alive in these past two nights than he had in twenty-three years. The aching and pain would lead back to strength, he knew. Even the mild slice across his chest felt like a mark of honor.

Whatever lay in the path before him, fighting was inevitable. He suspected that the task for which he was destined would either lead him back to his former life in England...or it would lead to his death.

More likely the latter.

Katarina's brother had not denigrated him for his lack of fighting strength. In fact, it seemed that all of the men had readily accepted his explanation that his return from death had resulted in a physical transformation. They regarded him with wariness, as if he possessed supernatural powers.

He had no answers to the thousands of questions haunting him. It seemed best to concentrate on gaining as much strength as possible in order to face what lay ahead. But would he be trapped in this place for the remainder of his years? It unsettled him to imagine it.

Eric trudged back toward the settlement, and Valdr met him along the way. "You cannot let the others see your weakness. They will lose all respect for you."

"I know this. But they did not cross back from death, as I did."

Valdr studied him, and his expression was troubled. "There is more that you have not told me."

Indeed. And if he did, he suspected Valdr would have him burned alive out of fear. He gave no answer, except to say, "There are many things I do not understand. I should have died in that storm, like all the others. But I was sent back for a purpose."

The older man's face was haggard and worn. "You have changed, Arik. But if you do not regain your strength, you will lose your place among our people. You must train each day, and become the fighter you once were. Or you will die. Leif *will* challenge you again, and you must be ready."

"I know this already." For he had no choice. He would never allow Leif to attack Katarina a second time.

Valdr regarded him closely, a weariness lining his face. "I am glad you returned to us, Arik. And the last thing I want is to watch you die." With that, he touched Eric's shoulder and walked away, accompanied by several of their kinsmen. His bearing was stiff, but within it, Eric recognized the unspoken message. Valdr had accepted him as his son. He *cared* and did not want him to fail. It meant a great deal to him, knowing that he had the man's support.

He was well aware of how the other men perceived him. He would have to be on his guard at all times, for any physical weakness made him a target. It was an impossible task to gain a Viking's strength with so little time, but he would work among them and hope for the best.

As he walked toward the small shelter he shared with Katarina, he realized one of the dogs was following him. He paused a moment to look back, and the animal's tail began wagging.

Without warning, the dog launched herself forward, whimpering with joy. Her tail wagged fiercely, and she jumped up to lick his face. He couldn't help but smile as the animal pranced in a circle, beside herself with happiness.

He remembered now that he had trained here, as a boy. The dog had been his constant companion while he'd been fostered with his uncle. And it was obvious that the animal had adored him. She sat back on her haunches, as if expecting something.

Eric reached into a pouch at his waist and found a bit of dried meat. He tossed the meat to the dog, who leapt up and caught it in her mouth. Then she trotted along at his side while he continued walking back to meet with Katarina. Even when he raised the leather flap entrance, the animal followed on his heels.

Katarina was stirring something in an iron pot, and the sight of her improved his mood. Her long blond hair was braided and hanging over one shoulder. When she saw him, she smiled and handed him a cup.

"I thought you might be thirsty."

He took it and tasted the ale. She glanced downward and saw the dog sitting at the doorway. "Where did the dog come from?"

He sat on a low stool and rubbed the hound's ears. "It belongs to my uncle, Dalla." The animal began licking his palm, and Katarina bent down to look closer.

Her smile faltered, and she met his gaze. "He remembers you."

"It's a female," he corrected. The animal rolled to her back, and Eric rubbed her belly. He thought back through the memories, searching for the right name. And then it came to him. "Her name is Oda, and she used to follow me everywhere when I stayed here as a boy."

"That's right. I remember you spoke of her a few years ago." She bent down to pet the dog, and his hand brushed against hers. He captured her fingertips and stared at her for a moment. Katarina froze at the contact, but then closed her fingers around his. Oda licked at her fingertips, and she smiled.

Eric kept Katarina's hand in his, and he drew her to stand up. He wanted her to feel at ease around him, but unbidden came the strong memory of her body beneath his. He could not deny the fierce attraction to her, but he would not press her for more. Instead, he wanted her friendship.

She was not an English debutante, like the ladies he had known. Katarina would never rap a wayward rake's knuckles with her fan—she would stab him first. The notion made him suppress a smile.

"What is it?" she asked.

"I was comparing you to the women I knew in England. That is, East Anglia," he amended. "You are very different from them."

Her expression grew shielded. "In what way?"

It was hard to describe it, but he offered, "They are concerned with what everyone else thinks. There are more rules about how to talk with women, and even how to dance with them. You are less formal, more open about who you are."

She kept her gaze upon the dog, not speaking. From her quiet demeanor, he suspected he should not have compared her to the ladies. To make it up to her, an idea came to him. He touched her waist, taking her hand in his.

"What are you doing, Arik?" she murmured.

"Dancing with you." He led her slowly into the steps of a waltz, keeping their circle small within the space. Her feet stumbled, but he demonstrated the steps, counting to three as he moved her body with his.

"This isn't how you dance."

"I learned this way when I was across the sea," he told her. "Try it." He slowed the steps, and she made an attempt to follow him. Her feet tangled together when he turned her in a circle, and he caught her before she could fall.

She started to laugh at herself. "It seems that the steps should be simple, but they aren't."

"Not at first. But once you understand the pattern, you will do well enough."

She tried again, stumbling in the footwork. Then she grasped his hand, regaining her balance. He moved her back, and she eyed him with chagrin. "I am terrible at this dance."

But he didn't want her to denigrate herself. "Look at me, Katarina." She lifted her gaze, and he continued moving her in a small circle. "I will guide you. All you have to do is follow my lead."

"It is possible that I might break your toes, as often as I have stepped upon them."

He kept his hand upon the small of her back. "I will take that risk." Eric slowed his pace, watching her eyes as he danced with her.

In time, she caught on, and her smile returned. "I've never danced like this before."

Eric slowed their pace and then stopped, still keeping one hand at her waist. He held both palms, and her cheeks flushed. He leaned in, resting his forehead against hers. The scent of her hair and skin was alluring, and he was caught up in the moment with this woman. There were no regrets at all about this arranged marriage; instead, it felt as if a missing piece of himself had been returned.

Katarina drew her hands up to his chest, tracing over his heart. The touch ignited his senses, arousing him deeply. He wanted so badly to hold her, skin to skin. She didn't seem to know the effect she had upon him. And if he didn't gather his control, he was going to capture that mouth and kiss her until she couldn't stand.

The dog broke the spell by yawning with a high-pitched noise. Then Oda crossed the space and sank down in front of the hearth. The dog was exactly the distraction he needed, and he caught his wife's hands, holding them away from his chest.

"I am hungry," he said by way of changing the subject. "Is there any food?" In truth, he hardly cared about food, but it was a means of avoiding the surrender to his impulses. He wanted Katarina so badly, he could hardly keep his hands from her.

Never before had any woman affected him this strongly. It was as if she belonged to him, as if he'd been waiting a thousand years for her.

"Yes, I have cooked a meal for us." His wife stepped back and went to fetch two wooden bowls. She ladled thick stew into the bowls and tore a small loaf of bread in half. "Come and sit."

He did, dipping the bread into the stew. He tasted chunks of venison and root vegetables. After the day of training, he was exhausted and it felt as if he'd never been this hungry before. When Oda sniffed the food, she trotted over and put her head in Eric's lap, sending him a hopeful look.

Katarina smiled. "I suppose she wants you to take pity upon her."

Eric tossed Oda a scrap of meat and finished the remainder of the stew. Katarina offered him more, and he took it gratefully.

"In the morning, I want to join you," she said. "While you train, I mean."

He doubted if she would find it interesting to watch. "There's not much to see. Your brother and Valdr are helping me, but it will take a few more weeks before I regain my strength."

She tore off a piece of bread and did not make eye

contact. "I mean that *I* intend to train, as well. I want to be able to defend myself better."

Her assertion surprised him, and he should have expected it. While he understood her feelings of vulnerability, he didn't want her to feel that she had to train unless she wanted to. "I don't intend to ever leave you unprotected, Katarina. All here will guard you." He might not have the strength yet, but there were half a dozen men who could protect her.

Katarina set her spoon down and reached out for his hand. "I know this. But I want to know how to fight, if there is a need. I couldn't defend myself the last time, and I won't allow that to happen again." Her face grew somber, and she confessed another fear. "What if you are killed? What will happen to me then?"

Her words hardened his mood, for they revealed her lack of trust. "Hrafn will guard you if I am not there." But he didn't want to face that possibility. He fully intended to see this through, no matter how long he had to train.

"My brother would give his life for mine," Katarina said softly. "But I don't want him to die. Leif would slaughter him if it meant claiming me, for he is not a forgiving man. And he believes that I belong to him."

"You don't." To emphasize his point, Eric caressed her cheek. "And I swear none of us will let him harm you."

She studied him for a moment and said at last, "I want to tell you everything that happened on the night Ingirún died. I think you should hear all of it."

A flash of memory intruded, of the young girl with darker blond hair, who used to follow behind Katarina. "You don't have to, if it's too painful to remember."

But she shook her head. "You need to hear all of it."

"If you want to." He moved closer to her and waited for her to continue.

"Hrafn was away on a hunting trip," Katarina began. "Ingirún was visiting with her friends, and they let her walk back alone at night. A group of men came upon her and attacked. She screamed for help, and I ran to her."

Katarina's eyes filled up with tears, and pain lined her face. "I couldn't save her. They forced themselves upon her, and before I could pull them off, they struck her head against a stone." Her voice grew quiet, and she admitted, "Then they tried to do the same to me.

"Valdr came, along with Leif, and they saved me before I met the same fate as my sister. It's part of the reason why I considered wedding Leif. I felt as if I owed him my gratitude for protecting me."

"Leif is dangerous," Eric said. And whether or not the man's drinking had caused him to behave badly toward Katarina, there was no excuse for it. The Viking was clearly a man who had wanted to control her, treating her like a possession.

"It's not over," she said quietly. "He will not forget what either of us did, and we are not safe."

Eric reached down to rub the dog's ears. "I won't let Leif harm you. And I agree that you should learn to defend yourself, in case I cannot be there."

A faint smile edged her mouth. "Thank you." She picked up the soiled dishes, and he joined her, pouring water into a basin. Katarina sent him a curious look. "What are you doing, Arik?"

"Helping you." He suspected that few Viking men would do such a thing, but he wanted a way to occupy himself.

"I can manage."

Eric knew that, but it took no time at all to help her wipe out the wooden bowls and put them away.

After they had finished, she regarded him with suspicion. "You are not the same as you once were, Arik."

"No," he agreed. "A great deal has changed. But I hope you are not displeased by the man I am."

A strange look passed over her face, but she shook her

head. "No. I am very glad you are here with me."

He drew a stool by the hearth, stretching to try and relieve some of the tension in his knotted muscles. He ached badly, but it was necessary to gaining more strength.

Oda curled up at his feet, and he reached down to rub the dog's ears. In the meantime, Katarina unpinned the brooches at her shoulders, removing her apron. She wore only a simple blue linen gown, and then she went to stand before the fire. Her body was silhouetted against the flames, and she began unbraiding her hair.

"What really happened to you in East Anglia?" she asked quietly. "I want to know. You said you would tell me."

He wished he could tell her the truth, that he was not from this era. That he had been stolen from his place, his soul switched with another man's. But he doubted if she would believe a word he said.

"Did Björn truly strike you down with a battle-ax?" she whispered. Slowly, she moved toward him and loosened his tunic, examining his back with her fingers.

He hesitated for a moment. "I do not remember much of the attack." He reached back into his memories, trying to put the pieces together. Though he didn't fully understand the images, he revealed what he saw in the visions. "I found Svala with Eyker. When I tried to kill him for touching her, his brother Björn struck me with his ax. I remember my men taking me on board the ship to die. There was a violent storm, and the moon was the color of blood."

The two visions blurred together and became one. Arik's fate and his own were intertwined during that same storm. "All the men were killed in the storm, except me. I do not know how I survived or why I was brought back." She reached out to touch his shoulders. Her hands were warm against his skin, and he enjoyed the feeling of her idle caress.

"There are moments when you do not act like Arik Thorgrim," she admitted, returning to her place by the fire.

"And at other moments, I want to believe you are."

She was treading dangerously close to the truth, but he said nothing.

"When you left for East Anglia," she began, "I was nothing to you. Hardly more than a little sister, for all that you looked at me. You were captivated by Svala." Her voice grew softer, and she admitted, "I wept when you sailed away, for I knew I would never see you again."

"You were wrong."

"Was I?" Her mouth curved in a sad smile. "Or am I simply believing what I want to believe? Arik Thorgrim would never have married me. He would have killed Leif and let me go. I never meant anything to him." She gripped her hands together and stared at him. "Who are you, truly?"

He held her gaze for a long time, wondering if he dared tell her everything. She was his wife now, and he owed her the truth. She had shared her own secrets with him.

After another minute, he took her hands in his. "I will tell you more of what I know. But as I said before, I do not think you will believe me."

Her expression held the burden of worry, but she tightened her grip on his hands. "Sometimes I think you are not real. That I may awaken one morning and find that this was all a dream."

"It is not a dream. I thought it was, too. But I found that what happened to me was real, in ways I could never imagine. And you are very real to me." He traced the outline of her face, still wondering how he could give her the truth.

She stood on tiptoe and kissed him. He'd never expected the gesture of trust, but he decided that she deserved the truth.

"My name is Eric Fielding, the Marquess of Thorgraham," he said quietly. "When I left East Anglia, it was the year 1811, a thousand years from now. I was traveling on board my ship, when the storm struck."

He felt the tension in her hands, but instead of disbelief,

he saw a trace of fear. Quickly, he continued, "I was washed overboard, and I knew I was going to drown. I prayed for more time. I regretted many of the choices I made in my life. But just as I was about to die, I heard a woman's voice on the wind saying, *Not yet.* I swam to the surface and arrived upon your shores."

She took a step back. "Then you are not Arik Thorgrim, just as I feared."

"No, I am not," he agreed. "I am Eric, Lord Thorgraham. The names are similar." He let her keep her distance and added, "When I saw you, I thought you were the most beautiful woman I'd ever laid eyes upon. But I also felt another man's memories within me. I knew your name and your brother's name. I knew your language, though it is not my own. It was as if my life and his were switched a thousand years in time. I believe Arik Thorgrim might have been sent to 1811, just as I was brought here."

She twisted her hands together and sat down on a stool. Her face lowered, and he said, "That is the truth, Katarina. I do not know why I was brought here, but it was nothing I did. Perhaps it was your gods or my own who used their power to twist my Fate."

He hunched down on one knee before her. "No, I am not the man you once knew. And I do not know how long I may live or what task lies before me. But I will not let Leif touch you while I am here. I will protect you, for as long as I can."

She would not look at him, and he gave her time to think about his words. There was no way of knowing what she believed or if she thought him to be a madman.

"I know that what I have told you may seem like a lie. I hardly believe it myself."

"No," she murmured. "I saw your clothing and the fastenings upon your tunic. It was like nothing I had ever seen." She swallowed hard. "You have no scars, as he did. And you cannot fight in the way he did."

Her words struck a blow to his pride, but he could not deny them. "Do you want me to take you to Valdr's house and leave?"

Her expression turned vulnerable. "No. I think I have always known you were not Arik. I simply...wanted to believe."

He tried to take her hand, but she pulled back from him. "What is it you want from me, Katarina? I know I wed you to protect you from Leif, but would you rather end our marriage? Would you rather go back to your brother?"

She stiffened and seemed to consider it. "No. It's what I *should* want, though." Her cheeks brightened, but she confessed, "Arik Thorgrim was the man I wanted to marry, even when I was a young girl. But I know that I was never the woman *he* wanted."

"You were the woman *I* wanted," he said quietly. "You befriended me and taught me your ways. And whether or not this marriage was meant to be, I hold no regrets."

There was something about Katarina that grounded him to this place. He was a thousand years lost in time, and his family and friends had not even been born. He could not tell her any of this, but in her, he had found an anchor. Her friendship and inner strength bound them together, and he hardly cared what had happened in the past. For him, there was only now.

But words would not convince her of his interest—only actions. He lifted his hands to cup her face and forced her to look at him. He traced the outline of her jaw, brushing his thumb against her full lips.

"This union was not one I anticipated," he said quietly. "But I am grateful for every single moment of it." He slid his fingers into her hair and kissed her lightly. "I wanted you from the first time I saw you. Each night, when I lie beside you, it feels right to have you with me. And though I will let you go, if you want your freedom, I desire you still."

He pulled back, giving her the choice of whether or not to continue. Her eyes were bright, and she appeared discomfited by his attention.

"I do not know what I want," she admitted. "The *volva* told me that I needed to be there for you. That we would…be together." She tightened her lips and glanced over at the bed furs. "But now, I think I understand the danger. If you are not from this world or from this time, you may be unable to stay with me."

He would not force her into anything. "The choice is yours, Katarina. If you want this to be a true marriage, I will not deny you. Or if you would rather end it, I will accept this."

She appeared shaken by his proposition, but he wanted her to be in command. They had no way of knowing whether or not the prophesies were true or how much time he had left. But he never imagined there was any possibility that he could stay here. And if that were true, he intended to make the most of every last day he had with Katarina.

Eric took a step back and granted her space. He stretched, rubbing at his sore muscles.

"You look weary," Katarina said at last. "I suppose my brother fought with you for hours after I left."

He recognized the tactic as a means of delaying her decision. "For a man with only one arm, Hrafn is fierce."

"He is," she agreed. Slowly, she took a step toward him. He didn't know if she had made a decision, but the single step gave him hope. "Arik—or Eric—I cannot say what I believe. It is a lot to accept, but I do believe that you are not Thorgrim." Her shoulders lowered. "What I do not know is what sort of man Thorgraham is."

"But you do know the sort of man I am," he countered. "I am a man who finds you beautiful," he said. "Brave, too— even if you did put your blade to my throat."

"I had a good reason for that."

"So you did." He took a step toward her but still maintained a slight distance. "As a boy, I always wanted to sail across the seas and explore distant lands. And now that I have, I wonder if it was because I was meant to find you."

Her expression remained somber. "I feel as if my life has been pulled apart, and I do not know what to say or do."

"Do you trust that I will never harm you?"

She nodded. "You have proved that, time and again. I suppose I can only trust what I do know of you." With a deep breath, she drew him to sit down. "Would you like me to ease your pain from the training? If it would help…" Her face flushed, and she added, "Your muscles may be tight after all the fighting you've done."

It was a gesture of peace, and one that he'd never expected. She had accepted his explanation without question, granting him her trust. Her offer to massage his shoulders was a dangerous temptation. If she touched him, he wasn't certain he could hold back his response.

But he would not refuse the offer, and she accepted his nod as an invitation. And when she began removing his belt and tunic, he held himself motionless.

Freya help her, Katarina didn't know why she had suggested this. But her husband was in pain; that much was evident. And surely she ought to be able to rub his shoulders and loosen the knots.

Yet when he removed his tunic, she found herself captivated by his bare skin. The scars of the past were gone, and she was shaken by his stories of traveling through time.

It was true—she believed him now, more than before. And whether he was from a thousand years in the future, reborn in the past—or whether he had been sent back as someone else, she found that it didn't matter. Eric Fielding,

Lord Thorgraham, was a good man who had fought to protect her. He had given her friendship and never pressed her for anything more.

Móðir Gerda had claimed that they would conceive a child. That might be the reason he was sent here. And every time she was near this man, she felt the physical urge to touch him. It went beyond human need, and after the past week when he had left her alone, she now knew he would never take what she did not want to give.

Katarina moved behind him and rested her palms upon his shoulders. His skin was warm from the fire, and she began kneading the tension from him. With her touch, she found the tightness and soothed it.

"Katarina," he breathed, as she massaged his back. She tried not to let it affect her, but she remembered their wedding night and the feeling of his weight atop her. It should have been terrifying…and yet, he had awakened feelings within her. She had yearned for this man since that night. And now that he was here, she didn't know what to do. There was no denying that she still cared for him, although he might not stay. And whether that meant his death or another journey back to his own time, she knew that if she lowered her defenses to this man, it would break her heart.

Her hands slowed upon his skin, and she questioned whether it was wise to tempt fate. He'd said he wanted her. For now, he belonged to her. He was hers to touch, hers to claim. But she was afraid to risk being with him.

She massaged his shoulders, noticing the shift in tension. "Am I hurting you?"

"No."

But she didn't miss the slight growl in his voice. Her hands did have an effect upon him, and she wondered if she should continue. Gently, she moved her hands to his neck, tracing circles upon his nape. "Is there somewhere else I should touch you? Somewhere else that it hurts?"

In one swift motion, he reached back and grasped her by the waist, pulling her onto his lap. Beneath her legs, she felt the hard ridge of his arousal. For a moment, he held her there, his eyes burning into hers. He claimed her in another kiss, and the heat of his mouth stole her breath.

"Yes," he murmured against her lips. "There is somewhere else I want you to touch me. If you are willing."

The wickedness of his tone made her blush, but he did not guide her hand lower, nor did he reach beneath her skirts. He simply held her on his lap, studying her face. "But I will never force myself upon you, Katarina. You can trust in that."

She understood, then, that he only wanted to show her his desire, to give her that choice. Her body warmed to his arousal, and she grew sensitive to his kiss, feeling the urge to give herself up and surrender to her needs.

She *did* believe that he would go to any lengths to protect her. And yet, she couldn't help but worry about the heartbreak that lay ahead. He would not stay, even if he wanted to.

She stood back, crossing her arms over her linen gown. Her body was aching, and she realized she had lowered the boundaries between them. Confusion roiled within her mind, for she didn't know if it was right to enjoy whatever stolen moments they had together. It would only make it that much harder to let go of him when he left her.

Arik stood from the low stool and took her hand, leading her toward the bed. She hesitated, slowing her steps. She was not quite ready to become his wife in body. He seemed to sense this and reassured her, "I only intend to sleep beside you. Just as I have every night since we arrived."

When she lay down upon the bed, Arik pulled her body into a light embrace with her back pressed to his chest. She had kept her linen underdress on, but she was well aware of his body heat. Nestled against him, she imagined for a moment what it would be like if she were naked. With nothing between them, she could easily envision him touching her.

Although the men had frightened her on the night they had attacked, Valdr and Leif had arrived before any harm was done. And with Arik, she had felt nothing but sensual attraction.

His breathing grew deeper as he fell into sleep, but her desire only intensified. She had enjoyed massaging him, taking pleasure in the power of touch. She wished she could have touched her mouth to his skin, exploring further.

Every part of her body felt alive right now, tingling with the closeness of her husband. Between her legs, she ached, wanting him more.

She reached up to the front of her gown, and her breasts were taut against the linen. Her nipples were so sensitive, and she bit her lip as a spear of desire flooded through her.

I want this man, she realized. She wanted him to touch her, to kiss her...to be inside her. And now he was here. He belonged to her, and she knew that he desired her, too.

From the moment she unlaced the top of her gown, she sensed him awakening. She pressed her bottom against his hips and felt the hard ridge of his arousal. Katarina remained still, waiting for him to touch her. But he kept one arm resting at her waist, the other arm beneath her neck.

And she realized that he would not touch her, for he had promised this. If she wanted him, she would have to make the first move.

Katarina lowered her bodice until it hung open, exposing her breasts. Her palm grazed the erect nipple, and a jolt of heat caught her between her legs. She let out a shuddering breath before she reached for Arik's hand.

She took his palm, gently resting it upon her bare breast. The pressure of his hand warmed her, and she imagined him rubbing her there. Her mind conjured up the memory of his hot mouth sucking upon her nipple, as he had on their wedding day. The thought made her arch against him.

His fingers moved in a soft caress upon her. "Are you certain you want this?"

"Yes." Her voice was barely above a whisper, and sensations rippled through her with aching pleasure. He gently traced the outline of her nipple, using his thumb to draw out the tip.

Arik paused a moment, and she guided his hand to her other breast in an open invitation. This time, wetness bloomed between her legs as he stroked her. With every touch of his fingers, she felt an answering tremble deep inside.

He shifted his position, cupping one breast while he drew his other hand over the outline of her body. He traced the curve of her hip and reached to the tangled hem of her linen gown, slipping his hand beneath it. For a moment, he paused, resting his palm upon her thigh. Then he moved it gently between her legs while his other hand caressed her nipple. Her breathing hitched at the sensation, and she pressed back against him, hearing his answering groan.

It felt so forbidden, wanting this man so much. He was right when he had claimed before that they were hardly more than strangers. She should have denied him, but the thought was unbearable when she needed him desperately. She knew where this would lead, and she hoped she could push back her fears of the night she'd been attacked.

His hand stroked the soft skin of her inner thigh. She froze, keeping her legs slightly apart. But when he continued to stroke her breast, she found herself beginning to seek more of his touch. It felt so good, as if he were worshipping her body with his hands. Gently, she parted her legs, and he rewarded her by cupping her intimately.

Katarina was wet with longing, caught up by how good it felt to have his fingers touching her. He seemed to instinctively know how to kindle the fire of her needs. It was even better than when he had touched her on their wedding day, and she craved the release she knew he could give her.

"Do you want me to stop?" he whispered, tugging at her ear lobe with his mouth.

"No." Her voice was breathless, and with that, he began to stroke his finger against her wet opening. Her reaction was almost violent as the arousal pulsed through her. A moan escaped her, and he slid one finger inside. The moment he did, he cupped her breast, stroking her nipple as he gently entered and withdrew with his finger.

By the goddess Freya, she wanted so much more. His thumb grazed above her entrance until she was breathing in rhythm to his intrusion.

"I want to be inside you," he murmured. "No matter how little time we have, I want to be joined with you, Katarina." To underscore his words, he continued rubbing her hooded flesh, shocking her with the intensity of the pleasure.

"Then do this," she bade him, trying to turn to him. "You are my husband, and it is your right."

He was silent for a time, though he never stopped touching her. She felt a tremor building deep within, and she begged, "Please, Arik."

"Not yet," he murmured. "But if you want me to touch you, I will."

Disappointment washed over her, but he moved her so that her entire body rested on top of him. He kept her back pressed to his chest, and he guided her hand between her legs. She felt shy about touching herself, but he ordered, "Put your fingers inside."

She did, feeling the moisture coat her flesh. Then he adjusted her gown until it was gathered against her waist. Her bare bottom rested against him, and he fumbled with his leggings until she felt the velvet length of his shaft resting against her spine.

"Let me touch you," she pleaded, but he kissed her neck.

"No. Another night, perhaps, but not yet. Keep your fingers where I told you to put them." Then with his thumb, he began to stroke her. She nearly came off the bed as the sensations caught her. The thickness of her fingers inside, coupled with the arousing touch of his thumb and his other hand pinching her nipple gently, was too much. She hardly recognized her own voice, as she let out a cry. The arousal crested into a wave that made her thrust against him, and the rhythm was unbearably pleasurable. She felt herself buck against his hand, and he rewarded her by rubbing hard, until a ripple of wild release shuddered through her.

She convulsed against him, feeling utterly boneless as the release swept over her. He gentled his caresses, and her body quaked with aftershocks.

Somehow, she was aware that no other man could have conjured these feelings. He'd known exactly how to touch her, sensing what she needed before she even knew it herself.

But when she tried to touch him in return, he refused to allow it. Instead, he held her tightly against his body. "It's too soon for this, Katarina. Sleep now."

What did he mean by that? They were already bound in marriage. And although she tried to relax, sleep would not come. Her body was alive, energized by the rush of sensations he had conjured.

Had he denied her because he did not want to join with her? Or was it because he was afraid of her conceiving a child? The gods had brought him back to her, but for how long?

She was afraid to even imagine the answer.

Chapter Nine

Eric awakened in a state of full arousal. His wife had snuggled against him after he'd touched her, and he'd spent a long night tormented by physical frustration. But it had felt right to have her in his arms. Even now, he didn't want to get out of bed. If they'd had a true marriage, he would have spent all night making love to her.

He gritted his teeth and forced himself to get up. He had nearly given in to his instincts last night, though it was wrong to do so. He was not a Viking who would follow his baser urges and claim his wife. He had no right to risk conceiving a child with Katarina—not when he might leave her even more vulnerable than she already was. Then, too, no child deserved to grow up without a father.

His mind drifted back to the duke. Although they had constantly argued, he missed Gregory. His father had been a bookish sort, never understanding why Eric had enjoyed learning boxing and fencing instead of immersing himself in Latin studies. He wondered what Gregory would think of Valdr. The former *jarl* bore a physical resemblance to his father, but he doubted if Valdr even knew how to read. And yet, both men believed they were always right.

He wondered if their similarity was a deliberate turn of fate—almost as if he'd been given a second chance to gain forgiveness from the man he'd abandoned. Or perhaps he was in purgatory after all, destined to face his mistakes and learn from them.

He dressed quietly, and Katarina woke up a moment later. The fire had died down, and he added more wood, coaxing flames from the glowing embers. She smiled sleepily as she ran her fingers through her hair.

"Good morn to you, Eric."

The use of his true name made him smile. "And to you." He watched as she put on a new apron and washed her face and hands from a bucket. She began preparing food for them, but he sensed shyness from his wife. He didn't want her to feel uncomfortable around him after their intimacy last night. It hadn't been his intention to touch her, but after her silent invitation, nothing could have made him turn her away.

"I will train alongside you this day," she said quietly. "My brother has taught me before."

He understood her reasons, but he warned, "Be careful. I do not want you to be hurt." The idea of her facing Viking warriors was not a welcome one.

"No man will hurt me. Not today or ever again." She spooned an oat mixture onto a heated stone, and he didn't miss the stubborn resolve in her expression.

"I agree." He came up behind her and kissed her cheek. "What weapon will you use?"

From her belt, she withdrew a small dagger. "This. I have fought with it before."

He examined the light blade and handed it back to her, hilt-first. "It will do well enough." Though the weapon was small, it was all she needed.

After Katarina put it away, she finished making their morning meal, and he ate alongside her. She rebraided her hair, tying it back with a leather cord. He helped her again with the dishes, and she seemed shy, refusing to meet his gaze.

"Is something wrong, Katarina?" he asked, when they were ready to leave.

She bit her lower lip, hesitating. He waited for her to speak, and finally, she caught his hand. She reached up to touch his nape and guided his face down to hers. Standing on tiptoe, she lifted her mouth to his, kissing him softly.

"I want a true marriage, Eric. Not a shadow of one."

Her invitation startled him, but he kissed her back, twining his hand in her long braid and pressing her against the wall. There was something to be said for a primitive life. Katarina cared nothing for propriety, and they both suspected that time was running out. He kept his kiss gentle, letting her take what he wanted. But he slid his tongue within her mouth, coaxing her into more. Her eagerness fired up his desire, and he felt himself growing more uncivilized with each minute, wanting to claim her.

He drew his hands over her body, pulling her so close, he could feel every curve. He ached to possess her, but a part of him considered the consequences. There could indeed be a child, which was too grave a risk.

With great reluctance, he pulled back. In her eyes, he saw a yearning emotion, before she veiled it. "We should go now, Katarina. We will speak more of it later tonight."

He opened the door for her and escorted her outside. But as they walked toward his uncle's dwelling, the pale moon was still visible over the horizon. No longer full, the shape had begun to wane. It was possible that he had barely a fortnight remaining.

A coldness slid over his spine, but he trudged forward. The future might be uncertain, but there was still a little time left.

It had been years since Katarina had trained in fighting. Hrafn had hung a heavy bag filled with grain, and she spent time lunging at the target, stabbing it with an upward motion. But although she worked until perspiration came over her skin, she was watching Eric all the while.

Her husband was more adept with the sword than the battle-ax. She now knew the reason—it was a weapon he had used in East Anglia—but she found it difficult to grasp that a man could cross through time.

He had discarded his tunic, and she noticed the healing nick across his chest. She stopped her training and watched him openly for a time. His chest held the lines of strength, and his stomach was lean and toned. For an idle moment, she remembered touching him and the feeling of his hands upon her bare skin.

He worked tirelessly with Hrafn while his uncle and father watched over him. She was unable to tear her gaze from him. He moved with purpose, and he never took his eyes off his opponent. Once or twice, he seemed to lose himself in the fight, and her brother was forced to retreat.

Eric glanced over at her, and she smiled at him, showing her approval. He sheathed his sword and switched over to the battle-ax. She tried to turn her attention back to her practice, but her mind kept drifting to her husband.

Everything had happened so fast, and yet, she admitted that she was enjoying the moments with this man. Tonight, she intended to stand firm, to be his wife in flesh as well as in spirit. The need went beyond all else.

Katarina's arms ached from the repetitive motion of stabbing, and so she stuck her blade into the bag of grain and crossed the small courtyard, signaling a *thrall* to bring ale. The young man returned with several goblets, and she went to wait for the men to finish their sparring. She drank while the men circled one another.

Although her brother only had one arm, he moved with swiftness and power. He struck out, again and again, and the sound of clashing weapons reverberated in the circle. Eric dodged one blow and followed up with his own attack, only to have her brother lash back with fury.

"Stop watching my hands, and watch my eyes," her brother demanded. "Else you will lose every time."

Hrafn wielded the heavy battle-ax and Eric raised a shield. The metal edge bit into the wood and before her brother could pull back, her husband spun and tripped Hrafn, disarming him as he tugged the shield back with the ax still embedded.

"Good," her brother said, accepting his hand and rising from the ground. "If you continue to fight like that, there may be hope that you won't be killed tomorrow."

The *thrall* offered ale to the men, and Eric drained his goblet, staring at her. She felt the heat of his eyes upon her body, and Hrafn was well aware of it, too. Her brother gestured for her to come forward. "Show me what you remember about fighting, Katarina."

She was about to return for her knife, but he shook his head. "No weapons." Instead, he came up behind her, and seized her with his one arm. "How will you break free?"

She slammed her head backward and twisted, moving away from Hrafn's hold. He rubbed at his nose and nodded to her. "Good. But most men will have two arms. Try it with Arik."

Katarina moved into position with her husband's arms wrapped tightly around her. His wrist rested against her throat, and she could almost imagine that he held an invisible blade. She could feel the taut strength of him, and she thought a moment.

"What are you going to do?" Eric asked against her ear. His voice resonated, causing a spiral of desire to wind through her body. She pressed her backside against him and felt the rise of interest from him.

A second later, she elbowed his ribs and used the distraction to try and twist against him. But her husband remained unmoving, his arms locked around her. She tried to knock her head backward against his, but he dodged the blow and pushed her to the ground, pinning her there.

"You've lost this battle." Eric stole a kiss before he let her back up. "But I will help you practice later." He lifted her to her feet and let her go.

Her cheeks burned with embarrassment, though she was accustomed to losing and wasn't entirely upset. She wanted him to regain his strength, and to be defeated by a woman would only cause him to lose face in front of Valdr and Dalla.

In the distance, she heard a dog barking and snarling. It sounded like Oda, but she had no idea why the animal was so unsettled. She started to move toward the noise, but Eric stopped her.

"No. Let Hrafn and me find out what it is. Stay here with Valdr and Dalla. They will guard you until we return."

The idea of staying behind didn't appeal to her. "I thought you wanted me to remain at your side at all times."

Eric's face hardened, and he shook his head. "It's safer for you here, among Valdr and the others."

If that was what they wanted, so be it. And yet, she had never heard Oda bark in that way before. Her instincts sharpened, and she handed her goblet back to a *thrall*. If the men did not return right away, she wanted to be prepared to fight. Katarina crossed the courtyard, intending to take back her blade.

Along the way, she cast a glance at Valdr and his brother, Dalla. The two men were speaking quietly, and it was clear that Eric was the subject of their conversation. She hoped that he had improved during this day of training, but from the unsettled expressions on their faces, it did not appear so.

Katarina walked toward the bag of grain, and all the while, the dog continued to bark. Strangely, her blade was missing.

She frowned and looked around to see if it had fallen, but there was no sign of the weapon anywhere. She had not sheathed it at her waist, so where could it be? She questioned the *thrall* who had brought the ale, but he only shrugged. Though it was only an ordinary blade with no particular value, she was certain she had plunged it into the bag.

She walked up the stairs to the platform where the two older men had been watching. Valdr's brother Dalla nodded in greeting. The man was younger, but his brown beard held tints of gray. "I understand that you married my nephew for his protection," he began. "But do you truly believe he can defend you?"

"He already has, when Leif attacked me," she said. Straightening, she added, "I believe all of his fighting strength will return."

It was true enough. Though it would take time, Eric had never faltered in his effort. Dalla inclined his head at last. "I offer my good wishes to you and my nephew. And may Freya bless you with many sons."

Katarina murmured her thanks and shielded her eyes against the afternoon sun. From her vantage point, she could see the longhouses and people moving about, but upon the grounds, there was no sign of her missing blade. She was beginning to wonder if it had somehow fallen into the grain from a hole in the cloth. Before she could go and look, the *jarl* caught her hand. "I've been wanting to talk with you about my son," Valdr said quietly.

From his tone, she detected a bleakness, and her suspicions rose. "What is it?"

"Do you think the gods truly returned him to us? Or is he one of Loki's shadows, meant to trick us into believing lies?" Valdr's expression turned grim. "He does not seem like the same man at all."

She would not tell him the truth, for if she did, it might mean Eric's death. The *jarl* was not a man who would take kindly to a deception. Instead, she kept her tone neutral, "He is different," she agreed. "What man would not be, after returning from Valhalla?"

"A man who is a liar," Valdr countered. "He does not fight in the same way he once did."

"He has changed, yes. But he is still a man of honor."

"I do not believe him," Valdr said quietly. "He does not remember our ways of fighting. No one would forget this, save an outsider."

"He is concentrating too hard," she said. "When he trusts his instincts, he has defeated Hrafn. I believe he can and will return to the fighter he once was."

Valdr sobered and said quietly, "There was another reason why I wanted you to wed this man. You have never made any secret of your interest in my son. And I thought that you, more than anyone else, would know if he was an imposter. A man cannot hide his true nature in his own home."

She held her ground, and insisted, "He is not an imposter." And although he was not Arik Thorgrim, she had found this man to be even better than the man she had once loved. He was kind and patient with her, whereas most men of her tribe disregarded a woman's desires. They would not have cared that she had been attacked and was afraid of men. Every last one of them would have consummated the marriage, crushing her beneath their weight while they claimed her body. But instead of doing this, her husband had given her choices. He had tempted her, teaching her that the intimate darkness held only pleasure. And because of that, she hungered for him.

Katarina looked back at the longhouses in the distance and saw her brother and Eric returning, along with Oda. The dog trotted by her husband's side, sniffing the ground as they neared the training grounds. She approached them, and when she reached Eric's side, he shook his head. "We found nothing. The longhouse was undisturbed, and the *thralls* saw no one."

"Then Oda was barking for no reason?"

"Dogs always have a reason," he said. "But we found no one there. At least, not when we arrived." But from the tone of his voice, she knew that his suspicions were on alert.

"My blade is missing," she said. "I had put it in the bag of grain after I finished practicing, but it's not there now."

"It could have fallen," Hrafn offered. "Or perhaps you mislaid it." He took a knife from his belt and offered it to her. "Use this."

She accepted his blade, but lifted her gaze to Eric. His eyes were clouded, and she saw the troubled look within them. But rather than worry, she said, "Let us return to training, and I may find it."

Over the next few hours, she sparred against her brother while Eric chose a different opponent. The dog lay sprawled upon the ground watching over both of them. Hrafn pushed her harder than he had in the past, and her muscles ached from exertion. She was beginning to wonder if they *had* seen something near the longhouse and had decided not to tell her.

Eric fought against one of Dalla's men, and from the vicious clang of weapons, she grew aware of the intensity. The fighting turned vicious, and her husband narrowly missed an axe blow to his upper arm.

"Keep your mind on this fight, Katarina," her brother warned. "You cannot afford to be distracted."

She nodded and clenched his knife, poised in a fighting stance. But all the while, she watched over her husband. Something had changed, and he seemed caught up within the fighting. There was a ferocity she hadn't seen before, and at one point, he seized a handful of earth and threw it at his opponent's face, blinding him before he took him to the ground.

"Good," her brother murmured.

Katarina wasn't certain what the difference was, but Eric had somehow transformed back into the warrior he had been. He had lost himself in the moment until nothing else existed, save the fight. The other warrior was on the ground, and Eric pinned the handle of the battle-ax against his throat. When the man yielded, he helped him rise, and then his gaze centered upon her.

His interest was unmistakable, and Katarina felt the blood rise within her. "That is enough for today," she told her brother. She was about to cross toward her husband, but she felt self-conscious from his open stare. When she reached his side, she offered, "Do you want to swim and wash off the dust?"

Eric nodded, but his heated expression made her remember what it was to have his hands upon her. A rise of nerves rippled within her, and she walked alongside him. He began leading her toward the lean-to where the horses were kept.

"Where are we going?"

He leaned in to her ear. "Further away from the settlement. I want to be certain that no one can threaten you. There are too many places a man could conceal himself in the rocks along the beach. I would rather take you out to the lake where there is nowhere to hide."

His reasoning was sound, and she helped him prepare one of his uncle's horses. Eric lifted her on and mounted behind her. He guided the animal eastward, and Oda followed them.

As they trotted, she was very aware of his body pressed to hers. His skin was warm from training, and she welcomed the closeness of him. Katarina rested her hands upon his knees, and he rewarded her by holding her waist with one hand. As they rode, she grew conscious of his arousal against her bottom, and it provoked her own rising needs.

"I enjoyed watching you fight," he said against her ear. "You are a strong woman."

"Y-you fought well," she stammered. "Especially toward the end when you stopped thinking about it."

He tightened his grip around her. "There is much to be said about trusting instincts. Or, in this case, Arik Thorgrim's memories." There was a trace of irony in his voice. "When I stop thinking, it's as if I become him. I feel more primal. The fighting becomes about survival instead of a sparring match."

"It has to be," she answered. "If you cannot defend yourself, you will die." But even as she tried to distance herself from the words, she felt a pang of fear. She didn't want Eric to suffer that fate, but neither could deny the risks facing them.

They rode in silence for a time, and after the first mile, he murmured in her ear, "Riding with you is torture, Katarina. I want to touch you. And I know that this is not the time or place."

She didn't agree with that at all. In answer, she drew his hand higher, guiding it beneath the apron pinned at her shoulders. She wore a thin linen gown, and the heat of his palm burned against the curve of her breast. He teased her nipple with his fingers, and the answering echo of desire made her ache between her legs. Her hands tightened upon his strong thighs, and she gave herself over to the swell of sensation. The summer air was warm, and when they reached the pond, a light breeze shifted the reeds growing along the banks.

Eric drew their horse to a stop and helped her dismount. Before she could take a single step, his mouth crushed against hers, hot and hungry. She kissed him back, reveling in the hard lines of his body against hers. She tasted his need and hardly cared that he was fumbling with the brooches at her shoulders, needing to free her body from the confining clothes. Right now she wanted him so badly, she was trembling.

She helped him unfasten his tunic and belt, dropping them to the ground. Once she stood in only her underdress, his eyes grew hooded with passion. Katarina felt the urge to tease him.

"You look like a wolf, about to tear me apart." She took a few steps into the water, raising the hem of the underdress. It was cool, and gooseflesh pricked over her skin.

"I might sink my teeth into you," he growled, removing the rest of his clothing. A faint sheen of sweat covered his skin, and he made no effort to hide his arousal.

Katarina laughed and moved further into the water, raising the underdress up to her waist. Beneath the water she was naked, and she walked toward the far edge of the bank. She would have to remove the garment to keep it dry.

"Are you running away from me?" he asked.

She lifted the underdress from her body, giving him a glimpse of her breasts before she tossed it onto the embankment. Then she sank beneath the water, hiding herself from him. "I am right here, Eric. Come and swim with me."

He strode into the water as if the frigid cold didn't bother him at all. Instead, he moved toward her like a conqueror, bent upon claiming her.

"It's cold in the water." Her teeth were chattering.

"Then I will warm you."

She smiled at her husband, waiting for him. Yes, she was afraid. But this man had saved her from Leif, and their marriage had been an unexpected gift. Over the past week, he'd trained hard, pushing his exertion to the limit.

For her.

Neither of them knew how much time the gods would grant them, but she could not deny that she wanted her husband. She stood in place, waiting for him. A moment later, there came a light splash as the dog dove into the water and began paddling toward them.

She bit her lip, trying to hold back a laugh. "I think Oda wants us to swim with her."

"She can wait." Eric drew her to him, skin to skin. He cupped the curve of her bottom, and she gasped at the rush of need that flowed through her.

"I've been watching you all day," he murmured against her mouth. "You are very good with a blade."

"I have a reason to fight. I don't want to be Leif's victim again. Or any man's." She moved her hands over his chest, feeling the pulse of his heartbeat.

"You won't be."

Katarina wrapped her legs around his waist, feeling the wildness rise within her blood. He was right—she hardly felt the cold of the water anymore. Instead, she was deeply aware of the water upon her bare skin and the touch of him.

After the day of hard training, she knew his body ached as hers did. She knew he wanted her, and she was no longer afraid to join with him. They were far enough away from the settlement that they would see intruders before anyone could interfere. Then, too, Oda would bark and alert them.

"Are you cold now?" he asked, nipping at her lower lip.

"A little." It was more of the temperature contrast between their bodies and the water. The shock of cold compared to the heat of his flesh was startling. But she was pressed against him so close, she was hardly aware of any discomfort.

Eric took a step backward, lifting her out of the water. His arousal rested against her damp curls, and in his eyes, she saw the rigid desire and a silent question.

"Join with me," she murmured. "I want to feel you inside of me."

The air was cool, but Eric carried her from the pond. "Do you?"

She did. In spite of whatever dangers lay ahead, she believed that their time together should be savored. When he stopped walking, Katarina still had both legs wrapped around his waist. She lifted her hips, guiding the head of him to rest at the entrance of her womanhood. He held her there, suspended, and her body ached to be filled.

"Please," she whispered. She kissed him deeply, trying to press herself lower. She needed to give back to him what he'd brought to her. And she knew that he would never take her against her will.

"What of the risks?" he asked.

His hands held her firmly, and she met his gaze with her own yearning. "I will take whatever risks there are. I want a true marriage with you. And I want your child, if the goddess blesses us." She drew her hands up to his face, tracing his features. "If the worst happens, I will have a part of you with me always."

He started to leave the water, but she pleaded. "Wait. Stay here." In this position, she was in control, and she had a feeling that he was still reluctant to claim her.

Katarina kissed him, and he relaxed, nipping at her mouth before the kiss turned heated. She lost herself in the kiss, but used the distraction to fit his shaft to her entrance. He tensed, but she continued kissing him, sliding her tongue against his.

Gently, she lowered herself, accepting his body. Eric didn't move, but she continued her shallow thrusts, feeling the slight breach of her innocence as he penetrated. Though it took time to grow accustomed to his shaft, she loved the feeling of their joined flesh. With him inside her, she felt the rightness of being brought together as one.

He bent down and took her nipple in his mouth, swirling it with his tongue. She felt a surge of wetness between her legs, and instinctively, she moved her hips, rising up and then sinking down against him.

He let out sharp intake of air, but he seemed to like it. "You steal my very breath, Katarina." A smile overtook him, and he remained embedded within her as he took her toward the banks of the pond.

To her surprise, he sat down and leaned back, letting her remain straddled upon him. "This wasn't quite what I'd intended," he murmured. "I had only planned to swim with you."

"I've been watching you all morning," she answered. "And after last night, I needed to touch you."

She inhaled as his hands palmed her breasts, stroking the tips. Awkwardly, she tried to rise against him, only to have him pull her back down. She kept him inside her, feeling the hard fullness of his body. "I don't know what you want me to do," she admitted.

"Ride me," he commanded. "Like this." He used his hands to lift her up and then guided her back again, plunging against her as she did. The motion evoked another quiver of longing, and she found her rhythm, moving against him as he caressed her.

She thrust upon him, over and over, and slowly, she felt the burgeoning sensation of desire rising. Beneath her, Eric's expression was fierce, his concentration locked upon her. He appeared to be fighting for control, and she wasn't certain he was enjoying this, from the rigid look on his face.

"Show me what I should do," she asked quietly. And with that, he moved her to the ground upon her back. He started to withdraw, and she protested, "I didn't mean for you to stop."

"I won't. But since this is your first time, I want to prepare you better." He withdrew fully and commanded, "Don't move."

He used his thumb to stroke the hooded flesh above her womanhood. A sudden tingling took hold, and she arched, feeling the arousal deepening. He brought his manhood to rest at the edge of her entrance. But when she tried to push against him, wanting to take his shaft inside, he held her back.

"Not yet, Katarina." He leaned over her, kissing her deeply while his hands moved upon her. His mouth licked a path down to her breasts as he stroked her in rhythm. She felt herself bowing against him, her hips arching, craving his invasion. His physical torment pushed her higher, making her tremble. She strained, wanting him so badly, until he slid in deep, and she gasped.

No longer did she fear this union. Instead of feeling dominated or conquered, it was a sharing of their bodies. She welcomed him, and as he gently entered and withdrew, he continued to arouse her with his thumb. He angled her hips upward, and she was caught up in his dark eyes.

Now that he was hers, she felt a stirring of emotion deep inside. *I don't want him to go.*

It seemed a cruel trick of the gods to grant her heart's desire and then snatch it away. She tried to shield her heart but feared it was impossible.

The tide of need swelled up inside her, and he held himself buried inside as she strained for her release. He rubbed her intimately, and she shuddered at the pleasure that rocked through her. She clenched his length as he kept up the rhythm, and urged him faster. At last, she broke apart, her body seizing at the fierce release.

He plunged deep, and she welcomed his invasion. She gripped his hair, meeting his hips with her own and was startled when she climaxed again, hot shivers racing through her body. Over and over, he thrust until his own fulfillment came upon him. He groaned, entering her a few more times before he collapsed atop her.

For a moment, they lay, flesh to flesh, with the grass beneath her and the sun overhead. Katarina had never imagined she could feel so close to someone, but with Eric, it felt right. Her heart continued to beat in a rapid tempo, while her body molded to his.

"Did I hurt you?" he asked, leaning down to steal another kiss.

She kissed him back and whispered, "No. I wanted this. I wanted to be with you."

He ran his hands along the edges of her body, and she reacted out of instinct, pulling him closer.

"We should bathe," he told her, "before we return."

She knew it, and yet, she wished they could remain here, away from everyone else. But he withdrew from her body and helped her to stand, before bringing her into the pond. The water was cold, but she swam to remove some of the dirt and dust from her training. And then she settled back to watch her husband.

Eric took long strokes through the water, and she admired his naked body. She held no regrets at all, and it struck her that this was what lovemaking should be. She found herself wanting to learn more about this man, how to please him, and how to be closer to him.

Oda swam with them for a time before she jumped onto the embankment and shook the water from her fur. She sniffed at the ground, and then lay down in wait for them.

"We should go back," she told Eric. It was growing late, and she decided it was time to get dressed and return to their longhouse.

"We will. But I am taking you to Dalla's longhouse this night." He strode out of the water and used his tunic to dry off, before donning his leggings and the damp clothing.

"Why? I thought you said there was nothing wrong at our dwelling."

"Whether or not we saw anything, there *was* someone who came to our longhouse. And if it was Leif, I don't want him finding you there alone at any time. It's safer to stay with my uncle."

She gave him no argument to that. After she dressed and Eric helped her back onto the horse, she said, "I do want to go back and retrieve our belongings first."

Eric agreed. He guided their mount back toward the settlement with Oda following behind. "We will. But afterward, Valdr has asked us to dine with Dalla and him."

"Is there any particular reason?" She wondered if this was about Eric claiming his place as *jarl*. It did seem that Valdr wanted his son to lead the tribe. And yet, she felt slightly nervous about it, knowing that the men did not completely trust his identity.

Her husband rested his hands at her waist while they rode back. "I do not know what they want. But be assured that no one will harm you tonight or any other night."

He returned the horse to the lean-to and helped her dismount. They walked together past the training field, but Oda stopped and sniffed the ground once more. Katarina grew chilled when she saw the dog stopping beneath the bag of grain where she had trained earlier.

Someone took the blade. She was sure of it. And the dog seemed to follow an invisible trail that disappeared over a hill.

"Let's follow her," she told Eric.

He took her hand and studied the animal as she sniffed her way back to the shelter where they had stayed the night before. She stopped in front of the doorway and sat back, scratching an ear with her hind leg.

"Someone *was* here," she told him.

He met her gaze and his mood seemed to darken. "I agree."

"Do you think Leif has come?"

Eric lifted his shoulders in a shrug. "If he has, I won't let him near you." He unsheathed his sword and shoved open the door. Katarina remained behind him until he beckoned for her to join him.

She took hesitant steps inside but was relieved to see no one there. The dog followed her inside, and let out a low growl. Katarina studied her surroundings, wondering why Oda was unsettled.

The fire. She saw that someone had lit the fire and rearranged the wood. A chill rose over her skin when she understood who had been here. When she turned around, her gaze settled upon the table…and there, she saw the missing knife.

§

"Leif followed us here."

Eric saw the terror rising in Katarina's eyes as she took the blade and sheathed it. Against the dying fire, she trembled, and he moved forward to take her in his arms.

"We knew he would. He was not going to give you up without a fight." He embraced her hard, caressing her hair. She held fast to him, and he resolved that he would guard her at all costs. He never wanted Katarina to be afraid—not while she was with him.

"I know he is only one man, but he frightens me. Especially after he took my blade and found out where we were staying."

The man had stealth indeed. But even so, Eric had no intention of allowing Leif to harm them. When he looked into Katarina's blue eyes, he saw the woman he was bound to protect. A woman who had offered herself and taken a part of him.

"He will not come near you," he swore. He tilted her face and kissed her, trying to comfort her. "I will help you gather our belongings, and we will join the others."

She took a breath and steadied herself. "Yes. I think that would be best."

He helped her take the clothing and supplies, packing them into a bundle that he carried for her. Outside, the sun had not yet set, but several torches had been lit, lining the outside of Dalla's longhouse. Several men nodded to him, and Eric murmured a greeting.

This life had enfolded him in ways he had never anticipated. Strangely, he felt as if he was losing the part of him that had once been a marquess. Even their language, which had seemed so strange at first, was now becoming second nature. Yesterday, when he'd trained, he had let go of civilized fighting and had reached into a ruthless part of him that he hadn't known existed. And whether it was memories from Arik Thorgrim, or whether it was his own instincts, he didn't know. But no longer did he feel like such an outsider.

He guided Katarina inside his uncle's longhouse. Dalla invited them to sit at their table to dine upon fish, bread, boiled eggs, and venison. He shared the best portions with his wife, but she only picked at her food.

Valdr kept Eric's cup filled, and the fermented beverage was stronger than he was accustomed to. It didn't surprise him—ale loosened the tongue, and undoubtedly, the older man wanted answers. He was careful not to drink too much, and his father noticed.

"Drink," he urged. "Else you will offend Dalla."

Eric regarded Valdr somberly. "I intend to keep my wits about me. Especially when an intruder is threatening my wife."

His father exchanged a look with Dalla. "There is someone who arrived a few hours ago," Valdr admitted. "Someone who asked to see you." He glanced over at Katarina and frowned. "I suspect it was the intruder you spoke of."

He raised a hand, signaling a *thrall*. Eric tensed, wondering if Leif had dared to come. When the door opened, he sobered at the sight of the woman approaching. Her long blond hair hung down to her hips, and her beauty was undeniable. Even so, he didn't miss the calculating look in her eyes. And he knew, before anyone spoke her name, exactly who it was.

"Svala," he said coolly. "I thought you had remained in East Anglia."

She smiled brightly and held out her hands in greeting.

"How could I stay when I learned that you survived your wounds?" Her gaze passed over him, and he detected a hint of apprehension, as if she were seeing a ghost.

Why was she here? And what did she want?

Katarina's face had gone pale, and she looked as if she wanted to skewer Svala. He didn't blame his wife at all, for this woman was to blame for Thorgrim's near death. When he thought back to the other Arik's memories, anger and frustration were foremost. Whatever the man had once felt for Svala had been overshadowed by hatred and betrayal.

Eric ignored the woman's outstretched hands and asked, "How did you come to be here?"

A hint of sadness crossed her face. "After I thought you had died, I could not…be with Eyker anymore. I made a terrible mistake. I needed to return home."

He didn't believe her. The tone in her voice sounded soft, guileless. Her eyes held back tears, tears he was certain she knew how to use for the maximum effect. He had seen women like her in the London ton, ruthless women who spoke lies to get what they wanted. He didn't know why she had come, but he held no trust in this woman.

"After they told me you were alive, I had to come. I had to see for myself." She moved closer, resting her hands upon the table before him.

"I imagine they also told you that I married Katarina." Beneath the table, he reached out and took her hand, to reassure her that he had no interest in the other woman.

Beside him, he saw his wife clench her eating knife. He wondered if Svala was aware of the danger. He'd stake a wager on his wife over any other woman—especially now, when they had spent the afternoon together.

Svala barely spared her a glance. "They told me you married to protect her from Leif."

As if that were the only possible reason why he would wed Katarina. Before he could speak, his wife answered,

"We married over a week ago." She clenched her blade, and his wife reminded him of a wallflower trying to face down a London debutante. Eric squeezed her palm in silent support.

But Svala dug in further. "It was kind of you to take pity upon her. When the danger is gone, I suppose you will end the marriage?" From the way she stared at him with a suggestive smile, her interest was clear enough.

Eric couldn't believe her boldness. Was she hoping that he would turn his attention to her?

"Why would I want to do that?" he mused. "Katarina is everything I could want in a woman." To emphasize his words, he leaned down and kissed his wife. She kissed him back, but her face reddened. Then she stood from her chair and rested her hands upon his shoulders.

"I am tired, Eric. I will wait for you in our bed." With a pointed look toward Svala, she walked toward the partition that divided the sleeping areas from the larger gathering space.

He was tempted to follow Katarina, but instead, he waited until she had gone. "What is it you really want, Svala?"

She reached out to touch his hand. "I want to make amends for what I did to you. I never should have betrayed you in that way." Her face softened, and she admitted, "I did love you, Arik. Whether or not you believe me, it is true. I don't think I realized how much I cared until I thought you were gone."

He pulled back his hand. "It is in the past, Svala."

Her face faltered with uncertainty. "Is it?" She folded her hands in front of her and regarded him. "My feelings have not changed."

He suspected that words would not dissuade her, so he decided to divert her attention. "Earlier today, did you visit the dwelling where my wife and I were staying?"

She gave a pained smile. "I did. But you were in the midst of training, so I left."

175

It was a possible reason for the dog's barking, but he probed further. "And what about Katarina's blade? Did you take it?"

At that, her expression turned confused. "I do not know what you are talking about."

Eric had his doubts, but he made no move to press the issue further. He knew better than to trust this woman. She had betrayed Thorgrim once and would do so again if it was to her benefit. But he would not allow her to cause trouble. He saw the true worth of his wife, and there was no comparison between them.

"It does not matter. You have seen that I am well and whole. If you have family, go back to them and leave us in peace." Eric stood, intending to return to Katarina, when he heard her cry out.

He bolted toward the partition, not knowing what he would find. When he reached Katarina, he saw that her hands were covered in blood. Fear iced through his veins until he realized it wasn't hers. She was holding the wolf pelt her brother always wore.

"What's happened?" he asked, hurrying toward her.

"Hrafn is wounded." Her voice was broken and she clutched the bloodstained fur to her gown. "Someone left this for me to find, and I don't know where he took my brother." Her voice revealed her terror, and though she made no accusations, Leif was likely responsible.

"We will find him." He took the wolf pelt from her and met her stricken gaze. Katarina was trying her best to remain calm, but he understood her fear. Hrafn was her only surviving family member, and she couldn't bear the death of another sibling.

Eric turned back to Valdr. "I will need some of your men to join in the search for Hrafn." He had no doubt that Leif intended to lure him into a fight. His enemy might be trying to draw him away from Katarina, in an effort to take her. But if Eric brought her along, she might face even greater risks.

He moved toward her and took her hand. "Do you want to go with me to find him? Or would you rather stay behind?"

"I am not remaining here while my brother is in danger." But she added, "I will stay at your side."

So be it. At least then, he would know she was safe. Katarina rested her hand upon her dagger and added, "If he dares to hurt my brother, I want him dead."

He agreed with her on that point, though he knew that he was not yet physically strong enough to defeat Leif. The moon was waning crescent, and despite the time he'd spent with the Viking men, he would have to rely on strategy instead of force.

He laced his fingers with Katarina's and signaled for the other Vikings to join them. This was the fight they had been expecting.

But he questioned whether he could win.

Katarina was grateful that Eric was leading the men to bring back her brother, though inwardly, her stomach clenched with apprehension. Her only consolation was knowing that Hrafn was not dead. If their enemy had intended to kill him, she would have found his body instead of the wolf pelt.

Even so, it unnerved her to think that whoever had done this had moved with stealth and cunning, sneaking past the guards into Dalla's longhouse. How had he taken her brother without making a sound?

She stood back as Eric assembled the men. Her husband moved with purpose and determination, and they followed his orders without question. As she watched him, she saw the man who had fought to earn their respect, the man who had sworn to protect her...and the man who had become her lover. No longer did she fear their joining, and her cheeks flushed at the memory of how he had pleasured her this afternoon. It made her realize that her fear for Hrafn was only a fraction of how she would feel if something happened to Eric. Somehow this man had stolen his way into her heart, no matter that he was not Arik Thorgrim. His very presence was a mystery, but she believed without question that they were meant to be together.

Svala moved to her side. "I will come with you." Katarina wasn't surprised that the woman had offered to join them. She wanted to be near Eric, even if it meant she was interfering.

"You are not needed," she told her. "Stay here with the other women."

"Why?" Svala asked softly. "Do I make you uncomfortable?" The knowing look on her face was irritating, and Katarina shrugged.

"If you want to be endangered, I care not." She turned her back, trying to shrug away the jealousy. Although she knew there was no relationship between her husband and Svala, she could not help comparing herself. Instead, she allowed her worry for Hrafn to push away all else. Her brother's life was more important than her bitterness toward this woman.

Eric approached them, but he ignored Svala. "Katarina, stay among the men. I want you surrounded by warriors on all sides." On his left arm he carried a wooden shield, and he had both a sword and a battle-ax sheathed at his waist.

Svala intervened, handing a dark woolen wrap to Katerina. She wore one of a different color and said, "Wear this. It will be cold tonight."

She didn't trust the woman's offering and was about to deny it, but Eric shrugged. "You might as well be warm." He moved to her and drew it around her shoulders and over her head, bringing her close.

Katarina lifted her gaze to his. "Be safe, Arik."

He leaned in and kissed her lightly. "I will." The affection was a silent reassurance that warmed her heart, for he would do everything possible to bring back her brother. He returned to the front and spoke to his father for a moment before they all took torches and walked outside.

As they continued toward the shoreline, Svala caught her arm. "I want to talk with you."

"I have no interest in hearing what you have to say." Especially when it involved the woman's interest in her husband. But she refused to be intimidated by her.

"Do you want him to live?" Svala asked quietly. "If the choice was yours, to sacrifice yourself for Arik's sake, would you do this?"

"What do you mean? Why would you ask such a thing?" Outside, the night was clouded, obscuring the moon. A coldness lingered in the air, and she wondered if Svala had something to do with her brother's disappearance.

She stopped walking and stared hard at the woman. The other warriors glanced back but continued on, leaving them at the settlement. "What is it you have not told me?"

"I know that Leif is here. He has come for you."

It wasn't surprising, and she had already guessed this. "I care not about him. I am married to Arik, and I intend to remain his wife."

Svala's tone turned cool. "And do you think Leif will let you go so easily? He is a proud man, and he will kill Arik by any means." Her face turned serious. "I don't want Arik to die any more than you do. But I fear for his life. You hold the power to save him."

"By giving myself up to Leif, is that it? You want me to surrender myself so that *you* can leave with Arik?" The woman's suggestion was ludicrous.

Svala shrugged. "If his life is about to end, you could plead for mercy. Leif might listen to you."

Katrina had no intention whatsoever of giving up. "Arik will defeat Leif. I hold faith in that."

The young woman's mouth twisted in a sneer. "I saw him on the training field earlier. You're wrong if you believe he can kill a warrior like Leif."

"Did you come here with him?" she asked. It would not surprise her if the pair of them were working together.

Svala shook her head. "He was already here. He has been watching you." Her attention centered on something behind her, and the hair on Katarina's nape stood on end. She knew without looking, who was standing there.

Footsteps approached, and when she turned, she saw the man of her nightmares, Leif Tormundsson. He wore leather armor, and the skin on his forearms was marred with burns. His eyes narrowed up on her face with a knowing gleam.

"Thank you, Svala," he said. "You can go and join the other warriors now. But take this with you." He stripped away Katarina's head covering and handed it to the woman.

Svala bound it over her head and hurried forward. If Arik happened to look back toward his men, he would only see a woman who looked similar. He might not even know his wife was missing.

So that explained Svala's offering. She had plotted this from the beginning.

Katarina remained frozen in place, unsure of what to do. If she tried to fight Leif, he would overpower her within moments.

"I should have known not to trust you," Leif said. "You always lusted after Thorgrim, didn't you? But you belong to me."

The malice in his voice went beyond anger—this was hatred. She couldn't understand why he seemed to loathe her.

"What do you want?" she asked quietly. Demure behavior had usually soothed his vanity, and she used it as her first weapon.

"You had no right to go to him or let him use your body. We were promised."

Katarina didn't apologize but instead faced him. *Arik, come back,* she thought silently. Surely he would notice she was missing and return for her.

But what if he didn't? She had no way of knowing whether Hrafn's disappearance had anything to do with Leif, or whether it had only been a distraction.

She started to walk back toward the jarl's longhouse, hoping that some of Dalla's men were still there. Even if there was no one, it was safer to be surrounded by the *thralls*.

But Leif caught her wrist and jerked her toward him, covering her mouth with his hand. "Come with me, Katarina. I want to have words with your husband before he dies."

His iron grip upon her wrist was hurting, and she called out for help. The moment she did, he backhanded her face, and she saw stars. Two of the *thralls* came running, but Leif never let go of her. When the first man charged, Leif swung his battle-ax with his left hand and sliced the man's throat. The second man held his wooden shield as he unsheathed a sword, but Leif seized the shield and kicked the man's legs out from under him. Seconds later, the warrior was dead. To the other men gathered at the longhouse, Leif said, "I am taking the woman back with me. If you try to stop us, you will join your friends in death."

The men hesitated, and Katarina shook her head in warning. She didn't believe Leif meant to kill her at this moment, but the *jarl's* men would die if they interfered.

Leif seized her by the arm and dragged her in the direction of the lake. Katarina hoped the men were watching and could tell Eric where she'd been taken.

She stumbled as he pulled her into the darkness. The crescent moon gave only the barest hint of light, but the sky was filled with stars. Katarina glimpsed the reflection of water in the distance, but he drew her further away.

"Where is Hrafn?" she demanded.

"Your brother is waiting for us."

After several minutes of walking, she spied the glow of a fire. The light blazed with an otherworldly fury, and the closer they walked, the more her heartbeat quickened.

Leif had bound her brother to a post, his head hanging low. He was unconscious, and at his feet, she saw stacks of wood and hay. Sparks flew from the fire, and she was terrified that one would catch hold of the hay and ignite it. Leif's purpose was clear enough—he meant to burn Hrafn to death.

Her blood turned to ice, and Katarina sent up a silent prayer for help. "What is this about, Leif? Why would you threaten Hrafn?"

He released her wrist, and she stood beside the fire, staring at the madness in this man. "Do you remember when I came to Rogaland, Katarina?"

She shrugged. "Yes. It was a year ago." She recalled that he had come alone, with hardly any silver, and he had used his fighting skills to gain a place among them.

"It was not the first time I came here. I was seven years old when my mother brought me to Valdr for fostering."

Since she had been a young child then, she never would have remembered it. But Katarina held her silence and waited for him to continue.

"Valdr turned her away. My mother pleaded with him, but he refused." There was a hard glint in his eyes as he continued. "She was forced to leave. Your father, Lars, dragged my mother outside, and she begged him to let her go back to the *jarl*. He shoved her hard, and my mother fell into one of the cooking fires. I can still remember her screaming. Her clothing caught fire, and they could not save her. She died within a few minutes." Leif's eyes hardened. "I lost my only family that day because of Lars. And I vowed that I would have my vengeance upon him and every child he sired."

Every part of her felt as if it had been turned to stone.

Katarina had mistakenly believed that Leif was acting out of jealousy. But this went far deeper than that.

"You killed my father, didn't you?" Her hands were shaking, but she forced herself to continue. "The day you found my father's body, you said he had died when a boar sliced open his stomach. But it was you."

Leif's expression held only satisfaction. "It was. And I told him before he died that I would kill every last one of his children." He stared over at Hrafn, who was starting to revive. Her blood ran cold when she understood how easy it would be for him to take her brother's life. She had to keep Leif distracted until Eric and his men arrived. Katarina prayed that her husband would discover her gone and come to help.

"If what you say is true, it must have been an accident," she told Leif. "My father would never have deliberately harmed a woman."

"I was there," he snapped. "I saw what he did." The fire of hatred burned in his eyes, and she faltered at the rage in his voice. "He gave no mercy to my mother, and I gave none to him. Or to his daughter."

A rise of nausea caught in her throat. By the gods, she'd been so wrong about this man. "On the night those men attacked Ingirún—"

A thin smile spread over his face. "I was the first to rape your sister before my men took her. And I watched as they smashed her skull against a rock afterward. I would have done the same to you, but Valdr arrived too soon. I decided I would pretend to be your rescuer instead."

She stared at him, horrified by his revelation. "But...I thought Geilir and Jokull..."

"They were with me that night. I hired them to help and then sent them away."

Shock was quickly replaced by fury. Katarina stared at Leif, feeling the anger rise up within her. All those weeks she had stared out at the sea, longing for vengeance, were for nothing. *This* was her true enemy, the man who had hurt her sister and was responsible for Ingirún's death. The man she had vowed to destroy was standing in front of her.

She had never killed anyone before. Perhaps she ought to be frightened or wary of it, but instead, she remembered her sister's sightless eyes and broken body. Leif was responsible for it, and he deserved to die.

Katarina eyed Hrafn, wondering if it was possible to free her brother first, before she attempted to kill Leif. She was not foolish enough to believe she could do this alone. But although she desperately wanted to cut Hrafn's ropes, he was still unconscious and might not be able to help.

There was hardly any time to act. She might be able to strike out against Leif in the darkness, but if he caught her, she would fail. There was no doubt whatsoever that he intended for her to die this night, along with her brother.

Her only hope for survival was the element of surprise.

Chapter Ten

"W here are the women?" Eric demanded of the *jarl*. "They were with us a moment ago." He had led the Vikings in the direction of the coast, only to find that both Katarina and Svala were missing.

"The men told me the women decided to stay behind. I agreed that they could remain at the longhouse," Valdr said. "It is safer for them there."

He was incredulous that the *jarl* could think this. Leif's very purpose was to find Katarina and take her. "I suppose this was Svala's doing?"

"It was. She told me their decision before she returned to the longhouse with an escort."

Eric was furious that Valdr could have allowed this to happen. "I brought them with us because Katarina felt safer with me. She wanted to find her brother, not stay behind where Leif might come for her."

"Do you doubt that our men can protect the women?" Valdr's expression darkened as if he didn't want to believe it. He lowered his voice and added, "Those fighters are better trained than you. She will be safer within our longhouse."

The remark was a direct blow toward his training, and it incensed him. "Walk with me, Valdr." Eric motioned for the men to stay back. It was time to speak with the leader and establish his own authority. This was his wife, and he was bound to protect her. But he would not shame the older man in front of the others.

"We are going back for them," he said, when they were alone.

"For women?" His father appeared irritated by the idea. "There is no reason for it. Our search is for Hrafn."

"We have not found him, and there is no sign of his whereabouts. I think it more likely that Svala tried to lure us away so Leif could take Katarina. We should return and try a different direction. Oda can track them."

The *jarl* stared hard at him for a moment before his shoulders lowered. "Over the past two weeks, I have considered whether you are truly my son, brought back from the gods. I wanted it to be true, but I have my doubts. Arik would never have let his purpose be distracted by a woman."

For a time, he met the man's gaze, knowing he had to choose his words carefully. When he studied the older man, he saw traces of regret that reminded him of Gregory. The burden of leadership had taken its toll over the years, and it was clear that Valdr wanted him to take the role of *jarl* among these people. And whether he wanted that place or not, it belonged to him by right.

He folded his arms across his chest. "My purpose is to ensure the protection of both Hrafn and Katarina. Svala betrayed me once before, and I believe she would do so again—particularly out of jealousy."

"The men will not follow you, if—"

"They will follow me if I command it of them." He had no qualms about cutting off the man. "No leader would take his men along a false path."

Valdr said nothing, and Eric kept his voice low, making his point. "I have crossed over to death and back. I may not have the physical strength I once had, but no man can take that journey and remain unchanged. What I do know is this—I left Rogaland because I denied my fate. I didn't want the responsibility of these men at that time. But it is mine, is it not?"

The older man let out a breath and nodded. "Only if they accept you."

He reached out and touched Valdr's shoulder. "I will be their *jarl,* but I would welcome your counsel and guidance. As a leader…and a father."

Valdr could not replace Gregory in his heart, but the strong physical resemblance and the similarities between the two men could not be denied. He had been brought here to reconcile a future he hadn't wanted to face, and now he saw the hope within it. As *jarl,* he could live with Katarina by his side, learning from her. She had pushed back the years of loneliness, teaching him what it meant to love someone.

Time was not his ally, and he didn't know if the *volva's* prediction would come true. But he would fight for this life with every breath he had.

"What guidance do you have to offer me now?" Eric asked quietly. "We have not found Hrafn. Do you agree with my suggestion?"

Valdr gripped his forearm, and gave a single nod. "We will look elsewhere and track them down." A faint softening came over his countenance afterward, and he added, "And after we have found them, we will talk about your future among us."

It was as close to a truce as they could muster. Eric squeezed the older man's arm in silent support. Being a leader was never what he'd wanted…but he understood that he would have Valdr's help for as long as it was needed. His own father would have done the same, had he welcomed the man's advice instead of fleeing responsibilities.

He continued toward the longhouse, with Valdr at his side, until the men fell in line behind him. The silence within the settlement only sharpened his suspicions.

There was no sign of Katarina, as he'd suspected. His mind blurred with fear, but he forced it back. He had to keep his wits about him, in order to find his wife. But he was unprepared for the primal fury that roared through him. Never would he allow anyone to harm Katarina, and he would track down the man responsible and slaughter him.

Near his father's longhouse, he found Svala sitting upon the ground. She appeared numb with shock, and beside her, two men had been cut down, lying in a pool of their own blood. When the young woman lifted her gaze to his, she admitted, "Leif took her."

Eric wasn't surprised to hear it, and his hand curved over the hilt of his sword. It was as if the years of civilization melted away, replaced by the savage need to kill his enemy. "Where?"

Svala lifted her shoulders in a shrug. "Toward the lake. But you should know, he plans to use her to lure you there. Send your men to save her, but you should remain behind."

Eric had no intention of behaving like a coward—not when Katarina needed him. Instead, he turned toward Valdr and the others. "I am going to bring back my wife and her brother. I would be glad of your help, if you are willing."

"They will go, if you command it," Valdr said.

Eric knew that, but he wanted them to make the choice. "If any man among you needed my help to save his family, I would give it, even at the cost of my own life." The moment he spoke the words, he heard the truth in them. He had lived among these Vikings for only a few weeks, but he now understood that their survival depended upon each other. "As a tribe, we fight for each other against our enemies," he said. "We stand together. But I do not command you to risk your lives. I ask you to make the choice."

He met the hardened stare of each man, one by one. "We have a traitor who has stolen my wife and likely her brother, our kinsman. Will you come and fight with me?"

The men were silent for a time, glancing at one another. Even Valdr stared at him for a long moment. The man's expression was unreadable, but at last he said, "I will come with you." The older man checked his weapons and joined at his side.

Eric picked up his shield and nodded to the men, uncertain if any would follow. But from behind him, he heard the sound of their footsteps. It gave him a measure of hope.

"Do you want horses?" Valdr asked quietly.

Eric didn't think it would be wise. "That might alert him to our presence. I think stealth would be best." He whistled for Oda, and after a moment, the dog came racing toward them. With a high-pitched whine, Oda sniffed the ground until she caught Katarina's scent.

The sky was fully dark now, and he ordered the men to put down their torches. "When we find her, I want you to surround them." Eric pointed to several of the men, instructing them on which positions to take. Oda kept her nose to the ground, hurrying toward the lake, and they followed in pursuit.

He could only hope that they would find Katarina before it was too late.

Katarina knew she was going to die this night. She knew it with a certainty in her bones. But if she chose the right moment, she might kill Leif and save her brother.

Strangely, she felt no fear at all. Instead, she took in the small details all around her. The shower of sparks from the firelight…the crescent moon that hung within the dark sky…the cool softness of the grass beneath her bare feet.

An aching caught her heart at the thought that this might be her last chance to enjoy these simple moments of life.

"Your *husband* will find us soon enough," Leif said. "But I want him to suffer before he dies."

Eric would indeed come for her. But she didn't know if he was strong enough or ruthless enough to defeat Leif.

"This is not only about vengeance for your mother's death, is it?" she said softly. "Your hatred goes deeper than that. Even if you kill us both, it will not be enough, will it?"

Leif poked at the fire with a long stick, and the red sparks shattered in the air. For a time, he did not speak. His expression grew clouded, as if thoughts preyed upon him. "Valdr should have fostered me. But he wanted no one but his trueborn sons to be *jarl.* Especially not a bastard son he'd fathered."

Understanding broke forth then. Leif's driving desire to command was born from a childhood where he had felt unwanted by his true sire. He was Arik Thorgrim's half brother, but he had never been acknowledged as such. He was a man who did not fit anywhere, and he had allowed hatred to poison his thoughts.

"You should journey across the sea," she told him. "Make a new place for yourself where no one knows you. Rebuild and start again."

She was doing everything within her power to stall him until Eric found her. Against her waist, she was conscious of the thin blade. Within her mind, she imagined sliding it up beneath his breastbone, directly into his heart. There would be only seconds to move, and she could not miss.

"I already started a new life, Katarina, when I came here a year ago. No one recognized me, and I let them believe I was a traveler." His expression darkened. "But I knew what I wanted. For them to see me as the man who should have been *jarl.*"

The longer he spoke, the more her mind calmed. He was waiting on Eric, and Katarina had no doubt he would come for her. When her husband arrived, there would be a slight distraction, which would give her the time she needed to stab Leif with her knife. But she was beginning to question whether a stab to the heart was the right place. Her blade might catch upon his breastbone, and it was a grave risk.

His throat, she decided. That was the best place to strike a killing blow before Leif would know what had hit him. But as she waited, her hands trembled.

Her brother began to regain consciousness, and he groaned aloud, lifting his head. The moment Hrafn realized he was bound to a post, he struggled against the ropes. Then his eyes focused upon her, and Katarina saw the confusion shift into violent anger. With his stump, he pushed against the ropes.

"Katarina, what has he done to you?" Hrafn demanded. "You need to get out of here."

"Leif will not let me go," she said quietly. "And even if he did, I am not leaving you. If our positions were reversed, you would never run."

Her brother's expression turned thunderous, and he directed his rage toward Leif. "I swear by the gods, I will flay the skin from your body and leave it for the crows."

"All I have to do is light this fire," Leif countered.

Katarina didn't miss her brother's uneasiness. But she would not risk fleeing this path she had chosen. Before the night was over, she intended to kill the man who had taken her sister's life. "Arik will come for both of us. I promise you, he will."

Hrafn's eyes held pity, then. It was the look of a man who did not believe it was possible for Arik to defeat Leif. Katarina rested her hand upon the weapon at her waist and sent him a long look. Her brother's mouth tightened, but he gave a faint nod of silent understanding. Even so, he did not like it.

She was well aware that Hrafn was discreetly loosening the ropes that bound him to the tree. Because Leif had been unable to bind her brother's stump, Hrafn adjusted the ropes each time the man's attention was elsewhere.

A rustling noise approached, and Leif unsheathed his battle-ax, facing the sound. Katarina stared out into the darkness but could see nothing. Her hand moved to the hilt of her blade, while she took a slight step toward Leif. If she moved now, he might swing the ax at her.

Her heartbeat quickened until at last, she knew she could wait no longer. In one swift motion, she unsheathed her knife and slashed toward Leif's throat.

But at the last second, he moved, and her weapon met nothing but air. She felt the sickening knowledge that he had anticipated her move, and his hand gripped her wrist, squeezing so hard, it felt as if the very bones were breaking.

She cried out in pain, and the blade slipped from her fingers. Leif shoved her to the ground and picked up the knife. "Was this what you were trying to do to me?" She watched in horror as he stabbed her brother's shoulder with the blade, leaving it embedded in his flesh. Blood welled up from the wound, but Hrafn never made a sound.

With horror, she felt his pain as her own. "I'm so sorry," Katarina whispered. It was her fault that Leif had done this— she should have waited longer.

"Or perhaps you wanted to slit my throat?" Leif ripped out the blade and brought the edge to the soft part of Hrafn's neck.

Katarina felt the bile rise up in her gut, terrified of this man. "No." Her whisper was so faint, she didn't know if her voice had made a sound.

"How does it feel to be utterly powerless?" he asked. Leif picked up a burning branch from the fire, holding it near to the straw at Hrafn's feet.

His taunt infuriated her, and Katarina bit her lip hard to keep from answering him. She would not reward him with obedience. With a sudden clarity, she understood that she would have to fight for herself and Hrafn. Leif was relishing his ability to hurt both of them. He would kill Hrafn soon, but what he craved was her reaction.

She lowered her face to the ground, and her action only provoked Leif further. "Look at him!" he roared. He jerked her to her feet, but she kept her head averted, refusing to play his game.

The grass rustled from nearby, and Oda appeared in the clearing. The dog lay down upon the ground, her flanks heaving.

Eric is here. She knew it with certainty. But only the gods knew whether he could stop Leif. She struggled against her enemy's grasp, hoping that her fight would cause enough of a distraction to aid her husband.

"Let them go, Leif," came Eric's voice. It was calm and commanding. She turned to look at him and saw that he had unsheathed a sword in his right hand, while he kept a shield in his left. Behind him stood Valdr and half a dozen of their kinsmen who encircled Leif on all sides. She wanted to feel relieved, but instead, her pulse quickened. Her brother was still bound, and she knew that Leif could kill them both before anyone could save them.

"You're going to watch her die, Thorgrim," Leif said. She could feel the heat from the burning branch he held in his right hand, while his left hand remained at her throat.

"Let her go," Arik countered. "It is finished. You cannot win this battle."

"I am not afraid to die, if it means slaughtering my enemies." Leif's hand tightened over her throat. "I care not if you kill me. Katarina and Hrafn will still die, and I will have my vengeance."

"The gods will judge you in the afterlife," Eric said quietly. "Do you not think they will punish you for this? Is an eternity in Hel worth it?"

"Yes," he answered. And with that, Leif tossed the torch upon the straw at her brother's feet.

A scream tore from Katarina's throat as she struggled to reach Hrafn, but the edge of the blade cut into her throat in a sharp sting. She froze, aware that she could do nothing to help her brother.

Dimly, she was conscious of the other men who hurried forward to put out the flames. Then she felt Leif's arm tighten across her throat. She couldn't breathe, and stars swam in her vision as she struggled to free herself.

Katarina's last thought was filled with heartbreak and regret, before the world went black.

A roar escaped Eric's throat as Katarina's broken body fell to the ground. He had sworn to protect this woman, and right now, he didn't know if she was alive or dead. They had only been together for a few weeks, but she had filled the emptiness in his life, making a place for herself. He had never imagined that he would come to love a Viking woman, but he did. He loved her beauty, her fiery spirit, and her soft heart.

Eric lunged toward Leif, no longer caring whether he died in this attempt. His mind was a flood of emotions, caught up with guilt, rage, and anguish.

The men tried to cut Hrafn free from the flames before he was burned alive. Smoke tainted the air and it was as if the world slowed down. He gripped his sword, releasing the instincts of a Viking barbarian. His enemy would die, and Eric would never cease until Leif breathed his last.

He gave in to instinct and charged forward, swinging his blade with both hands. Leif's ax arced toward him, but Eric dodged the blow. His sword bit into a wooden shield, but he tore it free, aiming for the man's head.

From deep within, he found a wilder side of himself that fought for every last breath. It didn't matter that this man was bigger and stronger. Nor did it matter that his training was unfinished. There was only this fight, here and now.

Leif swung his leg hard, tripping Eric. He stumbled to the ground and rolled, just as his enemy hacked downward with the ax.

Eric seized a torch from the fire, swinging it toward the Viking's feet. He was aware that his uncle's men had freed Hrafn and the man was still alive. Another man lifted up Katarina's fallen form, and it was all Eric could do not to snarl at them to leave her alone.

Above him, a reddish cloud slid across the moon, reminding him that he did not belong in this place. He was not of this time, but an anomaly meant to disappear. And despite his desire to live, to join with these people and make his way among them, he sensed it could never be.

"Mind yourself!" Valdr called out a warning.

Eric glanced down and saw Leif's ax slicing toward him. He lifted his shield to deflect the blow, and the metal sank into the wood. With a swift pull, Leif jerked the shield off his arm, leaving him defenseless.

The man's eyes were wild with battle fever, a thin smile on his face. He believed he could not fail in this.

Eric's anger intensified until it consumed him. He blamed himself for not striking sooner. And when the battle madness swept over him, he gave in to instinct, wielding his sword against Leif. The weapon was heavy, but he held it steady, releasing his hold upon Arik Thorgrim's memories. The knowledge poured through him, and he let go of all control, surrendering to the darkness inside him. No longer did he fight by the rules of Regency gentlemen—he gave in to Viking instincts.

His muscles flexed and he slashed, over and over, seeking a weakness within his enemy. Leif's brutal strength required

Eric to be much faster, and he sidestepped the fire, pouring himself into the fight.

The burn of exertion weighed upon him, but he ignored it. He had sworn to protect Katarina, and he would not fail in this. With a swift lunge, he stabbed his blade toward Leif's side, but the man deflected it with his battle-ax.

The men were watching the fight, none of them daring to interfere. He could feel Valdr's assessing gaze upon him, and Eric continued to push harder.

"When you die, I will become *jarl,*" Leif insisted. His voice was filled with the madness of a man who believed himself invincible.

But words were another kind of weapon. And Eric wielded them without mercy, striking out at the man's pride. "These men would never choose you as a leader. Not when you have proven yourself to be a murderer." He kept his sword in one hand and unsheathed his own battle-ax with the other. Over and over, he lunged at the man, until Valdr stepped in.

The Viking leader's interference was unexpected, and with a wooden shield, Leif backhanded Valdr, sending the old man to the ground. He lifted his battle-ax, ready to strike the killing blow, when the world seemed to slow.

"No!" The word ripped from his throat, and in Valdr's place, Eric saw his own father. The two men's lives appeared transposed, and in that frozen moment of time, Eric felt the sense of remorse. He had been selfish, ignoring his responsibilities in his own search for adventure. His father had remained at home, alone and worried about his only son.

Valdr had proven himself willing to sacrifice his life to save him. And Eric was not even Valdr's trueborn heir.

Before Leif could bury his ax in Valdr's flesh, he saw a glimpse of his father within the Viking man's visage. It was the kindly smile of a man who had loved him more than life itself. He knew with a certainty that he would never see

Gregory again. He would never feel his father's arms around him or hear the man's voice.

"I am sorry," Eric whispered. "Forgive me." He wished to God that he could see his father one last time, to speak the words he'd never said.

Instinctively, Eric dove forward, using his own body to shield Valdr's. And when the battle-ax cut into his spine, a flash of lightning split the sky in two.

Agonizing pain burned through him, and he gasped for air. He heard a woman scream, and Katarina rushed forward. Thank God she was all right. He felt his energy slipping away while his blood soaked the earth.

But this wasn't over yet.

Eric knew he was dying. Before he took his last breath, he intended to finish this. His hand closed around the blade at his belt, and he met Katarina's gaze. Her blue eyes were stricken with grief, but she gave him a nod to show she understood.

Leif's shadow fell across him as he reached for his battle-ax. In one motion, Eric used the last of his strength and embedded the dagger in his enemy's heart.

A look of shock washed over the man, and he stumbled backward. Katarina moved toward Eric, gripping his bloodstained hands. Within moments, Leif fell to the ground, and a scream tore from him as he fell into the fire. The flames caught his clothing, and within moments, he was dead.

The world was fading, and Eric understood that he had only a little time left. Katarina was beside him, tears falling over her cheeks.

"Eric," she wept, clinging to him. "Stay with me. Please."

He tried to speak, wishing he could tell her how much he wanted to. How beautiful she was and how he had been honored to be her husband, even if only for a little while.

He laced his fingers with hers, and murmured, "I am glad

I married you, Katarina." His voice caught, and he said, "I only wish we had more time."

No longer could he feel his body, and the world around him shifted and drifted away.

And when he saw the ghost of his father standing in the distance with an outstretched hand, Eric went to him.

CHAPTER ELEVEN

It felt as if her heart had been ripped from her chest. Katarina wept as Arik closed his eyes, and she could feel the life fading from him. Never again would she feel his kiss or the warmth of his embrace. She had never imagined she would feel so strongly for this man, but he had invaded her heart and stolen a piece of her soul.

She lowered her face to his chest, resting her cheek upon his heart. His pulse was ragged and weak, and after a moment, she could no longer feel it beating.

It wasn't fair. She wanted to rail at the gods, cursing them for stealing the man she had fallen in love with. And now he was dead.

The wind swelled, whipping at her hair while silence descended among them. Only the faint crackle of the fire broke the stillness. She was covered in blood, and she was hardly aware of anything except the loss of Eric. Time seemed to slow for a moment, and she glanced up, watching as a shadow crossed over the moon. A coldness slid over her, and when she lifted her hands, she saw that all traces of blood had disappeared. Seconds later, Arik's body disappeared from her arms.

She bit back her terror, not understanding what had happened. One moment he was there, and the next, he was gone. It was as if he had never existed, had never been here.

Because he did not belong within her time, the voice of reason insisted. He had been brought from a thousand years later, just as he had said. And although this man was not Arik Thorgrim, the man she had wanted, he had captured her heart by being the man she needed. He had fought to save them and had won.

When she looked back at Valdr, his attention was focused on Hrafn. Her brother was bleeding from his wounds, and the soles of his shoes had been burned by the flames.

She hurried toward him and demanded, "Are you all right? Did you see what happened?"

Her brother nodded and his face was grim. "I am glad you were strong enough to kill Leif."

She frowned, not understanding what he meant. She hadn't killed Leif at all, but perhaps in the midst of the fight, he didn't realize that it was Arik's blade. "I meant, did you see what happened to Arik?"

Hrafn's face twisted with confusion. "Leif must have struck you hard when you killed him, Katarina. Arik Thorgrim died in East Anglia, months ago."

She stared at him, wondering how he could say this. An icy chill washed over her and she looked over at Valdr. "But he was there just now. Did *you* see him?"

The *jarl* met her gaze and shook his head. "You must have glimpsed his spirit when you were fighting."

She sank to the grass, her whole body trembling. But when she examined her hands and her gown again, there was no blood anywhere—not even on the grass. Above her, in the night sky, the crescent moon shone down, as if nothing had changed. As if Eric had never been here nor even married her.

The old *volva* had been right. He had been given only a little time to be with her. And now she could not help but wonder if he had been a spirit all along. Perhaps that was why he'd had no scars. She had fallen in love with a man who was not real.

In the darkness, she stared at the fire, which had now consumed Leif's body. She had gained her vengeance on the enemy who had slain her sister, but only emptiness filled her heart now. She wanted to be in Arik's arms, to make love with him and be his wife in truth.

The tears would not stop, and she grieved for him, burying her face in her knees as her heart broke.

"Katarina," Hrafn said quietly. "It's over. I will take you home."

Although she knew he was right, it felt as if the world weighed upon her shoulders. Her husband was gone, and with him, the life she had dreamed of.

With reluctance, she followed the men back to the settlement. She saw Svala there, helping to tend the fallen bodies of the men who had defended them earlier. Katarina didn't bother asking the woman if she had seen Eric—if none of the others had seen him, why should she?

Hrafn led her behind one of the room dividers, to a bed of furs. She lay down upon it, hoping that sleep would take away the memories she didn't want to face.

Perhaps she was imagining it, but upon the bed she saw a cloak that Eric had worn. She brought it to her face, breathing in the scent of him. It was so real, she could hardly bear it. And when she closed her eyes, she could see his face before her.

As she drifted off into a hard sleep, her hand moved over to her womb, wondering if even their lovemaking had been a dream. Or whether the *volva* had been right, that they would conceive a child.

It might be the only piece of him she would ever have, and she prayed for it to be so.

All around him, Eric was surrounded by a gray mist. A part of him knew he was dead, but he felt as if an invisible barrier prevented him from crossing over. He was afraid to feel anything, not knowing what was real and what was imagined.

"My son," came Gregory's voice.

He saw his father's face emerging from the mist. No longer did the man appear haggard and world-weary. His gray hair was now a dark brown, and Gregory appeared to be a younger version of himself. The lines of worry were gone from his face, replaced by immeasurable joy. The duke embraced him hard, and his father's arms held a lifetime of love. The strong arms were real, and for a moment, Eric gripped the man in return. The years fell away, and he once more became a boy beloved by his father. He regretted the time he'd spent at sea, leaving this man to fear the worst.

"I never meant to hurt you in the way I did," he told his father. "I was reckless and selfish."

"You were young," the duke countered. "And I was unyielding." A quiet glimpse of kindness slid over the man's face. "I, too, am sorry."

Eric hugged his father, but despite the eternal peace surrounding them, he had no desire to join Gregory. He yearned to be with his wife, to hold her and know that she was safe. Even now he remembered the anguish in her eyes when he had fallen. Her fierce beautiful face would haunt him for eternity. And though they had only spent a little time together, he had known from the first moment he'd seen her, that she was the woman he was meant to love.

He had a thousand questions, and yet, he could feel nothing save desolation. He would surrender everything if he could go back to Katarina.

"What happened to me?" he asked his father. "Why was I sent back to the Viking era?" He felt certain that if he could understand the reasons for journeying through time, he might find a way to return.

Gregory's face turned haggard as he pulled back. "Your soul was switched with another man's. A Viking took your place, and you, his."

Eric nodded. "You speak of Arik Thorgrim."

"Indeed. He was brought forward through time to Juliana Arthur, the Viscountess Hawthorne. But he could not stay with her, either."

"So both of us are lost," he said. "There is no hope." The thought of an afterlife without Katarina was an eternity he didn't want to face.

His father's expression turned sympathetic. "What happened to both of you was part of a larger plan none of us can understand. But there is a legend that a man can only be saved from death if another takes his place." Gregory reached out and touched Eric's head. "I have made my choice. And you cannot walk the path I have chosen."

Upon his father's face, he saw the regret mingled with love. What did Gregory mean by this? "What have you done?"

"I am old and have lived my life," his father said quietly. "I was given a choice, and I made it freely. My life for yours."

The enormity of Gregory's sacrifice went beyond words. His father had accepted death in exchange for Eric's second chance at life.

"It matters not if you return to 1811 or if you remain among the Vikings. But after the phases of one moon, you will forget the other life you once knew."

A rush of hope filled up inside of him as he met his father's gaze. "Will I be able to go back to Katarina?"

Gregory nodded. "If that is your wish. But only because the child binds you to her."

It took a moment before understanding dawned over him. It was a paradox that never should have happened—a child born from a father in another millennium. And yet, it joined them in a way that could never be severed.

"I need to go back to her," he said. "She is everything to me." The intensity of his feelings blazed through him, making him desperate to see her face.

Gregory touched his forehead to his. "I never imagined you would be anything but my heir, the new Duke of Somerford. But my greatest wish is for your happiness." His mouth twisted in a faint smile. We will meet again one day in this afterworld. But not for a long time, my son."

And with that, his father's spirit vanished.

Katarina walked along the shoreline as dawn slipped over the horizon. The moon had gone through its phases, and during the past few mornings, she had awakened feeling sick. No matter what anyone else believed, she knew that her marriage to Arik Thorgrim had been real. She carried their child within her womb, and it was the most precious gift he could have given her. For a piece of his spirit would live on.

The morning mist clouded the edge of the water, and she watched as the sun's rays painted the surface gold. It was beautiful, achingly so. She turned back to walk toward the settlement, her thoughts preoccupied.

Oda had accompanied her, but abruptly, the animal grew agitated. She barked loudly, scampering in circles, while her tail wagged with enthusiasm.

"What is it?" Katarina bent down, but the dog took off in a full run across the beach. For a moment she watched the animal sniffing the ground before turning and leaping across the sand. She yipped at the silhouette of a man standing at the water's edge. The bright sunrise behind him obscured his features for a moment, but Katarina's heart began to pound at the sight of him.

For a moment, she touched her hand to her mouth in

disbelief. Was it possible that this was Eric, returned to her from death? Nothing was impossible for a man who had traveled through time. The gods could do whatever they liked.

She began running toward him, her eyes burning with tears. *Please let it be the man I love.*

When she knew it was him, Katarina threw her arms around him, crying with joy. Eric embraced her hard, kissing her until she was left with no doubt that he did know her. His mouth was hungry upon hers, reminding her of how much he loved her. The tears fell freely, and her happiness swelled so high, she thought she would break apart from it.

"Eric," she murmured, smiling as he wiped her cheeks. A blinding smile came over her face as she touched his hands. "You're alive."

He bent to kiss her again, and she needed no explanation from him. All that mattered was that he was here with her now. When he broke the kiss, she admitted, "For a time, I thought I imagined all of it."

He stroked her hair back. "I don't know what is real, Katarina. But I would cross over another thousand years to be with you."

She caressed his face, moving her fingers to the pulse at his throat. How could any man return from death? It seemed impossible, and yet, she could not doubt the steady beat beneath her fingertips. He was alive and whole again. She buried her face against his chest, holding him as tightly as she dared.

Then a terrible thought occurred to her. "Will you be forced to leave again?"

Eric shook his head. "A sacrifice was made, one life for another."

Though Katarina wanted to ask more, she decided it didn't matter. She moved her hands down his chest, tracing the shape of his torso. When she reached the hem of his outer tunic, she slid her hands beneath it, searching his back for scars. But there were none.

"Whose life was sacrificed?" she asked.

He caught her hands and drew them back. "The father I left behind in 1811." His voice was heavy, and she understood the grief he was holding back. Nonetheless, she would always be grateful to the man who had taken her husband's place in the afterlife.

"The *volva* told me I was brought here to change what was never meant to be," he continued. "And to bring back what was lost. For a while, I didn't understand her prophesy."

Katarina stroked his hands with her thumbs, feeling so thankful he was here. "What did she mean by it?"

"You were never meant to marry Leif. And I was meant to reconcile with my father, to take my rightful place as leader." His hand moved down to rest upon her hair. "I did see him again, for a few moments. And there is now peace between us, though for a time, we were lost to each other."

"He knows you love him," Katarina said.

Eric nodded. "I wish you could have known him. But he is similar to Valdr in many ways."

She rested her palms upon his chest. "Will you take your place as *jarl,* when the time comes?"

He nodded. "My father wanted me to be duke, and I thought the life meant being chained to responsibilities I didn't want. Now I see it as a chance to take care of these people and protect them." A rueful smile crossed his face. "Though I will have to continue training."

"No one remembers you," she said softly. "It is as if you were never here. You will have to reclaim your place, just as you did before."

"I have time now. And it is enough." He gazed back at the horizon and the sunlight gleaming upon the waves. "My father gave me a gift I can never repay—of sharing my life with you."

"You will understand a father's love even more, come next spring," she said, drawing his hand to her flat stomach. "When our own child is born." Tears of happiness rose once again, but she let them flow freely.

Eric lifted her up, kissing her hard as he swung her around. "You could have given me no greater gift, Katarina. We have been blessed beyond measure."

"Perhaps we will have a son," she mused, smiling as he set her down again.

"Or a daughter. And if it is a girl, we will call her Ingirún."

She hugged him tightly, so grateful that he understood her secret wish. And when he took her hand and they walked along the beach, she sent up a silent prayer of thanksgiving for this man.

"All my life, I never truly felt as if I belonged," Eric admitted. "I was searching for my place in the world." He studied her for a long moment. "Until I saw you."

She moved in to kiss him, and when his mouth touched hers, she felt as if her broken heart had come back together again. "I love you, Eric Fielding, Marquess of Thorgraham."

"I love you, Katarina." He embraced her, and then took her hand, kissing it in turn. She drew him in, needing to feel every hard line of his body, to know that he was hers.

"Will it be strange when no one remembers you?" she asked.

"*You* remember," he countered. "And it is enough for me."

She leaned her head against his chest, tracing her hand over his heart. "I do. And you will always be the man I want as my husband."

"I suppose I will have to marry you again," he teased. "If your brother will grant his permission."

"I will not give him a choice." She took him by the hand, eager to lead him back to the settlement. "You will be my husband, now and forever." With a teasing smile, she added, "If you will have me."

"I traveled across a thousand years for you, Katarina. And even a thousand years at your side would never be enough." He rested his hands upon her womb, kissing her hair.

As the sun rose above the horizon, Katarina sent up another prayer of thanksgiving for all the blessings she had been given—for this man and the love he had given her.

And for all the blessings yet to come.

Thank you for reading *A Viking Maiden for the Marquess!* Reviews are always appreciated if you want to let others know what you thought of the book.

Would you like me to e-mail you when I have a new book out? You may sign up for my newsletter at http://www.michellewillingham.com/contact. I only send e-mails when I have a new release, and you may unsubscribe at any time. Your e-mail address will never be shared with third parties or sold.

Did you miss book one in this series, about the fierce Viking, Arik Thorgrim? Enjoy an excerpt of *A Viking for the Viscountess.*

Excerpt from

A VIKING FOR THE VISCOUNTESS

by Michelle Willingham

CḣAPƬER ONE

He would die in an hour. Perhaps sooner, if the gods called to him.

Arik Thorgrim lay prone upon the deck of his ship, feeling his strength slipping away as the blood pooled beneath him. The battle-ax wound was too deep, and he'd already seen the grim looks upon the faces of his men. They knew, as he did, that his life was over and he would soon join his brother warriors in Valhalla.

The chill of the night air turned his skin cold, numbing him to the brutal pain. Though most men might fear death, he welcomed it. For this night he would claim immortality and leave behind the woman who had betrayed him.

He closed his eyes, trying to blot out the image of Svala's face. Her long golden hair had flowed against her hips, her beauty tantalizing the dreams of any man. A smile from her was beyond price, worth every last piece of gold he possessed.

And then, as if to taunt him, he recalled her bare legs wrapped around Eyker's waist, her head thrown back in mindless lust. Arik had stumbled upon them together when he'd returned to their camp after raiding the southern coast. He had believed Svala was a shy virgin, only to learn that she'd given herself to his enemy.

Her infidelity and lies had sliced deeper than any blade. But when he'd gone to murder Eyker, the man's brother had struck him in the back with a battle-ax.

So be it. There was a place in the frost-laden depths of *Hel* for a coward without honor.

The waves of the sea grew rougher, and dimly, he heard the call of his *böndr* as the ship tossed. The men had sailed with him over the past few months, leaving behind their families and farms to seek wealth. His brother, Magnus, had built a settlement along the northeast coast of East Anglia, and Arik had asked his men to bring him there. He could not survive the journey to Rogaland to see his parents again— but he could reach his brother's home within hours.

Magnus was his closest sibling, and if the gods willed it, he might look upon his brother's face before he died. He wanted his body to be buried with honor.

Arik lay motionless, letting the sea take him. The ship rolled him to his back, and the searing pain nearly sent him into a void of darkness. He stared up at the clouded moon, while it transformed into an orange haze of blood. A dark shadow eclipsed the surface, and his vision wavered.

Would that I could have another chance at life.

The icy hand of Death beckoned closer, and he felt his body trembling with the last fight to live. Regrets flowed over him, but there was nothing that would change his fate.

He'd have made far different choices. He wouldn't have left his father in reckless defiance to go a-viking. He would have taken a quiet woman as his wife. Then at least he'd have a son or daughter of his blood to live on. But now, only his brother remained.

When he blinked, there were no other clouds in the sky, and the night was clear. Strange for it to be so, while violent sea waves tossed his wooden vessel. He thought he spied another ship, a strange wooden boat that did not resemble anything he'd ever seen before. The mast towered over the deck, and he could only imagine how large the sails would be when they were unfurled. These men, too, were caught in the storm.

Although the ship lurched, Arik's wounded body remained motionless, as if an invisible hand pinned him to the deck. The swells crashed against the side of the boat, and he feared it was Jörmungand, the serpent of Midgard, rising from the depths to devour them all. Amid the roar of the sea, he heard the shouts of terror from his men before they were swept under by the frigid waves, their lives claimed as sacrifice.

Silence cloaked the night, and the agony of his wound began to fade. Arik took a breath and saw that the blood upon his hands was gone. When he reached back to touch the ragged skin where the battle-ax had cut him down, he found that it had healed completely. A coldness drifted over his skin, but he refused to let the fear gain a foothold.

He was dead now. There was no other explanation for his wound disappearing. No doubt his body now rested on the bottom of the sea. He had to finish this journey to the afterworld alone, and he suspected he would soon see the spirits of those who had fallen before him.

Not yet, he heard a woman's voice whisper upon the wind.

He blinked, wondering if he had only imagined the words. All was still now, and the sea had calmed. Arik rose to his feet, testing his strength to stand. At the front of the boat, he stared into the darkness, hoping for a glimpse of Asgard, where the gods dwelled. If there was land nearby, he couldn't see it. He leaned back to look at the stars, trying to determine his whereabouts. The waves bobbed his ship, but the motion was gentle. With his hand upon the rudder, he questioned whether to steer or let the sea guide him. In the end, he surrendered command of the vessel, for he had no way of knowing where the gods would lead him.

As the sea shifted and blurred all around him, he suddenly spied the prone figure of a body in the water. Her golden hair streamed around her, and his heart seized up, not knowing if it was Svala. Had she joined him in death? Or had the gods sent her to him, as a gift?

Whether or not she was real, Arik didn't hesitate as he dove from the ship to save her.

NORFOLK, ENGLAND
ONE THOUSAND YEARS LATER

Juliana Arthur, the Viscountess Hawthorne, tucked her son into bed, kissing his forehead. "Sleep well, Harry." The boy smiled up at her and snuggled deeper into the threadbare sheets. She had dressed him in two nightshirts and woolen socks, as well as a cap to keep him warm. Often at night, he would slip out of his trundle bed and crawl inside her own bed, while the wind rattled the shutters of their small house.

"Will we go back to Hawthorne House in the morning?" he asked.

"We might, if your father returns." She smoothed his hair and gave an encouraging smile. "Now close your eyes."

As soon as he did, her smile faded. She had been telling Harry the lie for months now. They could not return to Hawthorne House, no matter how badly she wanted to. For the past six years it had been her sanctuary. She loved every blade of grass on the estate, and it had become her home after the viscount had abandoned her there.

Juliana supposed she ought to be devastated that her

husband had gone traveling on the Continent without her. She did want William to come back—truly she did. But not because she loved him or because she missed him. No, she wanted him back to save them from this poverty.

God forgive her, she'd been so glad at first, when she'd heard the news that he might never return. She'd swept her infant son into her arms, hugging him with joy. No longer would William tell her how worthless she was, how fortunate she was to be with him. He wouldn't give her orders on how to dress, what ladylike pursuits to indulge in, or how she should best please him in bed. Her son would never know his father, and nothing could have dimmed her elation at that moment.

But then, a solicitor had arrived at Hawthorne House six months ago, informing her that her marriage was invalid and she'd been nothing more than William's mistress. Her husband's brother, Marcus, had swiftly stripped her son of his inheritance and title, and though she'd tried to fight back, he would not allow it.

"You were never his wife," Marcus said coldly. *"His mistress, perhaps, but nothing more."*

"But I was," she whispered. *"We eloped in Scotland. I signed the registry."*

"There was no registry. And no written record of the marriage." Marcus folded his hands, with not a trace of sympathy in his demeanor. *"My brother deceived you into believing it, likely so you would share his bed."* When she started to argue again, he cut her off. *"You're a practical woman, Juliana. Why would a viscount wed a fisherman's daughter?"*

He made it sound as if she was no better than a scullery maid. Yes, her father had been a common man, but her mother was nobility.

"My grandfather is a baron," she argued. *"And William loved me."*

"Whether or not he loved you is beside the point. You were never married, and your son is a bastard."

Her mouth moved to deny his words, but no sound came out. She clenched her knuckles hard, feeling as if she'd entered a nightmare from which she couldn't wake up.

"Didn't you ever wonder why he hid you away in the country, never bringing you to London? It was because he didn't marry you at all."

Deep inside, she feared Marcus was right. She'd spent months paying runners to search for a record of their elopement. And still, the search had come up with nothing.

Either her husband had lied to her, or Marcus was lying to prevent her son from inheriting. He'd escorted them out of Hawthorne House with hardly more than a trunk of clothes. To keep Harry from being afraid, she'd told him that they were going to visit his grandfather. She'd woven an elaborate tale of how they would spend a few months by the sea and he could build castles in the sand.

Her life had felt like that sand castle, crumbling to pieces all around her. Especially when her father had died a few weeks later, leaving her grief-stricken.

Quiet descended over the house, and her maid, Grelod, drew her chair closer to the fire beside the sleeping dog. The older woman had been with her ever since Juliana had been a little girl and spoke only a little English. She had sought work in London, after leaving Norway, and had found a position when the housekeeper took pity on her. Grelod had been a favorite servant of the baroness, Juliana's grandmother, for she worked hard and said nothing.

Keeping her voice low, the old woman murmured in Norwegian, "It's not right, the two of you living in a place such as this. It's hardly fit for a beggar."

"I have nowhere else to go, and you know this."

"Your grandmother ought to have opened her doors to

you." Grelod picked up the mending and muttered to herself, as she threaded her needle. "They might have cut off your mother after she wed your father, but that was no fault of yours."

"She did invite me to visit, but I would rather drown myself than accept help from her." Juliana moved her own stool beside the fire, watching the flames in the hearth. "Lady Traveston is a horrid woman."

"She did give you a Season," her maid pointed out.

"Only because it was my mother's last wish." And because her grandmother had wanted to mold her into a lady. Juliana had mistakenly thought that it would be a wonderful chance to meet a husband. She shuddered at the memory. The baroness had drilled months' worth of lessons and etiquette into her brain, as if she were preparing Juliana for war. And although she'd married a viscount, her grandmother had shown little satisfaction in the match. She'd never approved of William and had been aghast when they'd eloped.

A gust of wind blew through the crevices in the walls, and Juliana leaned over to bring the blanket up to Harry's neck. A bleakness caught at her heart. She had to do something to get her son out of this place. Soon, she would have no choice but to seek help from her grandparents. Lord Traveston might have abandoned his daughter and granddaughter, but she believed Lady Traveston would find a place for them to stay if Juliana groveled enough.

It was still a last resort.

Restlessness flowed within her veins as she paced across the cottage, worrying over how to find the evidence of her marriage. "Go out and have a walk," Grelod ordered. "You'll feel better for it."

"It's too dark," Juliana protested. "And I shouldn't leave Harry."

She started to walk toward the rocking chair, when

Grelod caught her hand. "You're troubled, and the night air will do you good. Go, and you'll find the answers you've been seeking."

"The moonlight won't solve our problems, Grelod," she argued. "Only William can put everything to rights." If her husband returned, he could bring them back to Hawthorne House, admitting that their marriage had been valid.

"His ship might return," Grelod admitted. "Give an offering to the gods, and see what happens."

"An offering?" She hid a smile at the old woman's superstitions. Grelod had always believed in magic and folklore. She had woven stories over the years at bedtime, legends that she was convinced were true, though Juliana now knew they had only been tales. Grelod's beliefs were a part of her, and she fervently upheld the old Norse traditions. At night, she often told Harry stories about the goddess Freya and her children of the moon. Though Juliana didn't believe in any of that, she saw no harm in indulging her maid.

"Give the gods a lock of your hair. Or a drop of your blood," the woman suggested. "Perhaps it will conjure up the help you need."

Juliana squeezed Grelod's hand, knowing her maid was only trying to help. She did want a chance to be alone, and strolling outside might clear her wayward thoughts. "I'll go for a walk. Watch over Harry and call out if he needs me."

Behind her, she heard the woman muttering incantations and words she didn't understand. Juliana sighed and reached for her cloak and bonnet.

The wind had stirred up, pulling the gray waves against the shore. She walked along the water's edge, while a full orange moon bathed the shore in a shimmer of gold. One could almost believe that a night like this could hold a bit of magic.

She drew her cloak around her, holding fast to her bonnet

as the night air buffeted it. Ahead, she spied her father's boat, and a pang caught her heart. He'd been a fisherman all his life, and the battered wood seemed to draw her closer.

When she walked to the edge of the pier, she stepped inside the vessel, remembering the days when he'd taken her out to the sea, teaching her to fish. Being here, she could almost smell the familiar scent of tobacco. He'd been the most wonderful father, and she missed him dearly. Sometimes if she closed her eyes, she could remember the warmth of his embrace and his quiet love.

He'd been her steadfast rock, all her life—especially after her mother had died. A tightness clenched her gut as she stared up at the moon. *What am I supposed to do now, Father? How can I support my son, when I don't know if William is alive or dead?*

The wind shifted, filling up the mainsail. Juliana frowned, for she hadn't untied it. How had it come unfurled? It was almost as if an unseen presence had emerged.

Don't be silly. There is no such thing as a ghost. She pushed back the thought, trying to find a logical explanation. The sail had been tied up when she'd climbed aboard the boat, but somehow, it must have broken free. She fought with the canvas and ropes, trying to bring it back down again, but another gust of wind made her stumble. The sail swung out, the wooden boom cracking against her forehead.

The vicious pain made her cry out, and she knelt down in the boat, lowering her head to fight the dizziness. She'd never expected a storm to be brewing, not when the night had been so calm.

A moment later, the vessel started to float away from the dock, though she couldn't understand how. Without someone untying the ropes, there was no way it could break free of the moorings. But the wind strengthened, filling up the sail as if an invisible force were pulling her out into the open sea.

Juliana fumbled with the ropes, fighting to reverse her

direction, but the wind was too strong. Even when she put her full weight against the sail, it didn't move. Panic sharpened within her as the boat sailed farther away from the dock.

No. She couldn't let this happen. She tore off her gloves, pulling with all her might. But even that wasn't enough to bring her back.

Her head ached, swelling up from the wound. Terror wrapped around her heart, for the boat was taking her too far away from the shore. And then how could she return to Harry? Though she didn't want to leave the safety of the boat, she saw no other choice but to swim back.

Steeling herself, Juliana slid both legs over the side of the boat, pushing herself into the frigid water. She strained with her feet to touch the bottom, but her head went underwater. What had happened? Now it seemed that the shore was twice as far away.

Impossible. She fought to swim back, though the weight of her clothes pulled her down. The waves sloshed against her face, and she began stripping away the layers, letting her cloak fall first. She tore off her bonnet and let it sink. The water was so cold, it froze her movements, making it harder to stay above the surface. As she struggled against the waves, the beach disappeared, leaving her alone on the sea.

Her heart was pounding with fear while her mind tried to make sense out of the impossible. Perhaps this was a dream and she was unconscious from the head injury. Dreams never made sense, and undoubtedly that was what this was.

The moon turned the color of blood, sliding back from behind a misty cloud. She tasted salt water, and her arms ached from swimming. But it did no good. The more she swam, the farther away land seemed.

It's not real, she told herself. *It can't be.*

The nightmare only worsened, and horror washed over her when she saw that the boat was now gone. If she didn't get help soon, she was going to drown. She cried out, though it was hopeless to think that anyone would find her on a night like this.

Her arms grew heavy as she swam, her hair drenched against her face.

And when she saw the outline of another ship in the distance, she prayed to God that someone would save her.

Arik swam against the current, a rope tied to his waist. When he reached the woman, her hair obscured her face. He didn't know if the gods had brought Svala to him, in spite of his death. Had she somehow crossed over, losing her own life? Her body was so cold, he didn't know if she was alive or dead.

He pulled her into his arms, but she remained limp and motionless. He kicked hard to stay afloat as he swam back to his ship. It was a struggle to bring her on board, but he managed to get her to the deck. She coughed hard, her shoulders heaving. Tremors shook her body, and a strange gown clung to her. It was dull gray in color, but high-waisted, with a square neckline and a slender skirt.

The moon slid behind a cloud, shadowing her face. He couldn't tell if it was Svala or not, but they were the same height and form. Her long blond hair was unmistakable. If he was on his journey to the afterlife, surely this was his reward. Eyker's brother had offended the gods by striking a blow at his back, and Arik felt certain that Svala had been given to him as compensation.

She was cold, her body shivering violently from the icy water. He carried her to the back of the boat, away from the oars. Carefully, he stripped away her wet clothing, cutting the strange girdle that was tied tightly to her waist before removing his own garments. Body heat was the best way to warm both of them.

He laid her down upon a rough fur and covered her with his own flesh, cocooning her with another fur on top of himself. With her head tucked beneath his chin, he held her close, stroking her smooth skin.

Her hair smelled the same as he remembered, like crushed flowers and sweet herbs. He rested his face against her cheek, inhaling the sweetness of her. Desire roared through him, along with the pain of Svala's betrayal. She'd given herself to Eyker, sharing *his* bed instead of Arik's. She'd offered him words and promises, but never her body.

The grim rage festered within his mind, making Arik want to punish them both. He wanted to touch her, to bring her such raw need, she'd regret giving herself to another man. Her bare breasts rested against his chest, and the tight buds of her nipples aroused him. Odin's blood, she smelled good.

In his jealousy, he wanted to show her what she'd spurned, that he was a man who would pleasure her in a way she would never forget. He lowered his mouth to the curve of her throat, kissing her. Then he filled his palms with her breasts and set to work on seducing the woman he'd yearned for.

Juliana tried to open her eyes, but dizziness and darkness clung to her senses. Her skin was warm. So very warm. Against her body, she felt the heat of a man's skin.

Had William come back? Or was this a dream? She thought about screaming, but his hands were stroking her bare back. It felt so good to be in safe, strong arms.

Yes, it was most definitely a dream. Ships didn't break free of knotted ropes, and land didn't disappear within seconds. She snuggled deeper into the man's arms and imagined that he was someone who adored her. Somehow she was safe within her own bed. The dreams of icy seawater and drowning were gone, and in their place was a fantasy she'd conjured in her mind.

The gentle touches moved from her spine to cup her breast. Against his palm, her nipples tightened, and she couldn't suppress the catch of her breath. The dream had become erotic, and she allowed her imagination to pull her into a deeper pleasure.

You will forget everything about him when I have finished with you, came the man's voice in a half-remembered language.

His words startled her. Was her dream man speaking of William? Juliana rather hoped so. She wanted to forget about her husband's demanding nature and the way he'd visited her bed, expecting her to scream his name or some other nonsense. What was there to scream about?

Her imagination settled back, enjoying the skilled hands that caressed her breasts, drawing out an echo of sensation between her legs. She had never felt this way before, with arousing liquid desires that raced through her skin. She reached out, not knowing what was happening to her, but her phantom lover bent to her throat, his mouth kissing her pulse point while his hands threaded through her damp hair.

A warning resounded in her mind, something about the cool water. Something she should remember...

But she didn't want to wake up from this dream. She wanted to see where it would lead and what her lover would do to her.

His mouth closed over her breast, wet and demanding. She arched hard, the exquisite pleasure tormenting her. He explored her flesh as if he wanted to taste every inch of her.

And God help her, she wanted him to. It had been six years since her husband had visited her bed, but William's touches had been rough, never arousing like this. She kept her eyes closed, afraid this dream would vanish in the morning light, and all of it would end.

Juliana held his head to her breast as he suckled and teased, his other hand reaching over to caress her breast's twin. Between her thighs, she grew wet and was startled that it had happened so easily. On the nights William had come to her bed, she'd lain naked beneath the coverlet, struggling to feel something.

She'd even touched herself a time or two before his visit, hoping to arouse herself. Anything that would make the lovemaking more comfortable and prevent her husband from criticizing her. But this dream was breaking past her meager knowledge of sex, leading her into so much more.

Again, a part of her grew fearful. As if she had to awaken, right now.

The fur beneath her had grown so hot, perspiration beaded upon her skin. She struggled to pull off the outer coverlet and felt instead the length of a male body. Conjured from her imagination, this man was firm, with taut muscles. Juliana traced his chest, her hands exploring by touch. Her lover was powerful, with broad shoulders that tapered down to a lean waist.

My, but her imagination had selected an excellent specimen.

His hips were hardened muscles, and she marveled as she learned his body in the darkness, moving her hands over his heavy thighs. His erection rested against her stomach, thick and hard. Out of curiosity, she took it in her hand, and he let out a low growl as if he liked it.

The dream shifted, and his mouth lowered from her breasts, down to her ribs. He tilted her hips up, kissing a path down to her intimate flesh.

She started to protest, for this was something she'd never imagined. She wasn't at all sure he should—

Dear God above. His mouth feasted upon her, his tongue sliding within her moist entrance. Inside, her body shook with tremors, her breath seizing at the shocking sensations.

She'd never imagined anything like this, and it took an effort to ignore the warnings in her mind.

She was shuddering, her fingers clenching at the fur while white-hot tendrils of desire drove her mad with need. He teased at the hooded flesh, provoking her toward the sensual pleasure she wanted so badly. And when she leaned into him, surrendering to her own needs, he suddenly pulled away.

Frustrated and upset, Juliana tried to bring him back, but instead, he replaced his mouth with the pressure of his fingers. The sensation was different, and when his mouth returned to her nipple, she felt the urgency roaring back.

Juliana leaned in, gripping his muscled shoulders as her body reveled in the glory of being touched this way. Instinctive tremors rocked her and she gripped his head as he forced her over the edge, a soaring heat of release pouring through her. Nothing in all the months of her marriage could have prepared her for the way her body craved his invasion.

Did Eyker touch you like this? he demanded.

Who was Eyker? Juliana struggled to open her eyes. The dark warning inside her was gaining momentum, urging her to wake up. Something was wrong.

It would have been like this between us, if you had allowed it.

He moved against her throat, speaking words she didn't understand. Between her legs, she felt his blunt erection probing. Her body was wet, aching to be filled by this man. She wanted to forget everything, to lose herself in a dream of pleasure. Abruptly, she gasped as his slick heat filled her. This was what she'd wanted from William. This desperate need to be taken and to shatter the boundaries between them.

Though she couldn't understand how her mind had created this fantasy, she wasn't about to lie quietly and let the dream disappear. No, she gripped him hard, meeting his thrusts while she arched her hips to receive him. There was nothing polite or quiet about the lovemaking—it was carnal lust, almost savage in nature. She grew molten as he sheathed himself. A part of her half-expected this lover to be barbaric, to thrust in a rhythm that would hurt.

But instead, he seemed to know when to quicken the tempo and when to slow down. She was frantic for another climax, desperate to make this man shatter in the way she had. The boat was moving, and the rocking motion echoed the surges of his hips against hers.

Within her, she sensed him seeking his own release, and she wrapped her legs around his waist, holding fast as he rode her. A cry ripped from her mouth as he held her bottom and penetrated over and over. She was coming apart, her body shuddering against the rhythmic pleasure, until the release shot through her in mindless lust. When her nails scored the man's back, he let out his own groan, his hard body growing slack against hers.

Juliana kept her eyes closed, stunned that she'd created such a vision in her mind. No doubt once she awakened, she would find herself back at home in her bed, with no man to share it.

It was a dream, and when dawn came, it would end.

Sparse rays of sunlight speared his eyes, and Arik blinked at the brightness. Although the morning air was cool against his bare skin, the woman in his arms was warm. His shaft hardened instantly, and he reached between her legs to prepare her, wanting the honeyed wetness against his fingertips. But when he rolled her over, his hands stilled upon her flesh. It wasn't Svala he'd taken last night. It was a woman he'd never seen before.

Uneasiness slid through him, and Arik wondered what was happening. Was she a slave girl, sent by Freya to tempt him? Was this a part of the afterlife? With his knuckles, he gently touched her skin. It prickled with gooseflesh, and she murmured something in her sleep. He didn't understand her words, and from the shape of her face, he guessed she was Anglo-Saxon. Yet the language was still foreign to his ears.

"Awaken," he commanded.

Her gray eyes flew open, and she let out a scream of terror. Gripping the furs to cover her nakedness, she looked horrified.

She started speaking words in a language he couldn't grasp, flustered words of panic and embarrassment. Her cheeks turned bright red, as if she'd suddenly remembered her actions from the night before. Arik folded his arms across his chest, waiting for her to speak words that made sense. When she gave none, he demanded, "Who are you?"

Her eyes narrowed, as if she'd suddenly understood his question. "You're...not English," she whispered. Her face furrowed as she spoke.

He didn't know what she was talking about, but he reached for his fallen clothing and covered himself. "I am called Arik Thorgrim, a *jarl* from the Ryger tribe."

"A what?"

"A *jarl*. I have lands in Rogaland, and my brother has settlements in East Anglia and Dubh Linn." He reached down and tossed her the discarded garment she'd worn the night before. It was a finely woven gown, one that spoke of her status. This woman was not a slave, but possibly a freewoman or a king's daughter. And yet, she wore no jewelry, save a small gold ring upon one hand. There were no jeweled torques nor bracelets to show her rank. He frowned, trying to determine more about her.

"What is your name? And what happened to your ship?" he demanded. If her family was searching for her, he would see to it that she was returned to them.

"I am Juliana Arthur, the Viscountess Hawthorne," she answered in his language, her eyes wide. "My father's ship broke free of its moorings, and the wind carried me out to sea. It was my own fault for climbing inside the boat."

"Then the gods did bring you to me." He studied her. "Clothe yourself and then we will talk further." Right now, he couldn't grasp what had happened. Though she wasn't Svala, her features were similar enough.

The sun had risen higher, casting light over the land nearby. It resembled the shores of East Anglia, but strange dwellings rested within the hills. He'd never seen anything like them, and more and more, he wondered if this was part of the afterlife.

There was no sign of Asgard, nor the Hall of Valhalla, as he'd expected. Arik sat upon one of the benches, resting his hands upon the oars. Was this a test? Since he'd been murdered instead of dying in battle, did he have to earn his place among the warriors?

Perhaps he truly *had* heard the words *not yet.* He didn't understand any of it, and the gods weren't known to explain themselves to mortals.

"Take me home," Juliana pleaded. He turned and saw that her gray gown was still damp, the fabric outlining her slender body and rounded breasts. It reminded him of the night they'd spent together and the way she'd welcomed him into her arms.

She hadn't been afraid of him then. He'd touched her, believing she was Svala. And though he didn't know why this woman had allowed a stranger into her bed, nothing had been done against her will. He remembered the way she'd clenched his head, arching against him as he'd tasted her swollen flesh.

His body hardened at the memory, but he forced it back. Clearly, there were reasons why the woman had given herself but now held regrets.

She was shivering hard, the gown doing little to shield her from the wind. He returned to their sleeping place and brought out a heavy fur. When he advanced toward her, she took a step backward. He let her retreat, ignoring her fear as he wrapped the fur around her shoulders.

"You live there?" he questioned, pointing toward the land.

"Yes." She held on to the edges of the fur, still staring at him.

"Then I will guide the ship to the shore. You will grant me food and shelter in return."

Her gray eyes turned suspicious. "There's no place for you at my house. I barely have a bed for my maid and my son."

A tension pulled at him when she mentioned a boy. "Where is your husband?"

She reddened. "I haven't seen him in six years. I think he's dead."

The traces of fear in her voice made him now understand her apprehension about the night they'd spent together. "And do you believe this?"

She lifted her shoulders in a shrug. "I don't know what to believe. But last night I was asleep... I never meant to—" Crestfallen, she stared at her feet, as if humiliated by what they'd done.

Arik took the fur covering with both hands, pulling her to stand closer to him. "I thought you were Svala, the woman who was promised as my bride."

Guilt stained her cheeks, but she raised her eyes to his. "What I did was wrong, and it won't happen again."

In her voice, he heard the firm resolution, and it irritated him that she'd dismissed him like a mistake to be swept aside. There was no doubt in his mind that he'd brought her pleasure last night, and by the gods, he wasn't without honor. He would never take a woman without her consent. But he wasn't at all averse to tempting her.

"It might." To remind her of it, he tilted her chin up and

kissed her. It was a kiss of possession, to place a claim upon her. But when he tasted the softness of her lips, he gentled his mouth upon hers. Her hands dug into his shoulders, as if to protest. But he caught her against his chest, pulling her closer. And whether or not she wanted to kiss him, she yielded to him like a temptation she couldn't have.

If her husband were alive, Arik would have understood her reluctance and honored it. But six years was too long to leave a woman like this behind. He had no doubt at all that her husband was dead.

Abruptly, she shoved him back, breaking the kiss. Her face flushed and she reminded him, "I have to go back to my son." She moved as far away from him as she could, and he saw the way her hands were shaking.

Arik moved to adjust the mainsail, then returned to the rudder, turning the vessel to make use of the wind. "Come here, Juliana of Arthur. Hold this steady."

She eyed him, but he stood firm on his order. He needed her help to steer the boat properly. After a moment, she climbed over the rows of benches until she reached the stern. Her face was pale, her lips swollen from his kiss. "You'll keep your word to bring me home to my son?"

"Yes." He stood and held out the rudder, guiding her hands. Juliana sat with her posture straight, not looking at him as she held the wood. She looked as lost as he felt. But he would bring her back to her home and learn whether or not she was telling the truth.

The path of his life had taken an unexpected turn. Never had he been given any reason to doubt his place in Valhalla. But...what if he wasn't truly dead? What if there was another purpose for him now?

He took his place on the bench, rowing toward the shore. Behind him, she remained silent. He glanced at the woman, and her expression held worry before she flushed at the memory of last night. Unlike Svala, she seemed embarrassed, as if she'd never expected to feel pleasure.

The memory of her passionate moans, the fervid touch of her hands, made him want to toss the oars aside and claim her body once again. But he understood her need to return to her son.

"Who are you really?" she interrupted, when he continued his rowing. "Did Marcus send you?"

"I know of no man named Marcus." He glanced back and saw the consternation lined upon her face.

"You're dressed like no one I've seen before, and you're speaking a language that I haven't heard since my maid, Grelod, taught it to me." Her fists curled at her hips. "What is it you want from me?"

He pulled the oars against the current, bringing them as close to the shore as he dared. "I might ask the same of you. You tempted me in your arms last night, trying to ensnare me before I could reach Valhalla in Asgard."

"I don't know what you're talking about. I nearly drowned last night."

"Or the gods brought you to me." He released the oars and stood before her. "Our fates are intertwined, so it seems."

"No, they aren't," she argued. "I've been through enough without needing another man to make me into a fool."

He sent her a dark look. "You should be grateful that I am willing to return you to your home instead of keeping you as my *thrall*."

She frowned. "I have no idea what you're talking about, but no man will keep me from my son." There was a cool tone to her voice that held a warning.

Arik moved to the bow of his ship and dropped the anchor near the dock. Juliana let go of the rudder and stood with her shoulders back, walking toward him as if he were her slave instead of the other way around. She reminded him of a Norsewoman, strong in her demeanor.

But she was sorely mistaken if she believed he was going to let her go. Somehow, she was tied to his fate. And he wouldn't rest, until he learned what his purpose was.

ChAPTER TWO

After the boat was secure upon its moorings, Juliana allowed Arik Thorgrim to lift her to the dock. His hands lingered upon her a moment too long, and his touch made her nervous.

"Thank you for your assistance, Mr. Thorgrim." She clasped her hands together, trying to distance herself from him, like a proper English widow. Not at all like a woman who had been intimate with a stranger.

The very thought set her cheeks on fire. She still couldn't believe that the dream had been real. She wasn't at all a woman of sensual desires. Hadn't William told her, time and again, what a disappointment she was? The day after their wedding, he'd told her that she needed to respond better to him, to grow aroused simply by looking at him.

But he'd had little effect on her—unlike this man, whose physical form reminded her of a Greek statue. He was tall, with broad shoulders, and she'd felt his ridged abdomen last night. His strong thighs had held not a trace of softness, like a warrior who had come off a battlefield.

His face seemed familiar somehow, and she tried to think of where she might have met this man. Long dark hair hung below his shoulders, and his brown eyes held interest, as if he remembered what they'd done last night. A stubble of beard lined his cheeks, and she thought of the way it had abraded her breasts as he'd licked and suckled her.

The thought sent a thrill through her body, making her respond against her will. No, she couldn't let herself be seduced again. The sooner she escaped his company, the better.

"Thank you for bringing me home. Now I'll bid you a good day." She nodded in dismissal and turned to leave.

"You will go nowhere without me, woman," came his reply.

Oh won't I? She stared at the man, disbelieving that he would have the gall to order her around. But he stepped out of the boat and tied it to the dock. It was a strange vessel, one that resembled a longboat from long ago. She hadn't seen anything like it. At the prow of the boat, there was a carved female face and a bronze weather vane.

Mr. Thorgrim strode across the dock until he reached her side. She suddenly realized how very large he was. Though she was taller than most women, the top of her head barely reached his mouth. Her eyes made direct contact with his muscled shoulders, forcing her to look up.

He wasn't dressed like anyone she'd ever seen. His woolen tunic was dun-colored, made in a primitive fashion. He wore darker trousers, a fur mantle across his shoulders, and leather braces upon his forearms. His dark eyes stared down at her with a hunger that made her shiver. He walked onto the shore with confidence, his leather boots striding through the sand. At his waist hung a long sword and a battle-ax. Arik Thorgrim almost reminded her of a…a Viking.

If you enjoyed the excerpt, you may purchase it at: www.michellewillingham.com/book/viking-viscountess.

Kindle bestselling author and Rita® Award finalist **Michelle Willingham** has published more than thirty-five romance novels and novellas. Currently, she lives in southeastern Virginia with her husband and children, and is working on more historical romance books in a variety of settings, such as medieval and Viking-era Ireland, medieval Scotland, and Victorian and Regency England. When she's not writing, Michelle enjoys baking, playing the piano, and avoiding exercise at all costs. Her books have been translated into languages around the world and are also available in audio. Visit her website at www.michellewillingham.com to find English and foreign translations.